THE ARCANE WARD

WARDENS OF ISSALIA, BOOK TWO

JEFFREY L. KOHANEK

FALLBRANDT PRESS

BOOKS BY JEFFREY L. KOHANEK

Runes of Issalia
The Buried Symbol (May 2016)
The Emblem Throne (October 2016)
An Empire in Runes (April 2017)

* * *

Rogue Legacy (February 2018)

* * *

Wardens of Issalia
A Warden's Purpose (May 2018)
The Arcane Ward (Sept 2018)
An Imperial Gambit (Dec 2018)
More coming in 2019…

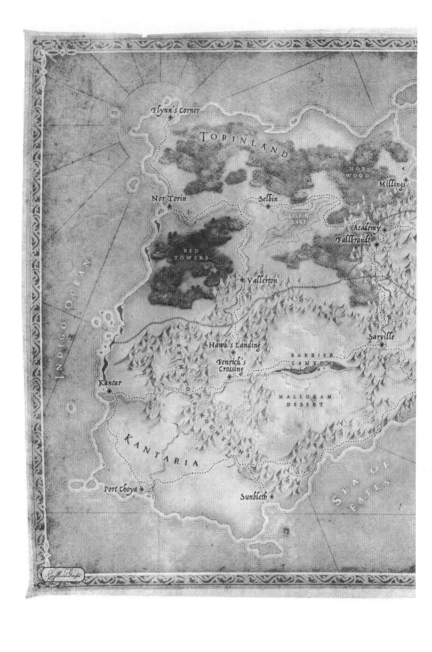

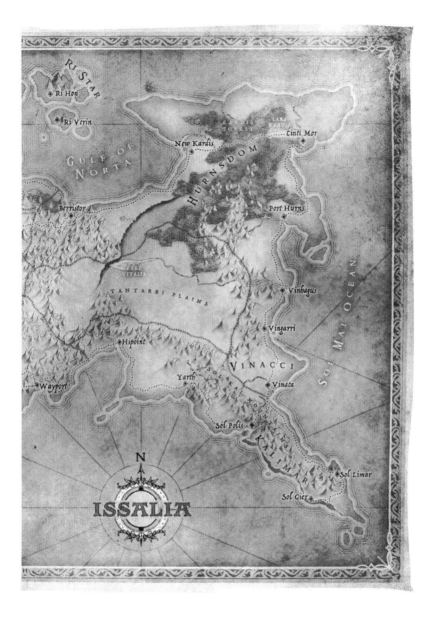

ISSALIA

PROLOGUE

Parker Thanes pushed the tavern door open, stepped inside, and was greeted by a cacophony of cheers and laughter. The smell of salt air mixed with stale beer and unwashed bodies made him grimace. *I don't understand why she likes these places.*

He pushed through the crowd as he headed toward the bar. Jostled sailors, spilled drinks, and a trail of curses followed in his wake. Ignoring the upset men, he scanned the crowded tavern until he approached his destination.

A hefty woman in her middle years stood behind the bar. The brunette filled a pair of tankards, turned, and placed them before two bearded men, one of whom had a pale scar on his tanned face, the wound running from his forehead to his cheek. After pocketing two coppers, she shifted her focus to Parker.

"Hello, Tess," Parker greeted the barkeep.

"I'm glad you showed. Things are getting out of hand."

Parker frowned. "Where is she?"

Tess flipped her head to the side. "Around back. You might want to hurry."

Stifling a sigh, Parker forced his way around the far end of the bar. He turned the corner and found a thick crowd – the source of the cheers that arose earlier. Another round of shouts erupted, fists pumping into the air. He forced his way into the mass of bodies, emerging to find the back area open but for two people.

A man – tall and sinewy, with shorn dark stubble on his head and cheeks – stood facing a woman. She was short, even for a female. With blond hair that ran to her shoulders, she was dressed in a simple tunic, cinched at the waist with a studded belt. Her brown breeches were tucked into tall black boots, each with a knife strapped to them, matching the knives strapped to each thigh. Between the two was a round table with a dozen mugs on it. The man lifted a mug and drank, foam running to his chin as he chugged the ale. When finished, he tipped the mug upside down and slammed it on the table, where it joined the other empty tankards. Cheers rose up from the crowd while the man shook his head to clear it.

As the crowd quieted, the woman grabbed the last full mug and lifted it to her lips, emptying its contents without pausing for a breath. When finished, she lowered it, stumbled, and blinked, her blue eyes glazing over. A mixture of laughter and mutters came from the crowd until she flipped the mug over and slammed it down beside the others.

The man scowled, twisting a tanned face marked by a gold ring through one nostril. "Now, we will see who is better."

He pulled a dagger from the sheath on his hip and gripped it by the blade. Turning away from the crowd, the man cocked his arm back and threw the knife, striking a hair below the intersection of an X carved into a wooden post fifteen feet away. He drew and threw another knife, which landed just above the first, the two hilts touching one another. When he turned back, his grin revealed the noticeable gap of a missing tooth.

"Your turn, Tenzi. Let's see if a sodden girl like you can even hit that post."

The woman moved toward the man, stumbling as she pushed him aside. As Tenzi stared at him, swaying, a satisfied smirk crossed the man's face.

"Watch this," Tenzi mumbled.

Her eyes seemed to transform, her half-mast lids narrowing with intensity as she stared at the man. Tenzi spun about, her hands a blur as a dagger appeared in each and flew toward the post. Without pausing, she unleashed the daggers strapped to her legs and they joined the first pair. A bend and a flick sent the two knives from her boots into the post. She then reached behind her back, pulled a blade from her belt, and flung it.

The seven knives perfectly formed an X, with the last blade landing directly on the intersection of the carved target, somehow fitting between the man's two thrown blades. The crowd fell silent, the moment lasting a few breaths before loud cheers and shouts erupted. Heads shook in amazement as the men and women surrounding Parker began exchanging coins from bets placed.

Tenzi held her open palm toward the man. "Pay up, Ridley."

The man snarled. "Leave off, Tenzi. I'm keeping my silver."

In a flash, Tenzi had a knife in her hand and pressed against the man's throat. "Didn't know I had a blade strapped to my upper back, huh? I find it wise to always have an extra, just in case."

With narrowed eyes, Ridley glared for a long moment before his lips pressed together and he slowly dug out a coin purse. Tenzi pulled the blade away and held out her other hand. After setting five silvers in her palm, he shook his head.

"Another ale and I would have had you."

Tenzi smirked, gripping the coins in her fist. "Perhaps. Not today, though."

The crowd began to disburse with many heading toward the bar for another drink. Parker shifted closer to Tenzi, frowning at her grin.

"Why do you spend time in these seedy places?"

Tenzi shrugged. "A girl's gotta have a little fun now and then."

Parker snorted. "I know you. Nothing you do is *little*."

She moved toward the post and began retrieving her blades. "Why are you here? I thought you were staying on the ship tonight."

"I was, but Joely and Hex came back early. They said that four others got into a fight at The Wind Sock tavern and were arrested."

Tenzi slid two daggers back into the sheaths on her thighs, rolled her eyes, and grabbed the last three knives. "Again? Why can't they stay out of trouble?"

Parker raised a brow. "I wonder who may have taught them to cause trouble."

"You're hilarious." Tenzi slid a knife up each sleeve and waved toward Parker. "Let's go. It looks like Ridley's silver is going toward bail money, straight from him to the city coffers."

Parker turned and squirmed through the crowd with the much smaller Tenzi in his wake. When he stepped out into the alley, the noise of the bar quieted and was replaced by a distant boom, followed by shouts and screams. With a furrowed brow, he led Tenzi down the alley and to the lit street.

People ran past in all directions, some heading toward the city wall, others toward the docks. Cries filled the air only to be engulfed by the boom of a distant explosion.

"To the docks!" Tenzi broke into a run.

Parker ran after her as she weaved her way through the foot traffic and around carts. They emerged from Downside – the portion of the Sol Polis that lay between the city wall and the docks – and found people crowding onto the pier. A flash of green flames erupted from a ship moored to the docks. People on the pier screamed and tried to reverse direction as the flames on the ship turned from green to orange.

"Flashbombs!" Parker shouted. "Someone is launching flash bombs!"

"That was a fleet ship," Tenzi said. "We have to get the fleet out of the harbor."

Fighting against the crowd, Parker and Tenzi pushed their way through oncoming traffic and onto the pier. An explosion blasted water into the air, sending two nearby ships rocking as seawater rained down on them. Running, Parker led Tenzi down the pier, running beside a handful of sailors trying to get to their ships.

"Why did we have to moor on the end this time?" Parker groaned as he ran.

They ran past the ship on fire. The flames had burned the length of the mooring rope and were licking the post tied to it. An explosion to the other side knocked them off their feet, Parker almost falling into the water as he gripped the pier edge. He sat up and turned toward the ship that had been struck. A wall of green flames raged upon it, turning orange as it spread. Burning debris lay scattered on the pier. Body parts as well. Tenzi cried out and frantically swatted the smoldering leg of her breeches.

Parker's focus shifted toward the shoreline, and he saw armed soldiers running toward the pier. His eyes widened and he grabbed Tenzi's wrist. "We need to run!"

Following his gaze, she saw the force collide with the crowd, cutting through them without resistance. Parker and Tenzi scrambled to their feet and ran toward the ship at the end of the pier. While Parker had never moved faster, he seemed be running in slow motion, the distance between him and the ship closing at an agonizingly slow pace. Until, finally, they reached it.

"What's happening?" Shashi called out from the rail.

"Sol Polis is under attack." Tenzi shouted. "Make ready to set sail!"

Parker reached the plank first and ran up it, heading straight for the pilot deck. Behind him, Tenzi shouted.

"I need Stein. Is he here?"

"Yes. Below deck," Joely replied.

"Get him up here. Now!"

Sailors scrambled about the ship, some untying it from the mooring while others began preparing the lines. Parker turned toward shore and found dozens of armed men charging the pier.

Joely reappeared with Stein in tow, the latter rubbing sleep from his eyes.

"Stein. We need to take down the pier before those men reach us." Tenzi pointed toward the soldiers and Stein's jaw dropped. Without a word, he ran down the plank.

Parker unshouldered his bow and drew an arrow. He nocked it and prepared to fire. His gaze landed on Stein and found the man kneeling on the pier, tracing a rune with a chunk of glowstone. An explosion sent a thump into Parker's chest as a wall of green flames blasted from the nearest ship. Again, flaming debris rained upon the pier and into the sea. Stein scrambled to his feet and ran up the plank as the enemy soldiers stormed down the pier. The moment Stein was on board, Shashi kicked the plank aside and it fell into the water. With its lines untied, New Horizons, the flagship of the Kalimar Navy, drifted from its mooring.

"Climb the rigging!" Tenzi called orders as she scrambled to the quarterdeck. "Raise mainsails!" She turned to Parker. "I'll steer. You shoot."

Nodding, he shifted away from the wheel and shot, the arrow arcing before it fell. A soldier in the vanguard stumbled to his knees and was bowled over by his companions. Another arrow launched as the rune on the dock began to glow a bright red. The rune pulsed while a third arrow found a target, striking a soldier who spun around and fell into the water. A fourth arrow struck an enemy soldier in the throat as the force reached the end of the pier. Archers stopped and raised bows toward the ship as the glow beneath them faded, the rune falling dark.

In a violent blast, the closest half of the pier exploded, launching debris and bodies into the air. Parts of both rained into the sea while angry red energy crackled and sizzled in glowing bolts that arced across the broken pier and the surface of the water. The portion of the pier that lay closer to shore remained, as did the soldiers who hadn't made it any further.

As New Horizons gained speed and sailed out from Sol Polis, another explosion emerged from within the city. Based on its location, Parker surmised that the tower of flames came from the citadel. The city was lost. The capital of Kalimar had fallen in surprise attack. Again.

PREFACE

From the journals of Benedict Hedgewick

Eighteen years have elapsed since The Horde was vanquished, the Ministry disbanded, and the Empire restored to the kingdoms of old. My inventions have changed people's lives, but not to the extent I had hoped. The secrecy surrounding enchanting has limited the dreams I held for a different future. Unfortunately, our fears regarding the abuse of the magic are well founded. One look at my compatriot, Elias, would prove this point. Chaos is a thing to be feared as much as a power to be held in awe. This is why we train arcanists in the academy, while simultaneously denying the existence of Infusion.

Still, the construction of the tower could never have happened without the assistance of magic. As a result, the Arcane Ward is a thing of wonder…and a home for the greatest secrets in Issalia. Most of the arcanists who had planned to live there have died or have moved on to live quiet lives. The tower remains largely empty as we seek the ideal individuals to fill it – those who have what is required to become Wardens. I will continue to do my part – to recruit, to train, to create, and to inspire the brilliance in our gadgeteers.

Recent events have forced ICON to alter its tactics and to accelerate its plans. King Brock and the other rulers fear the power that has risen in the east and have enacted an edict that ICON responds to this new Empire with stealth and alacrity. I believe that even Brock underestimates what it is we face. The rumors frighten me, for inside me resides a deep-seated dread that my discoveries may be turned against us in a manner I had never anticipated. In preparation for such an event, we must prepare ourselves to face the worst.

-Master Engineer, Benedict Hedgewick

1

SHAME

S hh, Cassilyn Talenz hushed her brother. *I'm trying to listen.*

Fine, Brandt sent back to her as he stuck out his tongue.

She sneered at him, her gaze locking with the green eyes that matched hers. Sunlight shone on his disheveled brown hair although his face remained darkened by the shadow of the castle. It would be mid-day soon, and that shadow would recede as the sun edged around the corner. While Brandt was technically her twin, he appeared more of a twin to their father, possessing the same compact, athletic frame and a noticeable intensity in his eyes.

Crouching, Cassie pushed her ear against the glass door again and listened. Although she couldn't see through the curtain, she suspected that only four people occupied the room. Her father and General Budakis were a given. The others had recently arrived at the castle.

"…lucky to escape." Parker paused telling his story and the room fell silent for a moment. From her other ear, Cassie heard a starfetch tweeting from a tree in the courtyard below.

Rather than Parker finishing his tale, Admiral Tenzi interjected.

"As our ship sailed beyond the breakers, another ship pushed off from the other pier. We could see the silhouettes of sailors scurrying up the masts, working eagerly to unfurl the sails." Tenzi's tone grew somber. "Then, the ship exploded in a burst of green flame. I felt the thump of it in my chest, my stomach souring while flaming bodies flailed and fell into the sea. The flames burned bright orange even as the ship sank beneath the water."

Silence followed.

Who would attack Sol Polis? Brandt's voice rang in Cassie's head.

I don't know. Just listen and maybe we will find out.

Cassie then heard her father's voice. "You mentioned soldiers wearing white tabards."

Parker replied. "Yes. With a blue rune of Issal on the chest and some sort of mail armor beneath."

"Hmm. Mail is heavy, difficult to move in."

"These soldiers didn't seem affected, Brock." Tenzi said.

"No Issalian kingdom wears white and blue...and certainly none would send out soldiers fighting behind that rune. How long ago did this occur?"

"Well," Tenzi said, "we sailed straight for Wayport to restock our stores. While we were there, I informed Duke Chadwick of what happened. His is among the nearest ports and is at risk. From there, we sailed straight here. I'd say it was nine days at the most."

Parker asked, "Do you know who's behind this?"

The sound of a drawer opening came through the door.

"I received this missive just last night," Brock said. "It appears that an old enemy has returned, declaring the entire eastern coast as their own."

The sound of paper unfolding preceded Tenzi's voice, reading aloud.

"Sol Polis has fallen, and with it, Kalimar is ours. A new regime rules the east coast, one with new laws – laws that restore order to Empire citizens.

"The borders between your lands and ours extend from Yarth, across the entirety of Vinacci, to the east coast of Hurnsdom. Any attempt to reclaim these lands will be treated as an act of war, as will the mere presence of an armed force approaching our borders. All trading between the Empire and the kingdoms of Issalia will cease until amicable trade agreements have been negotiated with each nation.

"Furthermore, know that we have reinstated the Choosing ceremony and have formally outlawed the use of the dark magic tied to Chaos. Anyone found to have the inherent ability to channel Chaos will be imprisoned. Any demonstration of this forbidden magic inside our borders will be met with swift execution.

"Take heed of these warnings. They are the last you will..."

Brandt sneezed, drowning out the last word. Cassie's eyes grew wide and she gasped.

Her father's voice came from inside. "Did you hear something?"

Quick. Over the railing, Cassie sent to her brother.

She turned and stood upright, her stomach twisting at the odd lack of gravity she felt. Lifting a leg, she climbed over, unable to resist looking down. Five stories below, a courtyard waited – a drop that would undoubtedly kill under normal circumstances. Despite the knowledge that she had nothing to fear, her stomach twisted again, this time from anxiety.

With one foot securely on the ledge, she stepped onto it and pressed her back against the castle wall as her brother scrambled to join her. The moment when they had both tucked in the recess, the balcony door opened. The sound of boots on the balcony caused Cassie to hold her breath in silence. Motion loomed in her periphery when the shoulder of her father's black coat came into view. He reached out and put his hand on the railing, leaning over it to look down.

"Odd," Brock mumbled. "I thought I heard something."

He turned and his footsteps faded into his study. When the door clicked shut behind him, Cassie released her breath.

Thank, Issal, she sent to Brandt.

That was close.

Yes, she agreed. *Let's get back.*

Shuffling to her left, with her back against the castle wall, Cassie eyed her target – a balcony thirty feet away. When she could move no further, she leaped. With her heart in her throat, she floated up, arcing high before drifting down to grab ahold of the rail. She climbed over and turned to watch her brother jump impossibly far and land atop the rail, grinning as he caught his balance.

Show off, she sent.

Jealous, he replied.

Cassie turned from him, opened the glass-paned door, and entered the room with Brandt a step behind. She gasped and froze in place.

Her father stood beside the interior door with his arms crossed over his chest. The man was dressed in a gold-trimmed black coat with a gold and red starburst emblem on his left breast. Beneath his barely tamed brown hair was a furrowed brow, distorting the two runes that marked his forehead.

"Aren't you two supposed to be taking a test?" Brock's eyes shifted toward the woman in the corner, her mouth hanging open, her head tilted back as she snored. "And what happened to Master Padia?"

"Sorry, Father. We were just..."

Cassie stopped talking when his eyes narrowed. Her gaze tracked his, looking down at the rune traced on the back of her hand. She covered the symbol with her other hand, but it was too late.

"You were abusing your abilities," Brock said, his tone accusatory.

Cassie glanced at Brandt. *Do you have any ideas?*

No...not this time.

What do we tell him?

The truth, I guess.

Cassie sighed. "When we learned that Parker and Tenzi had arrived...we were curious."

"We were bored and were only seeking excitement," Brandt said. "You must admit, those two always have the best stories."

"And what of the story they told today?"

Cassie suddenly felt ashamed. "It's...sad. It sounds as if many people died."

Their father stared at them for a long moment before sighing. "You now approach your seventeenth summer. While I understand your curiosity and your desire to seek excitement, you two must realize when it is appropriate and when it is not." Brock moved closer and opened his arms. "Now come here and give me a hug."

Cassie smiled and stepped into one arm as her brother took the other. The man abruptly gripped the back of her tunic and lifted her off the floor, doing the same to her brother.

Brock smiled. "You should also realize the negative aspects of the augmentation you used. Reducing gravity's effect on yourself also means that you have less mass for others to deal with."

He opened his fists, releasing them as they lightly touched down to the floor.

"We would use another augmentation, but you have only taught us one other and...it's useless," Brandt complained.

"Your instruction remains limited because of hijinks like this." Brock shook his head. "The ability to wield Chaos can be wonderful or it can be terrible. That type of power comes with responsibility and requires thought behind each action. Until you two prove you have matured, you'll not learn another rune from me nor from your mother."

Cassie found her eyes on the floor. *We must do better*, she sent to Brandt. Surprisingly, she felt his shame through their bond. Sensing emotion from him was no surprise, but she couldn't recall him ever feeling ashamed at his actions. And, Issal knows, he had done some very shameful things.

A loud snore came from the woman in the chair, drawing everyone's attention.

Brock frowned as he stared at the Padia. "What did you do to her?"

Cassie glanced at Brandt, who answered, "We put sleeping powder in her tea."

"As I suspected," Brock sighed. "What of your tests?"

Brandt shrugged. "Oh, we finished those by the time she fell asleep."

"I'm not surprised," their father said. "You two are clever, almost to the point of absurdity. Someday, you will learn to channel that cleverness into something positive."

He moved toward the door, opening it as the sleeping woman snorted a particularly loud snore. "Wake her up and apologize for your actions. The woman cares for you and does all she can to educate you. She deserves better."

The door closed, leaving Cassie and Brandt alone with their lore instructor.

2

RIVALRY

P ain throbbed from Brandt's nose and made his eyes water. He wiped it and found a streak of blood on the back of his hand. His gaze shifted to his opponent. A year older and slightly taller, the teen smiled, the look in his blue eyes one of confidence.

"What's wrong, little brother?" Broland smiled. "Having second thoughts?"

"Not at all. In fact, I have you exactly where I want you."

Broland grimaced. "Don't try to get in my head. I'll not let you goad me."

"Who says I'm not already in there, wading through the muck?"

The two teens edged toward each other, warily holding their fists up and ready. Broland's left hand lashed out and Brandt dodged. A jab with the right followed, which Brandt countered, striking Broland in the mouth. Broland stumbled back and wiped his lip, glancing down at the streak of blood on his fingers. His eyes narrowed and he shifted forward.

A fist flashed toward Brandt and he dodged. When the other fist drove toward Brandt's head, he twisted and grabbed his brother's wrist, bending at the waist and lunging to toss him over his back. Broland slammed into the dirt with a grunt and Brandt dove on top in an attempt to pin him to the floor, but Broland pushed him away before he got a grip.

As the two teens climbed to their feet, Broland rushed forward, slammed into Brandt, and drove him to the ground. A crack of pain ran through Brandt's head when it hit the dirt. Spots blotted his vision and he squirmed, rolling his shoulder up until he was on his stomach with Broland on top. Brandt gasped for air, blinked to clear his vision, and fought past the throbbing in his head.

Brandt pushed up, straining to lift himself off the floor with his brother on his back. Broland wrapped his arm about Brandt's neck and began to squeeze. With ragged breaths, Brandt strained as he regained his footing. Lifting his fist high, he drove his elbow backward into Broland's stomach, eliciting a grunt. Yet, the strangle hold did not loosen.

Brandt lumbered forward, dragging Broland with him step by step until he neared the wall. As expected, Broland changed tactics and pushed Brandt forward, seeking to drive him into the wall. Brandt pulled down hard while holding his brother's arm, and Broland's head hit the wall with a crack. The arm loosened and Brandt scrambled free. In the background, he heard his mother gasp.

Broland stumbled with his hand to his head. When he lowered it, Brandt found his brother's forehead torn open, blood dripping down. Before Broland could recover, Brandt spun and kicked backward, striking Broland in the midriff and causing him to bend forward. He threw a roundhouse punch, striking Broland square in the temple. The teen spun in a full circle and fell to his knees, wobbling and blinking in pain.

Wharton's voice rang out. "Match."

Brandt turned toward the man and beamed. "I won! I finally beat him!"

The captain clapped Brandt on the shoulder. "Yes. You possess your father's quickness, but you must remember to keep a distance from larger opponents. They can use their weight to overwhelm you."

Brandt turned to find his mother kneeling beside his brother with her hand on his arm. Broland inhaled a deep gasp, and a telling shiver shook his body when the gash on his head weaved shut.

Cassie moved close to Brandt, looking him in the eye. "Do you want me to heal you?"

"That would be wonderful if you can manage it."

"Have you been practicing your mediation, Cassilyn?" Ashland asked.

Cassie rolled her eyes. "Yes, Mother."

"Remember to remain calm," Ashland said. "Order is nothing like Chaos. You need to find your center, your own source of Order, before you can find your brother's."

"I know, Mother." Cassie put her hand on Brandt's forehead and closed her eyes.

He waited patiently, his head pounding in time with the beat of his heart. A full minute elapsed, and he was prepared to make a snide remark until he saw his mother glaring at him. The look on her face left his words unsaid. A wave of icy cold wracked his body, driving the air from his lungs and leaving him gasping for air. His headache was gone, his nose no longer sore.

"I did it!" Cassie blurted, turning toward her mother. "I did it!"

Ashland smiled and put her arms around Cass, hugging her tightly. "Yes, you did. I knew you had it in you." She released the girl and stared her in the eye. "Now that you have performed healing, it will become easier each time you do it."

While Brandt knew he should be happy for his sister, frustration surfaced. She must have noticed his frown.

Don't worry, Cassie sent to him. *You'll figure it out, too. Look how long it took me to make it work.*

Brandt sighed audibly. *I'm sure you're right. I'm sorry. I'm proud of you.*

And I of you…for finally beating Broland.

Brandt smiled. "I did finally beat him."

"You cheated," Broland grumbled.

"What?"

"Yeah. When you smashed my head into the wall."

"You tried to do it to me first."

Broland grimaced, but didn't respond.

Wharton gripped both boys by the shoulder, squeezing hard enough to make them wince.

"While such tactics appear unseemly, fighting is seldom a gentlemanly affair." The captain of the king's elite guard looked from Brandt to Broland. "If your life is on the line, you must be willing to do anything to overcome your opponent."

Broland nodded. "I understand."

"Good. If anything happens to your parents, you'll find yourself with a crown on your head. I can think of nothing that makes a better target for enemies than a crown."

Brandt's eyes locked with his sister's, but he kept his thoughts to himself. Oftentimes, he felt jealous of his brother's defined role as crown prince – the attention, the preferential treatment, the prestige. Then, there were times like this where he was reminded how much he valued the freedom of not having a crown hovering over his head.

3

THE SKY

"Turn around so I can see how you look." When Brandt turned toward her, Cassilyn smirked. "Aww. You're so pretty. If I was into girls, I might want to kiss you."

Brandt's brow furrowed. "But you're my sister."

Cassie laughed. "You know what I mean."

He chuckled. "Yeah, I do."

"This dress is even better than the last." Cassie eyed the skirts, yellow and ruffled. Her gaze rose and found curves, the chest stuffed to fill it out. Long curls fell over Brandt's shoulders, black and glistening, partially covering his face. "And the wig, where did you get it?"

"I found it in Duchess Illiri's room when she was here this winter." He couldn't contain his grin.

"You stole it? She had to notice."

"Oh, I'm sure she did. However, I knew she wouldn't make a fuss. To do so would have told everyone that her hair is fake." He chuckled again. "Illiri is far too vain to let that news out."

"True," Cassie agreed.

"Besides, she had two other wigs."

Brandt spun about, sending his skirts flaring with the twirl. Cassie suspected that he secretly enjoyed wearing the dress. It had been his suggestion, both this time and last. He grabbed a short black cloak and slipped it over his shoulders before pulling the hood up. When he turned toward her, his face was shadowed.

"How do I look?" he asked.

"While you look the part, your voice is too low."

Two octaves higher, he asked. "How do I look? Am I beautiful?"

When he batted his lashes and pouted, she laughed in response. "You are a vision to behold."

With his voice still high, he chimed, "Good. Now, let's be off."

He opened the parlor room door and peeked out before stepping into the hall. With an over-exaggerated sway to his hips, Brandt sauntered toward the door that led to the square outside the castle. Cassie turned, hurried down the corridor, and darted out the side door.

The courtyard beside the castle was covered in shadows, the sun now low, painting the clouds in orange and red hues. Sliding her hand from the sleeve of her gray cloak, Cassie examined the rune she had drawn, ensuring that every line was true, solid. She shut her eyes and latched onto the anxiety in her stomach, feeding it until she sensed a tumultuous energy surrounding her. With her mind, she reached toward the Chaos, embracing it as it came flooding in. Instantly flush from the heat of the raging storm in her veins, Cassie opened her eyes and stared at the rune on her wrist. Before the dam inside her burst, she opened it and let the energy flow out, into the rune. It glowed bright red, pulsed briefly, and faded.

A wave of exhaustion hit her, almost causing her to stumble. Her stomach then flipped as gravity loosened its grip. If not for the weight of her boots, the cloak, and the pack she carried over her shoulder, she knew that she would float into the air and be carried inland by the ocean breeze. She eased forward and peered around the corner.

Brandt, dressed as a woman in a black cloak and yellow dress, sauntered toward the guards at the gate. From across the plaza, Cassie heard a male soldier greet Brandt.

"Hello, miss."

"My," Brandt answered in his high voice. "King Brock employs such handsome guards."

"Um…Thank you…what's your name?"

"April. My name is April."

The other guard approached Brandt. A woman. By her posture, Cassie knew it would be trouble.

"Is that so, Miss April? I don't recall seeing anyone named April on the list of guests."

Brandt stopped and put his hands on his hips, feigning frustration. "Are you calling me a liar?" His head bobbed side-to-side with expressed attitude. "Do you not think I know my own name?"

The woman stepped closer. "I think your lies extend far beyond your name." She grabbed Brandt by the arm and reached for the hood, which he held tight.

"Help! Help! I'm being accosted!" Brandt screamed, sounding amazingly like a girl.

Cassie looked toward the wall and found the guards stationed atop it had shifted toward the main gate, both now watching the commotion below.

Brandt's voice rang in her head. *Now, Cass. Go now!*

She gritted her teeth, took a breath, and darted forward. Glancing to the side as she ran, Cassie saw the woman tear Brandt's cloak away, the wig coming with it. Brandt cried out and fell to the ground, flailing about like a fish on shore. All eyes were on him as laughter came from the guards.

Cassie turned to look at the wall, crouched, and leaped. Charged by a rune that left her at a fraction of her normal weight, her jump launched her up and over the three-story tall wall.

Rooftops came into view as she cleared the wall, covered in red-tinted clay tiles. She hit one of such roofs, tumbled across it, and fell off the far side. Her momentum carried her across the street and she struck the second story window of a house, her hands pressed against it as she faced the surprised children playing in the room. Then, she fell backward, snagged her foot on a planter, and spun to land face-down on the street.

She lay there for a moment, gathering her thoughts and thanking Issal that she had survived unharmed. When she rolled over, she found a man and a woman staring down at her.

"Where did you come from?" the man asked.

Cassie climbed to her feet and dusted off her breeches. "I was riding a cloud and saw the city below. It seemed interesting, so I decided to drop in for a visit."

The man's mouth hung open, and he turned to the woman, who had paled.

"What? A cloud?" he muttered as he peered up at the scattered puffy clouds overhead.

"I must be going. I have some shopping to do before the next cloud comes by." She waved to them and started down the street. "I don't want to miss it. There might not be another until tomorrow, and I have an appointment to keep in Sol Polis."

Cass resisted the urge to smile, instead filing the confused looks into a vault. *I have a story for you,* she sent to Brandt.

It better be good. I am on my way to Wharton's office, in trouble for another escape attempt.

Keep him busy. I'll be back inside an hour, before my augmentation weakens.

She had no worries. If Brandt possessed any skill, it was resourcefulness. She was good at scheming, but she considered him the master.

The street came upon an intersection with a larger street. As the main artery through the heart of Kantar, Center Street was also the hub of city business. Accordingly, the traffic thickened with people afoot and a passing carriage. Since she was still close to the citadel, the shops that lined the street were among the finest. Cassie knew that goods sold in the lower portion of the city were less refined, but she didn't need to visit that district. She followed Center Street past two more intersections and turned right after passing Finley's Fine Jewels. After a trio of doors that led to second-story apartments, she found a shop to her left and an Inn to her right. Above the shop was a sign marked *Andagan's Apothecary*. She approached the door and entered.

The waiting area stood empty, as was the counter that separated her from the front portion of the shop, consisting of a desk and rows of shelving that ran from the front to the back. When nobody greeted her, she rang the bell that sat on the counter.

"Just a moment," an old voice called from a back room.

A man emerged, shuffling down the center aisle with the aid of a cane, his wrist shaking with each step. The sight made her think of

General Budakis, the man suffering the after effects of an assassination attempt.

"Hello, young miss. What do I owe the pleasure?" the old man croaked.

Cassie gave him a smile. "I'm here for something to chase away the pain of life. Something that might…open one's senses to the sky."

The man frowned. "Why would a fine young lass like yourself need such an escape?"

"Oh, the drug is not for me," Cassie assured him. "It's for my uncle. He is in a bad way, in pain all the time from an old back injury."

The man gave a slow nod. "Very well. Even if I had such a drug, it would surely be quite expensive."

Withdrawing her coin purse, Cassie dumped a gold piece and five silvers on the counter, watching the man's eyes the entire time. His greed was apparent as he stared at the gold.

"Yes. Well, that would be enough for a small jar."

Cassie smiled. "Perfect."

The man gave her a nod, turned, and hobbled off to the back room. Moments later, he reappeared with a jar in his free hand, leaning on the cane in the other as he approached the front of the store.

"May I inquire, good sir…what happened to you? What malady leaves you using a cane this way?"

His frown returned. "It isn't proper manners to ask such questions."

Cassie smiled. "That's fine. I'm not a proper girl."

A huff of displeasure came from the man. "It was a thief."

"A thief?"

Grimacing, the man put the vial on the counter. "Yes, roughly twenty years ago. Stole my savings and left a scorpion behind. The critter caught me unaware. I'd be dead if I hadn't had the antidote in store and nearby."

With the swipe of his free hand, the man scooped up the coins. She gave him a nod and grabbed the jar, slid it into her coin purse, and secured it to her belt.

"Thank you, sir." She turned and opened the door. "Have a good evening."

When Cassie stepped outside, she found the sun had dropped

below the horizon, the sky growing darker. She hurried down the street, eager to return to the castle before someone discovered her absence.

Up Center Street, she went, weaving through traffic and avoiding looking anyone in the eye. Before drawing too close the gate, she turned down a side street and began seeking a way up. At the fourth house – the building next door to the one whose roof she had tumbled across – she found a second story balcony. With a leap, she cleared the balcony rail and almost tumbled over the far side. She righted herself and looked down to find a startled woman across the street, standing in her doorway with a pot of water in her hands. Cassie waved to the woman, climbed up on the balcony rail, and jumped. Her leap took her to the woman's rooftop, where she stumbled before regaining her footing. Without pause, she ran toward the citadel wall, easily twelve feet above her and twenty feet from the back of the house. A hearty leap launched her over the wall. As she sailed through the air and drifted toward the courtyard on the other side, she prayed that none of the castle guards happened to be looking in her direction.

4

THE GAME

A grunt escaped as Brandt scrubbed away the baked-on cheese. The stuff seemed to have bonded with the pan, refusing to let go. After a rinse of hot water and another round of diligent scrubbing, accompanied by yet another rinse, he examined the pot and decided it was clean. He placed it on the drying rack and wiped his hands with a towel.

When Brandt emerged from the scullery and into the kitchen, he found Sally and Vernes, the head cook, in quiet discussion. The room was otherwise empty.

"All finished, Grandma," Brandt announced as Sally turned toward at him. "This is my last day, so Bemini needs to return to work tomorrow evening."

"Very well, dear," Sally smirked. "While I would hope that a month of washing the dinnerware might teach you a lesson, you seem to spend almost as many evenings in the scullery as she does."

Brandt shrugged. "It's not so bad. Washing can be tedious, but it leaves time for me to think."

"Oh, my," Sally said with exaggerated alarm. "What new schemes have you come up with now?"

Brandt laughed. "I'm not always scheming, Grandma."

She guffawed, "You've been scheming your entire life, boy. While I hope you'll outgrow it, your little escapade in the dress proves that it hasn't happened, yet."

He responded with a shrug.

"Now, come here and give me a hug," Sally held her arms open.

He leaned forward and hugged the woman, having to bend down to meet her shoulders. When she released her embrace, she smiled.

"I saved you a piece of dessert."

Brandt grinned. "Dessert *does* sound good."

She grabbed a towel from the counter and unwrapped it, revealing a tube-shaped pastry with red sauce oozing from one end.

When he accepted the gift, he found it still warm. "Thank you, Grandma."

"You are welcome. Now, run along and try to find something to do that won't cause trouble."

"Don't worry. I'm off to Gunther's room for a game of Ratio Bellicus."

"Good. There's something to keep your mind occupied."

Brandt slipped out the door as he took a bite of the warm pastry. The crust was flaky and the fruity sauce inside full of flavor, leaving him smacking his lips as he headed toward the stairwell.

While ascending, he heard footsteps coming from above. Turning the corner was Chief Magistrate Filbert, dressed in the black robes of his office. The old man's wispy white hair wavered with each step, his wrinkled face in a grimace.

"Hello, Magistrate." Brandt paused at the landing to allow the man past him.

With the briefest of inflections, he paused to reply with naught but a breath, "My Prince." The man then swept past Brandt, his robes billowing behind him as he turned at the next landing and faded from view.

I wonder if that man has ever been happy, Brandt thought. With a shrug, he took another bite and continued upward.

A glowlamp on the low table lit the game board, the figures upon it casting shadows that flickered in the light of the fireplace. The map was one that Brandt hadn't yet tested, the field upon it divided into three areas by a deep, snaking ravine. Five bridges crossed the ravine, creating defensible choke points and a different twist to gameplay strategy.

Brandt watched General Budakis while the man surveyed the board. His bald head was smooth, shining in the blue light of the glowlamp, his graying goatee and eyebrows the only hair on his head. His cane leaned against the sofa, and his left hand remained curled to his chest. It had been years since Brandt had seen the old general use that hand in a functional manner. When Budakis reached toward the board, his right arm spasmed for a moment before it settled. The man grabbed a cavalry unit and moved forward nine spaces.

"Cavalry strikes your archer," Budakis said before tossing a pair of dice.

The melee attack put Brandt's archer at a disadvantage, so he threw one die and hoped for luck. It did not happen. With only two life disks remaining, his archer was defeated and removed from the board.

Reaching forward, Brandt moved an infantry unit forward three spaces, blocking the path to the bridge near his captain. Wincing, he pulled his hand back and stared at his thumb. His cut had reopened.

"What happened to your thumb?"

A frown crossed Brandt's face. "I cut myself in the scullery while washing a butcher's knife."

"You could have it healed, you know." Budakis moved an archer forward, beside one of his own infantry units that blocked another bridge.

"It doesn't hurt much."

The man stared at him for a long moment. "Why do you do it?"

"Do what, Gunther?" Brandt moved an arcanist up the edge of the board.

"Why continue to test your parents' patience? I assume you don't enjoy your time in the scullery." The man moved a cavalry unit beside another of Brandt's archers. "Cavalry attacks archer."

"It isn't that I actually enjoy getting into trouble." Brandt rolled one die while Gunther rolled two of them. "I guess I enjoy the challenge." He frowned at the roll with Gunther taking another of Brandt's pieces from the board. "I find that I also enjoy…the process, planning it all out and trying to predict my opponents' moves."

"Opponents?"

With Brandt's arcanist now exposed, he moved an infantry unit to guard it, joining another that protected the magic user.

"Well, that's how I see it. I have a plan, and they want to stop the plan."

Gunther moved his cavalry unit past his men, advancing toward his captain. "Libra Te is coming soon. I'm sure your father will warn you to restrain yourself."

Brandt smiled at the memory. "That day marks some of my best pranks."

"True." The general chuckled. "I clearly recall the year you released the greased pig in the crowd. Then, there was that time you dropped the fake body from the balcony over the platform while your father addressed the crowd. It dangled above his head for a good ten seconds before he realized why everyone was screaming."

The memories only made Brandt's grin wider. "Don't forget the year I put the dye in Burtles' shampoo."

The man's mirth dried up instantly. "To tell the truth…I recall very little of that year."

Brandt stopped mid-chuckle, his eyes turning away. "Sorry, Gunther. I forgot about the assassination attempt."

"I wish I could forget." He lifted his hand and held it before his eyes. It twitched for a short spell and then settled again.

Images of the moment flashed in Brandt's head as the game board before him blurred. An assassin in the crowd. Brandt's father diving atop his mother and driving her to the floor. The blade sailing past the couple to strike Budakis. The general going to the floor, his mouth foaming as his body convulsed. Brandt's mother urgently attempting to heal the man. Budakis had come within a breath of dying that day… from a poisoned blade intended for Brandt's father.

When Brandt's eyes lifted, he found Gunther staring at him.

"Regardless, I suggest that you put Libra Te aside this year. Just allow things to go as planned. Your father has enough on his mind without worrying about what you might do."

Brandt nodded. "Fair enough. I'll not sully Libra Te this year. I promise."

Gunther smiled, his grin somewhat frightening. "I'm glad to hear it."

Brandt tapped on his arcanist game piece. "Arcanist gives this infantry unit a Power augmentation."

Budakis frowned. "You do know your magic user is now immobile for five turns."

Rather than respond, Brandt stared at the board and waited. Budakis moved an archer into position. "Archer fires on arcanist."

They each rolled, with Budakis winning. Brandt removed three life disks from his arcanist, leaving only two remaining. One more attack and he would be dead. He reached for the augmented infantry unit, lifting the game piece over the gorge and placing it ten squares away, beside his opponent's captain.

"Infantry attacks captain."

The man grimaced and grabbed two dice while Brandt rolled all four, earning him a winning roll of fourteen to ten.

Budakis slid six yellow disks from his captain. "That hurts, but it leaves my captain with four health."

A smile crossed Brandt's face as he lifted the infantry unit, revealing the black disk he had slid into the base before the game began. "Not against my assassin. I win."

5

TOO FAR

C assie eyed herself in the mirror, twisting her head for a better view of the bun at the back, secured with a green ribbon that matched her dress. A few rebellious brown curls hung loose, just enough to suit her. She spun around and held her arms out.

"What do you think?"

Ashland smiled. "You look gorgeous, Cass. I can't believe how fast you've grown." She rubbed a tear away. "My baby is becoming an adult."

Cassie's brow furrowed. "Baby? Brandt is only a few minutes older than I am. Even Broland is only a year older."

Her mother moved closer and cupped Cassie's cheek. "Sorry, dear. You will always be my baby."

A sigh and an exaggerated eye roll from Cassie elicited a chuckle from her mother. Ashland pulled her close for a hug and then stepped back. "Perhaps you should pull the dress up just a tad. It's better to leave more to the imagination."

Cassie eyed her mother's black dress, the neckline low enough to expose a little cleavage. "What about your dress, Mother?"

"I'm a grown adult...and I'm the queen. It is my prerogative if I want to express my womanhood."

"Fine." Cassie executed another eye roll while making the requested adjustment.

After settling her crown into her brown curls, Ashland headed toward the door. "We should go or we will be late for dinner. You don't want to upset Burtles...or your grandmother."

She held the door open, and Cassie stepped into the hallway. "Is Grandma Sally joining us for dinner?"

Ashland closed the door and turned toward the stairs. The two guards at the top of the stairs followed as mother and daughter descended. "No. She and Milan will eat with my parents. Our table will be full with the visitors."

A flicker of anxiety knotted Cassie's stomach. This was the first eve of Libra Te that she and Brandt were to dine with the royalty of Kantaria. While Cassie had met each of the Dukes and Duchesses, she did not know them well. Most had only been to Kantar during the annual meeting, and she had yet to visit any of the other duchies. She began to question Brandt's plan. While the prank was epic in concept, the reality of it approaching left her uncertain of the repercussions – whatever they may be.

Down the stairs they continued, not stopping until the third landing. Ashland and Cassie then led the two guards down a hall lined with ornate paintings and lit by glowlamps in sconces every ten strides. After passing a series of closed doors, they came upon a pair of doors that stood open, a hum of conversation carrying through them.

The king's dining hall was a spacious room, occupied by a long table down the center and an arched fireplace along one wall. Glowlamps on a chandelier over the table lit the room, bathing it in soft blue light.

Ashland paused just inside the doorway and gestured for Cassie to take a seat. Of the six chairs at the near side of the table, only the farthest one remained unoccupied. Cassie headed toward the chair and sat beside Brandt, giving a nod to those who paused their conversation to glance in her direction.

I was wondering when you would get here, Brandt sent.

Women require more time to prepare for this sort of thing. What do you have to do? Wet your fingers and rake your hair to the side?

Jealous.

Show off.

Cassie then recalled their plan, the thought sending a flutter in her stomach. She turned toward Brandt and found him grinning. In the chair beyond him, she spied Broland in conversation with Duke Harvin of Port Choya. The duke's wife, Filma, and his daughter, Halima, sat beside him. Filma was conversing with Duchess Illiri while Illiri's husband, Duke Chadwick of Wayport, whispered something to the overweight man beside him. Jerious, the duke of Sunbleth, chortled at the man's comment, his jowls flapping as his head bobbed.

Sitting beside Jerious was the man's likewise overweight son, Hurien. A year older than Cassie, the boy seemed more fixated on her each time they had met. As she suspected, Hurien stared at her, his face in a grin that turned her stomach upside down. Worse, he was seated directly across from her chair, and Cassie feared that his unwashed smell might spoil her appetite.

The sound of a throat clearing called everyone's attention toward the door. A man, with white hair and a waxed mustache to match it, stepped into the room.

Burtles said aloud, "Presenting…King Brock and Queen Ashland, the rulers of Kantaria and your gracious hosts for this evening."

Conversation stopped as everyone stood to receive the king and queen. The head of the castle staff moved aside, and the couple emerged from the corridor, arm in arm. Brock wore a fine black doublet, trimmed in gold with a gold belt to match. Bright red rubies on the belt reflected the flickering light from the fireplace. His hair was properly combed, and the crown of Kantaria, gold with a red starburst of rubies at the heart, rested upon his head, matching the one that Ashland wore upon hers. Her brown curly hair was tied in a bun atop her head, and a pair of carefully chosen curls dangled beside her ears. Ashland smiled at Brock, her bright blue eyes meeting his green ones. They entered the room, Brock walking Ashland to the far end of the table before he pulled out her chair. She eased in front of it and gave him a nod of thanks before he strolled to the other end of the table.

Brock slid in front of his chair and smiled. "Thank you for joining us. I rather enjoy our yearly get-togethers. Please, sit." He sat and everyone at the table did likewise, some with more grace than others. "Burtles," Brock called over his shoulder. "Please bring us some wine."

The man with the white hair bowed, holding his white-gloved hand to his chest. "Very well, Sire."

Burtles clapped his hands and two stewards entered, a man and a woman – the man in a black dinner coat and white tunic, the woman in a black dress with a white apron. The man leaned over the table and poured deep red liquid into Brock's chalice while the woman did the same into Ashland's cup. Both Cassie and Brandt held their hands over their cups, indicating that the woman pass them.

When the woman filled Broland's cup, Brandt elbowed him. "Why didn't you cover your cup?"

"I'm an adult now. I'll drink wine if I choose to do so." Broland's voice carried a haughty tone.

Brandt snorted. "Suit yourself...exalted Prince of puffiness."

Cassie bit her lip in an attempt to restrain a grin, a battle that she lost when Chadwick chuckled at the comment. His wife, Illiri, gave him an icy look, and the man lifted his hand to his bearded face, hiding his mouth although his bobbing motion made it clear that he was laughing. When Cassie's gaze landed on her mother, she found Ashland glaring at Brandt – the look on her face speaking volumes. A third steward entered with a carafe of water, filling the cups of those who had passed on wine.

"So," Jerious said with his deep voice, "How does trade fare in Wayport these days, Chadwick? Have things slowed down for you as much as they have for me?"

Now recovered from his laughter, Chadwick took a sip of his wine and said, "Worse, I suspect. Nearly half of our port trade was with Kalimar. With the new regime in place, every eastern port from Yarth to Cinti Mor is barred from receiving Kantarian goods." Chadwick turned toward Brock. "My King. Please tell us that an accord will be struck soon."

Brock met the man's gaze, holding it for a lengthy period before responding. "I understand your concerns regarding trade with the eastern cities. However, I had no part in the current embargo. This... Empire...they appear to dance to the beat of their own drum and their motives are unclear to us. I have sent an envoy with a request to negotiate, but I have no response at this time."

After a sip of wine, Brock added, "Their extreme views against magic give me much concern, as does the nature in which they displaced the rulers of Vinacci, Hurnsdom, and Kalimar."

Duchess Filma put her hand on Brock's. "It will not lead to war, will it, Your Majesty?"

Glancing down, Brock flipped his hand and gripped hers. "I pray to Issal that it does not."

Illiri burped, drawing everyone's attention. "Oh, my." She covered her mouth with her hand. "Pardon me."

The woman appeared embarrassed and took an urgent drink of wine, emptying her glass. The steward stepped forward, filling the glass and then refilling the others around the table.

"Is it getting warm in here?" Jerious asked as he loosened the collar on his purple doublet.

"Does anyone hear that?" Duke Harvin asked.

Filma replied, "Hear what, dear?"

"That buzzing." He looked around, seeking the source.

With the wine carafes empty, the stewards left the room, trailed by Burtles, likely off to ensure dinner was on its way.

"I hear music," Ashland mumbled, the queen's eyes glazed… distant. "It sounds so lovely." She stood and turned from the table, swaying to some tune that Cassie could not hear.

"It's so bloody hot…" Jerious now had his doublet unbuttoned to his belt, struggling to free it. He pushed his chair back and feverishly worked at the belt.

A howl rang from the far end of the table. Cassie turned to find Filma down on the floor. From her hands and knees, the woman's face pointed toward the ceiling as she howled again. Her husband's chair tipped over backward, the man scrambling to swat at something only he could see. Their daughter rose from her chair with her eyes on Brandt.

Oh, no. Brandt's voice rang in Cassie's head.

Halima climbed over the fallen chair, almost stepping on her mother as the woman crawled beneath the table.

"Oh, Brandt," Halima held her hand to her breast. "I have missed you so."

The girl's arms opened wide as she stumbled to her knees.

Serves you right for your dalliance last Libra Te. Cassie sent to her brother as she scrambled from the girl.

He replied, *The girl is pretty enough, but she lacks personality – she has no spark.*

As Brandt backed away from the girl who shimmied across the floor on her knees, ruining her fine evening gown, Illiri climbed on her chair and then, onto the table, knocking her wine glass over.

"I am a pretty bird...the prettiest bird." Illiri thrust her ample chest out and bobbed her head while flapping her elbows.

Likewise, Broland climbed upon the table and began to strut. "No. *I* am the prettiest bird." He then began to cluck in time with his bobbed head, like a crowster attempting to impress a mate.

All the while, Chadwick laughed with raucous energy, slapping the table while his eyes watered. Cassie and Brandt joined the man's laughter.

"This is the best one, ever," Brandt said, chuckling as he looked about the room.

She was about to respond when she spotted Jerious, the pale skin of his vast body exposed but for his smallclothes. The man then laid down on the stone floor and began rolling around. "So much cooler...it feels so good."

Meanwhile, Brock had been sitting in a daze, staring into the air. He suddenly jumped back, his chair tipping to the floor with a thud. "Stay away. Don't make me hurt you!" he bellowed.

At that moment, Burtles entered the room. "What in the name of Issal is happening?"

His gaze swept from the king, attempting to defend himself against the fireplace, to the queen as she spun and danced to music only she could hear. Harvin swatted invisible flies and his wife howled like a cat in heat while his daughter crawled after Brandt. Broland had climbed onto the chandelier, clucking loudly. Illiri strutted on the table while Chadwick laughed so hard he fell out of his chair. Jerious began squirming across the floor, claiming to be a worm. His son just stared at Cassie with his tongue hanging out, drooling. Burtles then turned toward Brandt and Cassilyn, the bewilderment on his face morphing to a scowl.

"You miscreants caused this! What did you do to them?" Burtles howled.

What do we say? Cassie asked.

Let me take the lead.

Brandt shrugged. "Perhaps the wine had gone...bad?"

The deep red of the man's face was a stark contrast to his white hair and beard. "You'll not get away with your prank this time, young man. I know you two are behind this."

With that, he scurried out of the room and shouted for guards.

Cassie glanced at Brandt and wondered if things had gone too far. When her father kicked his leg into the fireplace and came away with his boot on fire, she gasped. Brock began shouting and kicking frantically, the flames only growing worse. She grabbed her water cup and Brandt's before running around the table. With a lunge, she poured them on the flames as her father hopped about the room. The king then tripped over Jerious, who still thought he was a worm, and his head hit the floor with a crack, sending his crown rolling across the room. Cassie hurried to her father's side and began to seek her center.

Long, slow breaths calmed her as she ignored the commotion around her. Deep inside herself, she found the soft blue presence of her own source of Order – her life force. Through her contact with her father, she extended her consciousness toward him and found his source of Order, dim and damaged. Bright red, angry symbols stirred within his head and his foot, while dimmer ones churned throughout his body. Using her will, she stoked his life force and commanded it to smother the red symbols, drowning them with the blue light until they dissipated to nothing.

Brock gasped, a shiver wracking his body. Cassie opened her eyes as he sat up and looked about the room.

A deep voice bellowed. "What is happening here?"

Wharton entered the room with Burtles and a pair of guards. The captain of the king's guard bent down and picked up Brock's crown, frowning at it before glancing toward Brock.

With certain dread, Cassie knew their little prank had, indeed, gone too far.

6

THE ARCANE WARD

C assie fidgeted with her hands on her knees. The sofa vibrated steadily, shaken by the constant movement of her brother's fidgeting feet pumping up and down as they waited in quiet. The two siblings were trapped in the sitting area of their parents' bedroom suite, caught between their pacing father and the glare from their mother. A glance to the side found Brandt's fingers tapping his thighs and she reached out to him.

How long will they make us sit here?

This is some sort of sadistic torture, Brandt sent. *I suspect the penance for our actions will be something beyond washing dishes. Otherwise, we would be on our way to the kitchens by now.*

A chance glance toward her mother lasted a mere moment when she saw Ashland staring at her from the opposing sofa. Her eyes shifted toward her father, still pacing before the fireplace with his hands clasped behind his back, as he had been doing since they were first called to the royal suite. The room had been dimly lit by the rising sun at the time, but now it was as bright as mid-day. Cassie was unsure of how long they had been waiting, but each passing minute had been excruciating.

Brock finally stopped and stared at Ashland. Her parents' eyes met, and Cassie sensed something pass between them unsaid. When

Ashland nodded, she turned toward the two teens and cleared her throat.

"You two are aware that those who have a high affinity with Order can use it to heal others. Cassie has already performed this miracle, and I suspect it is simply a matter of time before Brandt can do it as well."

Cassie sent, *Why is she talking about this?*

Brandt shrugged.

Ashland smiled briefly before continuing. "What you do not know is that Order can be used in other ways. The magic can manifest numerous abilities, some that are more common than healing. The simplest such skill related to Order is divining, a method of seeking inherent talents that reside inside an individual. Beyond that, Order can unleash various forms of prophecy, ranging from near-term glimpses into our own future to powerful visions of world-changing events in a more distant future.

"Of course, there are other skills that are far less common." She looked at Brock again. "Rumors are that Tantarri elders possess the ability to walk among dreams, and, along with that skill, share visions with other individuals. Then, of course, there is telepathy."

Cassie glanced at her brother. "Telepathy?"

Ashland replied, "The term refers to individuals who are able to communicate with their minds, regardless of distance."

Cassie's mouth dropped open, and her brother gasped.

Their mother leaned forward and placed her hands on the short table between them. "You two possess this ability, don't you?"

When Cassie turned toward Brandt, she found him chewing on his lip. *How do they know?*

I'm not sure. Perhaps they don't know, he replied. *Perhaps they are just guessing.*

The ability had been their secret for years…something that Cassie had always wished to keep secret. Now, she found herself pressed to reveal it and was reluctant to do so…even to her own parents.

Ashland sat back and crossed her legs while resting her hand upon her knee. "I sense your reluctance to admit what you can do. Trust me, I understand. Not only is the skill exceedingly rare, but it is also some-thing you *should* keep private. You see, there are very, very few people who are aware of what your father and I can do. The less who know, the better."

Brandt frowned. "What do you mean?"

Brock stopped pacing and responded. "Your mother is trying to tell you that we can communicate telepathically."

Cassie gasped as it hit her. The silent looks between her parents, the consistency of the two sharing the same opinion, those times where Brock and Ashland had outmaneuvered the schemes Cassie and Brandt had conceived...they had been communicating telepathically... just as she did with Brandt.

"Wait a minute," Brandt said. "You two aren't even related by blood. How can you do this?"

Ashland shook her head. "Blood relation isn't relevant. The ability manifests when two people possess a strong ability with Order and develop a close relationship...*very* close."

That's why we can do it, Cassie thought.

Now it makes sense, Brandt agreed. *I'm going to tell them.*

Cassie didn't respond. She could tell that his mind was set, and she knew that nothing could stop him once that happened.

"It began about seven years ago," Brandt said, his tone one of telling a longer tale. "Remember when I crawled through that high window into that storage room in the dungeon level? When I dropped into the dimly lit room, I never dreamed that the door would be bolted shut with no way to open it from the inside. I tried to stack items into a tower so I could climb out the window, but the crates and chair I used crumbled from my weight, the wood old and rotted.

"I then pounded on the door and screamed as loud as I could. Hours passed, and after screaming myself hoarse, I sat on the floor and cried for a long time. A realization came upon me as I considered the situation. Based on the condition of the junk down there, I feared that years might pass before anyone happened upon me. I saw my own dust-covered bones on the floor and I became...desperate. Closing my eyes, I reached out for the person I knew best – my twin. For some time, I thought it a trick of my imagination when she actually responded.

"Of course, Cass didn't hear me yelling with her ears. She heard me in her head. Over this connection – which I still didn't believe was real

– I told her what had happened and where I was. She concocted the story you already know, using it to lead Wharton to the room and he freed me."

Cassie stared at Brandt while he told the tale, it ending with him looking her in the eyes. She turned toward her mother and bared herself. "Once we had done it, speaking to each other with our minds became…normal. I often do it without even realizing that I didn't open my mouth. There were even times I feared others discovering our secret when we would have a private conversation that I thought was said aloud."

Brock moved to the sofa and sat beside Ashland. "This ability you have…it is special. Very special. It is not something to squander, which is what you have done with your entire lives thus far."

Ashland grabbed his hand, squeezing it. "It's time for you two to grow up. This family is not like most others. We have a responsibility to the people of Kantaria…and even to people beyond our borders. Your older brother's role has always been clear, having been groomed his entire life to become the next king should anything ever happen to us. You two, on the other hand, seem to lack the direction required to take advantage of your abilities."

Brock patted her hand and took over. "You both are already strong in your ability to channel Chaos. The fact that you established the ability to communicate telepathically at such a young age shows that your potential to utilize Order is also likely to become quite powerful. And then, there is your endless scheming and pranks…something that is partly the fault of your mother and me."

Cassie's brow furrowed. "Your fault?"

The king nodded. "Yes. It demonstrates the need for more challenge in your lives. The instruction you have received while living at the castle has prepared you well, but it apparently came too easily. That will soon change."

Brock stood and again began to pace. "I have arranged transportation for you to go to Fallbrandt. There, you will find a new sense of purpose."

Brandt sat forward and looked at Cassie. She sensed his excitement through their bond. "We are to attend the magic academy?"

Brock paused his pacing and shook his head. "No. Not quite." He resumed pacing and continued to speak. "There is something else I must tell you, another secret you must hold close and share only with careful thought.

"Within the school is a highly restricted tower. We tell others that master arcanists live there, practicing magic – dangerous magic. Under this guise, other things occur, for it is the headquarters of a secret organization known as the Issalian Clandestine Operative Network, or ICON. You two will travel to Fallbrandt to join this group. There, they will train you to become wardens."

Cassie turned toward her brother with an odd feeling in her stomach, excited at the idea of traveling to Fallbrandt and experiencing something new, yet she felt apprehensive.

"What, exactly, is a warden?" Brandt asked.

Brock smiled. "You'll find out."

A frown crossed Cassie's face. "What's that supposed to mean?"

"It means that your precise role has not yet been defined. Regardless, you should know that your new home is a wondrous but dangerous place. Your past antics will not sit well there, and you had best respect the powerful magic and inventions you will be exposed to."

As Cassie considered her father's warning, she wondered what mysteries awaited them. "This place you mention – our new home. What else should we know about it? Does it have a name?"

"It is the home of the most powerful secrets mankind has ever discovered," Brock replied. "As for the name, ICON's headquarters is known as the Arcane Ward."

7

TRAINING

J acquinn Gulagus leaped. A whoop of joy emerged as she sailed up into the air at an incredible speed, reaching the apex of her jump four stories later. One hand reached out to grab a metal bar, and she swung herself forward to land on a platform thirty feet away. Without pause, she ran down a narrow beam, fifty feet above the Atrium floor. When she approached the end, she launched herself again. Up, she arced through rays of sunlight streaming through the windows above. The beams that supported the skylights drew closer until they were less than eight feet away, and then she began to descend. When she looked down, her breath caught in her throat. The drop was terrifying, deadly under normal circumstances. However, she was hardly normal at the moment.

She grabbed ahold of a thick rope that dangled from the ceiling, gripping it with one gloved hand as she swung forward. With her target in sight, she released her grip and flew toward it...to land upon the platform with a thud and a few quick steps to stop her momentum.

Already upon the platform stood an eighteen-year-old boy with a nest of black hair on his head. His most notable features were the contraptions strapped to his legs – mechanisms that gave him the ability to walk.

Quinn stood and beamed at her brother.

"Show off," Everson said.

Still grinning, Quinn responded. "You seemed overly proud of your new invention. I thought I would prove that there's a faster way to the twelfth floor."

He chuckled. "We don't all have the advantage of a Power augmentation. In fact, you will rarely have the ability yourself."

"I know. But the augmentation is so fun! It makes me feel invincible."

She thought of Iko, wishing she could face him while charged by Chaos magic. With such an advantage, it would be impossible for him to stop her. Losing to him in their duel during the TACT games still annoyed her. A sigh slipped out when she thought of Iko...and the murders he and Percy had committed. The sting of his betrayal had faded, but her resentment toward him had not. Nor had the tear he had rendered in her heart.

Everson's voice interrupted her thoughts.

"Would you like to be the first person to get a ride down?"

Quinn blinked, regained her focus, and smiled. "Sure, Ev. Jumping from this height while endowed with a Power rune probably won't kill me, but it may hurt...or even damage the floor."

Everson snorted. "I doubt it would damage the floor. Those tiles have all been Infused with an Elastic rune. They cannot crack, nor can they break."

"So you tell me. I can't say that I really I understand, but I trust you."

Rolling his eyes in response, Everson flipped the lever and it engaged with the rod that ran up the wall. The motor below began to whirl, joined by the squeaking of the massive pulleys above. The platform began to move downward at an even pace – the four ropes secured the platform rails moving with it.

Quinn turned and gazed out at the Atrium interior, brightly lit by the mid-day sun. The elevation platform that Everson had built stood in one corner of the indoor space, five hundred feet from the adjacent corners. The Jungle – an odd conflagration of beams, poles, and ropes – stood on the opposite side of the space. Rows of balconies slid past them as the platform drifted toward the Atrium floor – a grid of square stone blocks that appeared like a giant Ratio Bellicus board.

As they neared the bottom, the people waiting below came into view. Rena stood beside Masters Elias Firellus and Benny Hedgewick. The trio began clapping in applause, the sound growing louder as the platform slowed and stopped.

Quinn bowed and addressed them with a grin. "Thank you. I do what I can to impress my fans."

"Sorry, Quinn," Rena said with a wry smile. "The applause was for Everson's invention."

Her brother moved forward, his mechanical legs whirring as he opened the platform gate and descended the stairs with Quinn following behind.

Master Hedgewick patted Everson on the shoulder. "Well done, Everson. This lift will make trips to the upper levels much easier for everyone."

A grin formed on Everson's face. "Thank you, sir."

Elias grunted. "If anyone deserves thanks, it's you, my boy." He waved his cane about, pointing it toward the upper floors. "All the blasted stairwells have been my enemies since they built this place. Your lift is a gift from Issal himself, if you ask me."

Everson glanced toward his own legs. "Trust me. I understand, Sir."

Quinn understood her brother's reference. Having lived most of his life relying on braces to bolster his legs and canes to help him walk, Everson had a perspective few others could appreciate. However, his brilliance had solved that problem by inventing the mechanical legs… and by discovering the energy source that powered them.

Hedgewick pointed upward and asked, "What happens if someone down here needs to use the lift when the thing is at one of the upper floors?"

Everson glanced up. "I considered that. I plan to add a lever at the top and bottom floors that will enable a user to call the lift to them." He pointed toward the two chains of metal rods that ran up the length of the lift track. "Those metal rails are conductors for the Chaos that drives the lift. All I need to do is add a means to activate the down-ward drive at the bottom and the upward drive at the top."

Everson smiled. Hedgewick nodded at the idea while Elias shuffled up the steps to the lift. The expression on Rena's face informed Quinn that the girl was as clueless about the conversation as she was. Yet, Quinn was used to Everson speaking in that manner, as if engineering were a language unto itself, something beyond what normal people like her understood. Her thoughts drifted back to moments earlier, recalling her superhuman ascent to the top of the Atrium – a display that nobody would consider normal.

Hedgewick patted Everson on the back as they joined Elias on the lift. "I'll be interested to see your next application for Chaos Conduction."

Everson closed the gate and turned toward the control panel. "Well, the first Flyer upgrade should be ready in a few weeks. Flying should become far less work...and it may be faster as well."

The teen engaged the lever and the lift began to rise, the motor below the platform whirring as the pulleys lifted toward the upper floors. The conversation faded and Quinn turned toward Rena.

"I think I'll play for a bit. I have some time before the augmentation wears off, right?"

Rena nodded. "Yes. It should begin to fade around an hour after it was applied. Until then, have fun."

Quinn returned the girl's grin. "I will. And, thanks. I love this augmentation."

"It was my pleasure."

With a nod, Quinn leaped for a platform that waited forty feet above her.

A foot flashed toward Quinn's face. She ducked beneath it, spun and kicked, her boot grazing Nalah's backside. As she came around, the woman's fist lashed out and Quinn swatted it away while throwing a counterpunch that was blocked. They traded a flurry of blows, high and low, until Quinn grabbed Nalah's wrist and chopped down on the woman's arm with her elbow. Nalah grunted in pain, jabbed Quinn in the kidney twice, and tore her wrist free. When Nalah spun away, she held one arm close to her side, her face twisted in a grimace.

Quinn eyed her opponent and wiped her swollen lip, leaving a streak of red across the back of her hand. Nalah eased forward with caution, feinted with a spinning kick, completed the pirouette and leaped. Quinn's attempt to avoid the low kick left her open, and the woman's boot connected with her cheek, sending her spinning and stumbling to the Atrium floor. Landing on her hands and knees, Quinn shook her head clear and turned as Nalah kicked toward her midsection. Quinn spun away while swiping her hand beneath Nalah's boot, lifting hard enough to pull the young woman off balance. Nalah fell backward, rolled with her momentum, and stood as Quinn rose to her feet.

Pain throbbed in Quinn's cheek. Anger filled her for allowing the kick to connect, the fury reshaping itself into determination. With narrowed eyes, she eased toward her opponent and then burst forward. Leaping high into the air, she kicked as Nalah dodged to her right, protecting her injured side as Quinn had expected. Quinn had already pulled her kick in to ensure a stable landing. By the time Nalah, had spun about, Quinn's foot was sweeping low and connected with the woman's knee with a solid crunch. Nalah cried out as she collapsed, and Quinn dove on top of her.

"Match." Nalah said as tears clouded her eyes.

Quinn smiled as she stared down at the woman. "I won!"

"Yes. Now get off me," the woman replied between clenched teeth.

Rising to her feet, Quinn shifted away while Nalah clutched at her knee. The sound of applause attracted Quinn's attention. She looked up and found a man ten years her senior leaning over the nearest balcony – the one that led to his room.

Delvin stopped clapping and gave her a grin as his hands settled on the balcony rail. "You've improved, Quinn."

"When did you get back?" Quinn asked.

"Last night. Late."

Motion in her periphery caused Quinn to glance to the side as Rena strolled in and knelt beside Nalah. *It's nice not to be the one requiring healing*, Quinn thought before turning toward Delvin again.

"Where were you, anyway?"

He stood, smoothing his dark hair. "You know better than that."

She shrugged. "A girl can try."

That earned her a nod. "True. There are bits that I *can* tell you, but that will have to wait. I'm off to meet the others for a debriefing. We have some decisions to make."

Quinn frowned, her bloody lip responding with a twinge of pain. She had discovered an exhilaration from being included in secrets. Her exclusion felt quite the opposite. Since both were parts of her new life, she knew that she would have to take the good with the bad. However, accepting and knowing are not necessarily equivalent.

8

SECRETS

E verson Gulagus leaned over the table, sketching the plans for his next creation. As he scrawled the lines, his tongue stroked across his upper lip – a habit he had carried his entire eighteen years, a habit he seldom noticed. Warm afternoon sunlight streamed through the glass-paned balcony doors and lit the diagram before him. Slowly, the image in his mind began to form on the paper and excitement brewed inside him, forcing the pen to move faster and faster. Once he had traced the last line, he stared at the image in satisfaction.

Shaped like a disc with a short metal rod sticking from it, his invention began to crystalize – at least the prototype. Bent metal conduction strips ran from the rod to a glass encasement in the middle, where the Chaos-charged stone would sit. Staring at it sent his thoughts drifting back to the discovery and the events that led him there.

The secret to enchantment was the lure that had led Everson and Jonah to the ovens in the academy kitchens. The Heat runes inside the ovens gave them a clue, but when they tested the rune in the old quarry behind the academy, the rock had flared up with an intense heat that burned for over an hour and then subsided. All that remained was a blackened rock, so dark that it seemed to absorb all light. Weeks later, they returned to the same rock and tried again. With the second attempt, the rock itself drank the Chaos rather than it charging the rune. That stored energy remained weeks later and had led Everson to discover Chaos Conduction. The charged chunks or rock proved to be an immense power source...but not an endless one. The more power that was drawn, the faster the Chaos would expire, requiring a new charge or a new chunk of charged rock.

A knock on the door echoed in the recesses of his brain, the sound unable to penetrate his concentration. A second knock – louder this time – successfully intercepted his focus. He looked up, and his eyes shifted toward the rack he had built to hold his prized invention. The mechanical legs stood there, waiting for him to don them again. Hence, a trip to the door seemed rather inconvenient, so he answered from his seat.

"Who is it?"

A voice he knew well responded. "It's me. Can I come in?"

"Yes. The door is open."

The door swung open, and his sister entered the room. Matching him in height, she had an athletic build with lithe muscles and a confident gait. Her blond hair was two shades darker than normal, clearly wet. The girl's face was normally pretty, sharing expressions that ranged from a wry smile to a steely defiance. Instead, Quinn's face was marred by red and purple tones, her cheek swollen such that one of her blue eyes was barely visible.

"What happened to you?" he asked from the table.

She strode toward him, and as the lighting grew better, her appearance grew worse.

"I was sparring with Nalah earlier." Quinn pulled out a chair and sat with a grunt.

"Does her face look as bad as yours?"

"Oh, her face looked far worse before she was healed. I also broke her arm and destroyed her knee." When Quinn grinned, Everson saw a gleam of pride in her eye. "I'm finally getting it. The form of fighting Kwai-Lan teaches was difficult to learn. After ten weeks of frustration and all those times she beat me bloody, it was rewarding to get the better of the woman."

"If she was healed, why didn't you get healed as well?"

"Rena offered. Since there was no real damage, I told her *no*. Bumps and bruises will heal, given a few days." A grin crossed Quinn's face.

"Nalah didn't seem to like it much. I suspect she thinks I'm showing off, attempting to prove my toughness."

He snorted. "She doesn't know you that well if she thinks that. Everyone knows you're tough. However, *I* also know that you don't care what she thinks."

Quinn's grin grew wider. "True."

"So why do it? Why not let her heal you?"

She shrugged. "When I'm on a mission, I may not have access to a healer. I am choosing to get used to minor pain now, so I'm prepared to handle it in the future."

Everson stared at his sister as he considered the statement. He knew her well, better than anyone did. Quinn tended to walk a line between eagerness and boldness. Both had likely been gnawing at her over the past few days.

"You're anxious to be assigned a mission." He said it as a statement of fact.

Quinn nodded, showing no trace of her previous mirth.

He added, "It's driving you crazy that Chuli was selected for one first."

Again, she nodded.

"I'm sure you miss her. I miss Jonah as well," Everson sighed. "This apartment is nice, but living alone feels strange, even after just two days. Before coming to the academy, you and I roomed together our entire lives. Since then, I have roomed with Jonah for almost a year – ten weeks here in the Ward and far longer while at the academy."

"I do miss her." Quinn's gaze shifted toward the Atrium beyond the balcony. "And…I guess I understand why she was chosen for this mission. After all, she *is* the best with a bow. Delvin tells me to focus on developing my skills until I receive an assignment. All I can do is just continue training so I'm prepared when I am called upon. I just wish…I wish I knew when it was coming."

Everson looked down at the image on the paper. "When it comes, I hope that my next invention will be ready. If it works, it might be of help to you."

She leaned forward to peer down at his plans. "What is it?"

He shook his head. "You know better than that."

Quinn rolled her eyes. "Really? You and your secrets."

"Remember, we *do* work for a clandestine organization. Secrets are at the core of our very purpose."

"Yes, but not from each other."

He laughed. "Still, I prefer to unveil my inventions when they are complete and not before then."

Quinn turned toward the Atrium again. "The lift you created is quite impressive. You continue to find uses for your discovery."

"Chaos Conduction." The discovery frequently occupied Everson's mind. "Having access to an energy source like that changes everything. We can create things that move on their own...but that is just the beginning. I believe there are uses for it we have yet to discover."

"Well, if anyone can find a way, I place my bets on you."

"You are too kind...and you're my sister, which skews your perspective. The other gadgeteers here are brilliant as well. If they weren't, they wouldn't have been brought on as wardens."

The creations Everson had seen in the Forge still amazed him, as did the application of Chaos to enhance them. However, he had been tasked with finding ways to utilize Chaos Conduction and had not yet been exposed to the secret of enchanting. All he knew is that it remained among the most closely kept secrets in ICON.

Quinn pushed herself from the table and rose to her feet. "I need to rehearse for my next performance."

"I can't wait to see it."

Quinn snorted. "I hope I won't get tripped up by anything this time."

"You've improved each week. I'm sure you'll do great."

She gave him a sidelong glance as she headed toward the exit. "If you aren't busy, I will stop by in an hour and we can go to dinner together."

"I would be happy to join you. I've been feeling kind of lonely. With Jonah gone, the apartment seems so...empty."

Stopping with her hand on the door, Quinn said, "I wonder how they're doing...and if they're safe."

"I hope so, but the mission sounded dangerous. With more than a dozen deaths now tied to this thing, hunting it down and destroying it certainly seems necessary." Everson took a deep breath. "What worries me is that, sometimes, the hunter becomes the hunted."

9
VALLERTON

C huli Ultermane rolled her eyes as Jonah rattled on with his complaints.

"...think I will ever be able to sit again. Why don't they make these saddles with more padding?" he groaned.

Wyck, who rode at ease in the saddle, turned to look back at Jonah. "Are you sure you're a warden? If so, I didn't realize that we had ones who specialized in whining."

Chuli covered her mouth to hide her smile but the hunch of her shoulders revealed the laughter she tried to conceal. Over the past ten weeks, she had grown to like Everson's roommate. Two days of riding had erased much of that feeling. In obvious misery, Jonah's usual clever quips had been reduced to a string of complaints that wore on her – and, apparently, on Wyck as well. Somehow, Thiron seemed to ignore the boy.

Amazingly, Jonah didn't reply to Wyck's comment. When Chuli looked back, she found Jonah frowning, his face shadowed by his hood. Despite the warm day, he wore his travel cloak with the hood up, claiming that he burned quickly because of his red hair and skin tone. Chuli shook her head when she spotted Jonah's white knuckles gripping the reins. *How can these silly outlanders not know how to ride?*

You'd think we were moving at an urgent gallop rather than an easy trot. They crested a hilltop for their first view of the valley beyond.

Pines covered the foothills before them – pines standing a fraction of the size of the ones they had passed. The Red Towers still amazed her. When Jonah had first described the massive trees, she had been reluctant to believe him...until they reached the edge of that wood. Chuli had never been among trees that made her feel so tiny, so insignificant. They were towering monoliths that had existed before man ever stepped foot in their shadows, and they would likely remain long after mankind faded from Issalia.

Without the use of a bridle, she guided her mount with the pressure of her knee, and Rhychue shifted accordingly, giving her a better view of the mining town below. *Vallerton*, she thought.

With Thiron in the lead, the riders continued down the road as it descended into the valley. The ranger was a quiet one, even compared to the Tantarri. At thirty-six summers, Thiron Hawking was the eldest in the group, twice the age of Chuli and Jonah and ten years Wyck's senior. As the most seasoned, he had the honor of leading the mission, one that suited his skills well. Like Chuli, he wore a full quiver over one shoulder and a longbow over the other. The dark-skinned man's eyes searched the surrounding woods, watching warily. From the side, his hooked nose reminded Chuli of a bird of prey, as did his intense glare.

Motion from Wyck drew her attention as he took a drink from his water skin. Tall and blond with dark scruff on his face, Chuli thought that the man might be attractive if not for his arrogance. Like Thiron, Wyck was dressed in a sleeveless brown leather jerkin, but his exposed arms were thickly muscled and marked by visible scars. The shield on his back, longsword on his hip, and bracers on his wrists made it clear that his skills were different from those of the ranger.

She turned her attention toward the sun, now past the mid-point in the sky. With an early start from Selbin, they had made good time, affording the party hours of daylight after their arrival.

As the ground leveled, the first building came into view. Built of logs, the house and neighboring shed stood beside a field fenced by split logs. Freshly cut rails revealed a section recently repaired. A small herd of cattle – white with black spots – huddled at the edge of the field as they ate in the cool shadow of nearby trees. A man emerged from the shed wearing a wide-brimmed hat. Upon seeing the horses, the man stopped and stared toward them. Jonah waved and the man waved back. Chuli considered waving, but rather than mimic Jonah, she held back like Thiron and Wyck and instead turned away.

Other buildings soon came into view as the party emerged from the forest and entered the mining town. Built of logs and aligned in rows, the small houses mirrored one another, as if all were built by the same person. When they crossed a road that led east, Chuli saw a sprawling excavation cut into a hillside marked by red-tinted rock. *The ore mine*, she nodded, knowing she was correct. A fair portion of the ore used to forge steel came from Vallerton.

The houses gave way to larger buildings, mostly storefronts with second-story apartments, all lining the dirt road. A wooden path, covered by an awning, connected the buildings and ran the length of the street. Chuli noted a cobbler, a baker, a butcher, a tailor, an apothecary, a glass blower, and an inn – all typical businesses in one place. At the end of the street was a building with black smoke rising from its chimney. The ring of a hammer carried from the interior, informing Chuli that it was a smithy.

Thiron pulled on his reins and guided his horse toward the inn. The sign above the awning depicted a bucket and the words *Wishing Well Inn*. He dismounted and tied his stallion to the hitching post, Wyck doing likewise. When Chuli settled on the ground, she patted Rhychue and spoke quietly.

"Remain here." She pointed toward the trough, half-full. "Drink some water. I won't be long."

"I still don't think that horse knows what you're saying." Jonah grimaced and slid off his horse.

"If she doesn't understand, why does she do as I say?"

Rubbing his backside with one hand and holding the reins with his other, he turned toward her. "Perhaps she does it out of habit...or training. Someone has to train your horses, right?"

"Tantarri horses do not require training. They grow with the Tantarri, as the Tantarri grow with them."

Jonah snorted. "I should have known you would have an odd response."

Chuli smiled. "Odd is a matter of perspective."

He gave her a wry smile in return. "True."

"If you two are through, we should secure rooms."

Hearing Thiron speak, Chuli turned toward him and nodded. He climbed the two steps to the wooden platform in front of the building and entered the inn with the other three close behind.

Four small windows along the front offered dim light to the inn's interior. A dozen tables occupied a common room with a stone fireplace at one end, a bar at the other. Now at the midpoint between lunch and dinner, the room stood empty and quiet.

With Wyck beside him – the big man's hand resting on the pommel of his sword – Thiron headed toward the bar. Chuli and Jonah followed, him still rubbing his backside while she restrained a chuckle. Other than Jonah, the group looked like hunters, which was the point.

Thiron knocked on the bar and called out. "Hello!"

"On my way." A voice carried from beyond the back door to the room.

A moment later, a man emerged. He was balding atop his head, surrounded by a ring of short brown hair and a beard to match. Of average height, the portly man weighed much more than average. He gave them a grin as he wiped his hands on his apron, leaving streaks.

"I'm Barley, the inn's owner. What can I do for you?"

Thiron replied, "Well met, Barley. We're in need of rooms for a night or two. Meals are required as well."

The man nodded. "We have two rooms vacant."

Thiron glanced at Chuli. "Can you fit three of us into one of them?"

"Yes. I'll have my daughter bring up a cot."

"Fine. How much per night?"

Barley's eyes shifted as he considered his response. "Two silvers per night."

Wyck slammed his hand on the bar, and Barley jumped with a yelp. "Are you trying to rob us? Should we get the constable?"

"Um…I…" Barley stammered while kneading his thick hands. "I meant one silver per night and was assuming you were staying two nights."

Thiron planted a silver piece on the bar. "Done."

Wyck grinned, the expression lacking humor. "Where can we find the constable, anyway?"

"But, but..." Barley stuttered.

"Don't worry." Thiron said. "We're hunters, here to take down the beast that has been wreaking havoc in the area. We wish to speak to the constable for information."

Barley exhaled and wiped his brow. "Well, then. You'll find the keep at the south end of town, past the smithy."

Thiron said, "Very well. We will be back soon. Have our rooms ready."

He spun about and crossed the room while Wyck lingered, grinning at the barkeep. "I'll see you soon."

Before the man could respond, Wyck slammed his hand on the bar again and the barkeep jumped with a start. Wyck then spun around and headed outside to join Thiron while Chuli and Jonah trailed behind.

Rather than riding, Thiron led his horse by the reins and headed south. The others did the same, save for Chuli, who simply held palm against Rhychue's neck as she walked.

When they circled the smithy, they spotted a building made of stone. A wooden palisade encircled the building, the logs sharpened to points at the top. The gate stood open, so Thiron led them through and found a hitching post in the courtyard, already occupied by a piebald mare. They tied their horses up and approached the dark green door at the front.

Thiron's knock echoed inside. A moment later, the door opened, revealing a tall, thin man holding a sword.

"Greetings," Thiron gave the man a nod. "I'm seeking the constable."

"I'm Constable Hardy. State your business." Something about the man's tone seemed forced.

"We're hunters. We hear there's a bounty."

The man's blue eyes shifted to look beyond Thiron, landing on Jonah. "He doesn't look like a hunter."

Thiron looked back and shook his head. "No. He certainly does not." He turned back to the man. "Among other things, the boy is our cook. He's not very good at it, but he's my sister's whelp, and I promised to give him a job and to attempt to keep him out of trouble." Thiron leaned closer and whispered just loud enough for Chuli to hear. "The kid is a thief. He'll steal the smallclothes right off you while you're asleep if you're not careful."

Hardy scowled when Jonah pulled a coin from his pocket and began flipping it across the back of his hand, the coin dancing from finger to finger.

"He best not steal while he's in Vallerton."

"I'm trying to change his ways, good sir." Thiron replied. "I'll keep him busy, so he won't have time for mischief."

"Good. See that you do." The man eyed Thiron. "Now, about this bounty. I assume you've heard the stories?"

Wyck leaned against the wall and gave the man a look that said everything. "Surely, you can't believe all that rubbish."

"I wish it were otherwise...but I've seen it." The man's face took on a haunted look. "The beast is massive, fast...evil. Vernon's farm, just north of town...it attacked there a few weeks back. Tore up three cows and left only parts behind. Broke his fence and everything."

Thiron raised a brow toward Wyck. "What exactly are we talking about? A bear? A bacabra?"

"Like a bacabra, but worse. Just as big, perhaps bigger. It has red eyes, too – glowing in the darkness as it hunts." Hardy stared at nothing while he spoke. "It's as if the nastiest thing in the forest became ten times bigger and ten times nastier."

"But what is it?"

"A beast – a monster that has already killed thirteen people, a half-dozen horses, two dogs, and three cows." His focus shifted as he looked Thiron in the eye. "If you can kill it, you deserve the bounty King Cassius has offered. I suspect he would deal with it himself if he were able. Before the king's...incident, he and one of his sons hunted a stag in the Red Towers. The thing had gone mad and had killed hunters and travelers alike. They say it was massive, ten feet tall and a thousand pounds. It was also reported to have had eyes that glowed in the dark."

"Never mind the stag," Wyck grumbled. "I'm worried about the bounty...and finding this beast. Where have the attacks occurred?"

The man's forehead furrowed in thought. "To the north and to the west." He nodded as if convincing himself. "Yes. None south or east of here."

"Well, that's something to go on," Thiron said. "Is there anything else you can tell us? When was the last attack?"

"Like I said, about two weeks back, at Vernon's farm. It was the closest attack to town, and it left the people here more on edge than ever."

"Does it always attack at night?"

Everyone turned to look at Jonah.

"What?" Wyck asked.

Jonah shrugged. "Night. It's dark. Have the other attacks occurred at night?"

Hardy scratched his head. "Now that you mention it, I can't recall any that occurred before sunset."

10

THE HUNTED

The forest was dark, despite the sun's position well above the western horizon – at least, that is where Chuli assumed the sun to be. Now, somewhere deep amongst the Red Towers, there was scant chance to see the sky and confirm her assumption.

The surrounding trees were massive, some ten strides in diameter. When she peered up, the forest canopy stood hundreds of feet above her. Here and there, thin beams of sunlight shone at an angle, a rare drink of light for the ferns that covered the forest floor.

They happened upon a narrow bubbling brook, the water's gurgling the only sound in the area. Thiron dismounted while the other three stared off into the forest, watching for movement. The man squatted and touched the ground with his fingers.

"These tracks match the ones we saw yesterday." His gaze scanned the forest floor. "These are fresh, no more than a day old. Whatever this thing is, it went that direction." He pointed to the northwest, the opposite direction of Vallerton.

Even from atop her horse and ten strides away, Chuli could see the indentation of a paw print and deep claw marks. "The paws are huge. Are you sure this isn't a bear?"

The hunter stood upright and shook his head. "No bear has claws that big. Whatever this thing is, we had best not let it get near us."

"If we want to be back before it's dark, we should turn around," Jonah offered.

Thiron walked to his horse and put his foot in a stirrup before climbing on the stallion. "Our job is to hunt this thing, not sit in the tavern and tell stories."

"What about nightfall? Think of how dark it will be in this forest."

Thiron looked back at him. "If we're not back by then, you'll give us some light." He then nudged his horse into motion.

Although Jonah grimaced at the man, he let the issue drop.

Following Thiron's lead, they rode through the eerie forest, scanning their surroundings. The sound of running water faded, leaving the trampling of forest undergrowth and the occasional snort from the horses as the only sounds.

When the forest seemed to grow even darker, Chuli looked around to determine if it were just her imagination. The beams of sunlight had faded, losing intensity. *Clouds must be blocking the sun*, she thought.

The building anxiety twisted Chuli's stomach, and her back itched. It felt as if someone – or something – were watching from behind. Wyck's horse stepped on a fallen branch, and the loud crack made Chuli jump. Thiron stopped and glared at the man for a long moment.

"Let's dismount," Thiron said as he slid from his horse. "We must now place stealth above ease of travel or speed. We are nearing this thing, I can feel it."

The others joined him on the forest floor. Chuli patted Rhychue and requested that the mare remain while the others tied their horses to the branch of a downed tree, the trunk marked by a series of deep gouges. Nobody needed Thiron to note that those were claw marks. Chuli stared at the shredded trunk and tried to imagine what beast wielded talons that could render gouges that thick. She recalled the stories told by Constable Hardy and now understood what the man had meant. Images of shredded humans emerged from the recesses of her imagination.

When Thiron slid his longbow from his shoulder, Chuli did the same. Wyck swung his shield from his back and slid it on his left arm before drawing his sword. Rather than draw his belt knife, Jonah unhooked a pack from his horse's saddle and gave Thiron a nod.

They advanced slowly with Thiron in the lead, the man kneeling to examine the forest floor every twenty strides. Chuli found herself wishing the clouds would move along and allow the sunlight to sneak back into the woods. Then, she spotted something odd to the southwest.

"Thiron." He stopped and turned while Chuli pointed. "Over there. What is it?"

The man peered with narrowed eyes toward the dark shape. Without a word, he headed in that direction, not making a sound. They circled a massive tree, eight strides in diameter. Deep gouges, each consisting of four parallel lines, marked one side of the trunk. Once past the tree, it became clear that the dark shape was a mound of dirt. Moving slowly, they edged closer until Thiron stopped and stared at the dark maw before them.

It was a tunnel, twelve feet in diameter, and it angled downward.

"Hold on," Jonah whispered as he opened his pack.

He removed a rock the size of his fist, the rock glowing with a soft blue light. Winding up, he tossed it into the hole. The rock rolled down the hill, its nimbus eating away at the darkness as it advanced. It stopped forty feet away – a beacon of light with darkness beyond it.

"I wonder how deep it goes." Jonah muttered.

Thiron reached behind his back and grabbed three arrows. By the time he glanced at Chuli, she already had her arrows ready, the middle one nocked in her bow.

Without a word, the man stepped into the hole.

"We're going in there?" Jonah asked.

Wyck nudged Jonah with his shield. "Yes. Now, be quiet."

As they crept toward the darkness waiting beyond the glowing stone, terror slipped a noose around Chuli's throat, tightening the rope as her breathing became ragged. Thiron shifted around the stone while keeping his bow pointed forward. A step behind him, Wyck turned toward Jonah and gestured toward the glowing rock. Chuli shifted to the side so he could pick it up.

A nightmarish sound came from the forest behind them...a scream in the distance. Chuli spun toward the tunnel opening, a dimly lit doorway to the forest beyond. She turned toward Thiron and found him frowning as his head turned to look deeper into the hole and then back again.

"I have a bad feeling about this," Jonah muttered.

"Out. Now. Run."

The words came from Thiron's lips, and Wyck burst into a sprint toward the tunnel entrance. Chuli glanced at Thiron, hesitating, as did Jonah.

The man pushed Jonah back. "It's in the forest. Get out or we'll be trapped!"

Jonah scrambled toward the exit, tripping in the process. When Chuli jumped forward to help him, something massive eclipsed the entrance.

Oversized in every way, a hairy beast with red eyes lunged and swiped at Wyck, slamming him against the tunnel wall. The big man crumpled in a heap, the back of his leather jerkin shredded, as was the flesh beneath it.

"Shoot!" Thiron cried out as he began to loose arrows.

Chuli raised her bow and shot in a fast, repeated motion, striking the monster with all three arrows. The beast flinched and snarled but did not retreat. Jonah then stepped past her and threw his glowing rock. It landed near the tunnel mouth and provided light that had been lacking.

"It's...it's a badger." Jonah said.

While Chuli agreed that the monster had the appearance of a badger, it was many times the size of a badger. In fact, it was three or four times the size of a bear. She grabbed three more arrows and shot. In seconds, both she and Thiron had the thing's face full of arrows. The beast darted forward with amazing speed, stepping right on Wyck's prone form. Desperate, Chuli aimed, fired, and struck the monster in the eye. It stopped just shy of Jonah, who had fallen on his backside. As Jonah scrambled backward, the beast released a massive roar and backed out of the tunnel.

Chuli watched Thiron, who began to ease forward with his bow ready. She drew another arrow and advanced while Jonah rose to his feet. Her gaze flicked down toward Wyck, whose back was a bloody mess, the bone of one arm poking through his skin. Jonah scrambled past her and knelt beside the injured man. He put his boot against the exposed bone, grabbed the man's arm and snapped it back. A weak cry of pain came from the man and he fell limp. Still gripping his arm,

Jonah closed his eyes, and all fell silent. Wyck's body shook visibly, his wounds closing as he gasped for air. Without waiting, Jonah withdrew a chunk of glowstone from his pack and began tracing a rune on the man's shoulder.

Thiron snuck forward, sliding past Jonah and Wyck, and approached the tunnel entrance. Chuli followed as the rune on Wyck's arm flamed with red light.

Emerging from the tunnel, Thiron scanned the area with his bow, ready for movement. The thump of Chuli's pulse sounded like a drum in her ears as she edged forward. She sensed movement behind her, about to glance back when a dark shape fell from above the tunnel, the beast landing atop Thiron. She fired her arrow at the monster's back-side, and it roared with the ranger pinned beneath it.

A blur sped past her as Wyck smashed into the beast with a thrust of his shield. The impact launched the gigantic badger across the clearing. It slammed into a tree so hard that the branches, hundreds of feet above, waved wildly. Chuli lowered her bow as Wyck advanced past Thiron's bloody body.

The monster rose to its feet and shook its head, the shafts of the arrow in its snout now snapped off, the one in its eye covered in blood. With the remaining red eye narrowed, the monster glared at the approaching warrior and slowly shifted sideways. Wyck crouched and leaped, his magic-enhanced jump arcing thirty feet over the beast. The monster's head followed the man, spinning to face him, and it attacked when he landed. Wyck raised his shield to block the swipe of a massive paw, each foot-long claw like a curved dagger. The force of the strike sent the man stumbling to the side before he leaped forward and sliced, taking the beast's fore-foot off clean. The badger howled, the sound a raging trumpet of pain that shook the forest. Wyck struck again, cleaving a three-foot slice along the side of the badger's neck. The beast stumbled to the ground, and the man leaped toward it with an overhead stab, driving his sword deep into its ribs.

Wyck staggered backward his chest heaving with each breath as the beast shuddered, groaned, and fell still.

Jonah ran past Chuli, emerged from the tunnel, and knelt beside Thiron. The man's face was a bloody mess, his scalp half-torn away, his chest and shoulder torn open.

"Help me." Jonah cried as he pushed the man's scalp back into place.

Dropping her bow, Chuli scrambled to the man's other side. "What do I do?"

"Try to push this wound together. I can heal him if he still lives."

Moving quickly, Chuli pushed the damaged flesh back into place. It felt warm and wet to her touch. Blood was everywhere. Jonah closed his eyes while holding the man's scalp to his head. Nothing happened. The man's body just lay still beneath her grip. Right when Chuli feared they were too late, the man's body shook and his back arched for a long moment. He then fell limp, his breath coming in rapid gasps, but he did not wake.

Jonah sat back and raised a blood-soaked hand to his forehead. He released a sigh, his hand shaking.

"Are you all right?" Chuli asked.

Jonah opened his eyes and blinked. "I'm spent...and hungry."

Hearing a grunt, Chuli turned to find Wyck standing over them with his bloody sword in hand. "I feel like I could eat that thing we just killed...the entire thing."

Jonah nodded. "Yes. Your injuries were significant. That type of healing leaves you hungry. The Power rune should help for a while." Moving slowly, Jonah stood and wiped his hand on his breeches. "Thiron's injuries were even worse. He'll likely not wake for a day or two."

"In that case," Wyck walked over to the dead badger and wiped his blade clean on the beast's fur before sheathing it, "I suppose I could carry the man for you. At least until the augmentation fades."

With the forest growing darker, and night almost upon them, they returned to where they had left the horses. To Chuli's horror, corpses waited for them. She said a prayer to the Spirit of Nature, hoping that she would reward the horses with another chance to run upon the plains. Rhychue was missing and had likely fled when the other horses were attacked.

They retrieved what they could from the torn saddlebags and headed southeast.

It was a long hike back to Vallerton. When Wyck's augmentation wore off, they stopped and built a makeshift litter for Thiron, with Chuli and Jonah taking turns helping Wyck carry the man. Through the forest, they trudged until they reached the hills. The forest canopy relaxed as they left the Towers behind for normal-sized trees. Clouds in the sky hid the stars, and Chuli found herself praying that they were heading in the right direction. Their exhaustion grew to a crescendo as they carried the unconscious man up a rise, over a hilltop, and down the backside. The gaps in the trees became wider and a clearing gave them the lift they needed. With their trail rations consumed and hunger still raging in their stomachs, the sleeping town of Vallerton came into view.

It was well past midnight when they finally arrived at the Wishing Well Inn. As they approached the building, Chuli spotted a dark silhouette standing beside the hitching post. A grin found its way past her weariness when she saw Rhychue sleeping over the water trough.

11

DEPTH OF CHARACTER

The pale light of a waning glowlamp lit the corner of the room. Beneath it was a wooden table with four worn chairs, two of which were occupied. Quinn sat on one side of the table, across from the man who had preceded her arrival.

For this particular mission, she had made an effort to roughen her appearance. Tight breeches and a short sword at each hip joined her drab brown leather jacket – open at the front to reveal a stained tunic beneath it.

Caught in a conversation that had been going on for several minutes, she turned the man's question over in her head and gave him a sideways glance, intentionally allowing a moment to pass before responding.

"Word on the street is that you're seeking assistance."

The man leaned back in his chair and crossed his arms. Dressed in a sleeveless black leather jerkin with multiple knives visible and dark bangs hanging over the Custos rune on his forehead, he carried the appearance of a ruffian. His grimace added weight to that image.

"Why would I need assistance?" Kirk replied. "I'm pretty sure I can take care of myself."

Imitating the nonchalant pose she had seen so often from Delvin, she examined her fingernails, rubbing them with her thumb. "Could be that someone of certain skills might be of use to you."

That earned her a grunt as the man took a drink of his ale. He put the tankard down and wiped the foam from his lips. "I'm not unskilled myself. There is little I find myself lacking."

Frustration began to bubble inside Quinn. "Your pride will do you no good if you are dead or locked up in a cell."

Kirk eyed her with suspicion. "How do I know I can trust you?"

Quinn leaned forward and slammed a leather pouch on the table, the contents inside jingling. The man's eyes narrowed as he stared at it. He clutched at his hip, feeling for an item that wasn't there.

"Is that my coin purse?" he asked.

"Rather than waste my time talking to you, I could have just left with this. I would be five silvers and a few coppers richer…and you'd be none the wiser." Quinn sat back and glared at the man. "I've spent my entire life doing small jobs, stealing enough to get by. Houses, shops, a drunk in an alley here, a coin purse there. I have yet to be caught. I'm through with just getting by. My sources tell me that you're planning something significant, and I want in."

Kirk took another drink from his mug, his glare never straying from Quinn's face. When he put the mug down, he leaned forward. "Suppose I decide to entertain this offer, there will be no going back. Once you're in, you remain in. A change of heart in this case could become fatal…as could being caught."

Quinn pressed her lips together and pretended to turn the consequences over in her head. "Life is full of risks. There are seldom guarantees. One thing I *can* guarantee is that you'll not find anyone more determined than I am." She spat in her hand and held it out to the man. "I am committed if you are."

He glanced down at her hand, hesitating before spitting in his palm and extending his.

"Hold on, Kirk."

Delvin emerged from the shadows and approached their table.

"As your partner, I deserve a say in who we accept." Delvin pulled out a chair and sat, bringing his fingers to his chin as he stared at Quinn. "I have a few questions for the young lady."

A frown crossed Quinn's face. *What are you up to, Delvin?*

"What's your name?" He asked.

"As I already told Kirk, my name is Kaylin."

"And your last name?"

"Griggs."

"Fine, Kaylin Griggs." He leaned forward. "Where did you grow up? Where do you live now?"

Quinn responded with confidence. "I grew up in Port Hurns, but I ran away from home when I was fourteen. I lived in Vingarri for a while, then Yarth, and most recently in Wayport."

"I also am from Port Hurns." Delvin shared a sly smile. "Who were the other children you grew up with?"

Quinn's frown returned. "I...what?"

"Your childhood friends. I need their names."

Like tendrils of a creeping vine, confusion and doubt spread throughout Quinn's mind and began to squeeze. She struggled to come up with a response...names...an excuse...something, anything. Her mouth opened and, rather than words, a stuttering groan came out. Delvin sat back, crossed his arms, and glared at her.

Quinn glanced toward the audience who sat in the shadows – Master Firellus, Master Hedgewick, Everson, and a few fellow wardens-in-training. Her focus returned to Delvin as he rose to his feet.

"You have talent, Quinn. Your portrayal of a thief-for-hire was solid, and you did well in becoming the character in a convincing way." Delvin's eyes were intense, lacking their normal levity. "I need you to take it further. You must completely flesh out your character's history and consider all possible questions. You must be able to react naturally and not find yourself tripping over your own lies. When in the field, these small things define the line between success and failure. You have valuable skills. I would hate to see you killed because you missed some seemingly innocuous detail.

"This is why we interrogated you and your brother before you were offered the position of warden. The fact that two siblings in two different schools were both involved with Empire spies just seemed too coincidental. We had to know the truth before we could expose our secrets. Once you and your brother each relayed your tales, it became obvious that they were truly genuine. Even with the truth rune present, there was the chance that cleverly phrased responses would enable you to skirt the truth. However, it is far more difficult to build an entire false life, filled with detail and depth. That detail is what you must strive for with each persona.

"I'll assign a new role for you, along with a different scenario and another partner. After you receive your objective, develop your character's background, personality, history, goals, morals, habits, and anything else that might come into play. Prepare well, for your first mission may come soon."

12

ANYONE

A hammer struck iron in the distance, the ring repeating every other breath. Grinding sounds came from the other direction, joined by the hiss of released steam. Everson ignored the sounds and focused on his project. With gritted teeth, he used the ceramic tongs to place a shard of Chaos-charged rock into place, watching the entire process through his magnifying spectacles. He then slid the dome of glass over it, careful to align the slots he had ground from the glass so the conductors fit snugly within them. Lifting the goggles to his brow, he stared at his creation and considered how he might test it without risking his life. *I will need to do it outside where I won't destroy anything if things go haywire.*

Everson pulled the goggles off his head and rested them on his workbench. When he stood from the stool, his mechanical legs whirred. A glance to the side revealed Ivy and Henrick working on the modified flyer. Although Everson was confident in their abilities, he moved closer to inspect their work. Despite being two years older, Henrick was forced to follow Everson's lead, as was Ivy. Both had been brought in as gadgeteers at Everson's request. Henrick was among the few engineering students from the Academy whom Everson admired. Ivy was among the few whom he trusted, both as a fellow warden and as a friend.

He squatted beside Ivy, the cylinders of his mechanical legs hissing as air expelled from them. "You've done a fine job."

The dark-haired girl turned toward him and adjusted her spectacles while a shy smile spread across her face. "Thank you, Everson. I'm glad you approve."

Everson put his hand on her shoulder. "You don't need my approval, Ivy. You're smart, skilled, and are here on your own merits. I merely pointed them out to people who would listen."

She chewed on her lip, her eyes flicking to the side before returning to focus on him. "I want to thank you again for that as well. I never dreamed that a place like this might exist...that I could be part of something so important."

"I know what you mean." Everson looked about the Forge while he spoke. "This building and the things we can create here exceed anything I could have hoped for. Having a greater cause to work toward only makes it that much more grand."

Henrick grunted. "When we're through retrofitting this flyer, I have something of my own I want to work on."

Everson turned to look at the boy, who stood a half head taller and weighed twice what Everson weighed. Although he had never said it aloud, Everson believed that Henrick didn't enjoy deferring to Everson. Rather than kick the beehive, Everson sought to ease the situation with a little honey.

"Yes, of course. Once this flyer is finished, you both can have a few weeks to work on your own projects. While I have other ideas in the works, they can wait. I would rather that you have time to express your own creativity and see what you might dream up."

Henrick's eyes narrowed toward Everson as he swept his blond bangs aside. "What have you been working on over there, anyway?"

Everson grinned. "Something of a lark, but one that will be wonderful if it works."

Henrick raised a brow. "If it works?"

Rising to stand upright, Everson said, "The invention is based on a theory. And like any theory, it is nothing more until proven."

Henrick returned his attention to the bolt he was tightening. "Well, I've seen your theories come to fruition before, despite their outlandish nature."

"Would you like to see how this one works out yourself?"

He looked up and shrugged. "Sure. When?"

"Now," Everson said. "I could use some help."

"Me, too?" Ivy asked.

He laughed. "Of course."

Everson returned to his workbench with Ivy and Henrick following close behind. Upon reaching it, he gripped a handful of thin metal rods, each four feet in length, and lifted them with a grunt. The metal felt cold in his grip, the weight solid despite each rod being no more than half an inch in diameter. He held the rods toward Henrick.

"Carry these, please."

Henrick accepted the rods and stepped back. Everson grabbed a handful of metal sleeves and a pair of pliers before handing them to Ivy. With those items addressed, he scooped up his creation, cradling it in one hand as he turned from the workbench. Walking in the lead, Everson observed his surroundings as he headed toward the exit.

Two fellow engineers were using a pair of clamps while applying heat to a pole as they began to bend it. Beyond them, an arcanist sat before a metal plate marked with a Heat rune. The metal glowed with a crimson hue as the woman worked on her enchantment. As usual, Everson found himself staring in wonder, wishing he understood the process.

After passing the inlet pipes that routed steam to the various machines in the building, the trio reached the door at the far end. Everson opened it, entered the corridor, and held the door open for Ivy and Henrick. They then made their way toward the rear of the building, turning at the next bend to exit through a pair of thick wooden doors, stained black.

Everson paused when he emerged and found himself squinting in the afternoon sunlight. The stable stood to his right, the south wall to his left – the same wall that divided the Ward from the Fallbrandt Academy of Magic and Engineering. The solid black gate in the wall swung open, held in place by an armed guard. A horse walked through the opening, a Tantarri chestnut mare with a shock of white on its chest, ridden by a girl Everson knew.

Chuli sat in the saddle with obvious ease, guiding her horse without a bridle, as was the way of her people. Three males on foot trailed behind her. Everson's brow furrowed at the sight as dark-skinned Thiron led them, the man wearing a green tunic rather than his usual brown leather jerkin. A step behind was Wyck, who appeared almost barbaric without a shirt, his tanned and heavily muscled body glistening. Oddly, the man's leather bracers remained on his forearms as the only item of clothing above his waist. Trailing the group was Everson's roommate, appearing worn and ragged as his footsteps dragged, scraping the gravel and stirring up a cloud of dust with each step.

"What happened to your horses?" Everson asked, his voice fighting with the clopping hooves.

Already possessing tanned skin, black hair, and angled eyes that marked her as Tantarri, Chuli's face darkened further and she frowned at Everson. Without answering him, she rode Rhychue through the open stable door and disappeared into the shadowed interior.

"What did I say?" Everson muttered.

Wyck approached, "Step aside, twerps. I'm starving."

Everson shifted to the side, and Wyck walked past him to enter the building with Thiron a step behind.

Jonah stopped before Everson and wiped his brow. "It's hot. Are you hot? I'm hot."

Everson noted, "It *is* a tad warm, but we just stepped outside."

Lifting his water skin to his lips, Jonah took a long drink. He then wiped his lips dry, smacked them, and responded. "Chuli's upset."

"I've noticed," Everson said, looking toward the stable. "Why was she the only one riding?"

"That's why she's upset."

Everson blinked in confusion.

"That doesn't make sense," Henrick said.

Jonah glanced toward the stable. "She's Tantarri, and she's taking the horses deaths as if she lost family members...maybe worse."

"Deaths? Your horses?" Everson said

"Yes. All three were slaughtered by the beast we were sent to hunt," Jonah said. "Chuli's mount wasn't tethered, and it was able to escape. We found her mare waiting for us when we got back to Vallerton."

"It sounds like your hunt was dangerous," Everson noted.

"Just a bit," Jonah snorted. "Wyck was attacked, torn up, and left unconscious. Thiron was even in worse shape, and he nearly died. Chuli stuck a quiver full of arrows into the thing, but it was massive and each shaft may as well been a thorn. I was scared out of my mind but was able to heal Wyck and give him an augmentation in time to save Thiron, who I also had to heal. After those close calls, we somehow survived, only to find our horses dead."

"Well, I'm glad you made it back safely," Everson gave his friend a smile of encouragement. "If you aren't in a hurry, perhaps you would like to join us?"

Jonah gazed down at the device in Everson's hands. "What crazy experiment are you doing this time?"

A grin spread across Everson's face. "Come along and you'll find out."

Jonah stared at the door to the Ward, silent for a moment. As Chuli emerged from the stable, Jonah gave Everson a shrug. "I guess my meal and bath can wait a few more minutes."

"Mine cannot," Chuli said as she approached the group. "My stomach longs for a decent meal and my body needs a hot bath. Neither can come soon enough."

Everson turned toward the tall Tantarri girl. "Hello, Chuli. I'm sorry about the horses…"

She paused briefly. "Greetings, Everson. Yes, I am saddened at their loss, even if they were not true Tantarri stock." Chuli then slid past them and entered the building.

Everson waited for the door to close and then turned to his friends. "Come on. Let's get to work."

The other three followed, Jonah carrying his pack while Henrick and Ivy carried the components of Everson's experiment. Circling behind the stables, Everson discovered the thick stump of an old oak tree. *That should work*, he thought as he led the group toward it.

He placed his invention atop the stump and reached into his tunic. When his hand emerged, a white sheet of cloth trailed it. Upon the cloth, was a rune drawn in black.

Henrick's brow furrowed. "What's with the rune?"

"Increase Gravity," Jonah said.

Everson nodded. "Exactly. It should be a harmless rune…at least as harmless as Chaos can be."

The mechanisms strapped to Everson's legs whirred as he squatted and tacked the cloth to the side of the stump. He then stood and retrieved his prize creation.

"Let's connect the poles together. Henrick, please press one end of the first pole against the rune. Then lay down the other poles and Ivy can add sleeves and clamps to each junction. When you're finished, the poles will be thirty feet in length."

Henrick stared at Everson for a moment before he began laying out the poles as requested, the tip of the first pole poking into the rune on the cloth. Then Ivy slid the sleeves onto the pole ends and clamped the poles together into a single assembly. When finished, they reached the location where Everson waited with Jonah.

"Now, we will see if my theory proves true."

"And, what theory would that be?" Jonah asked.

Everson grinned in response. His heart thumped in his chest as he knelt and placed the contraption in his hands on the ground. The stone under the glass at its core was so black that it drank every ray of sunlight, dull and non-reflective. He chewed on his lip and slowly moved the contraption toward the butt of the nearest pole. When the conductor sticking out from his machine contacted the pole, red energy sparked from the conductor. His eyes shifted toward the rune on the cloth and found it glowing hot. He pulled the charging unit backward, and the sparking ceased, the rune at the far end pulsing as it faded. The cloth suddenly tore away from the tacks and crumpled to the ground.

"What did you do?" Henrick asked in a hushed voice.

"Can't you see, Henrick?" Ivy smiled, her eyes alight. "Everson charged that rune with Chaos."

"It can't work that way, can it?" Jonah asked.

Everson stood and stared at the cloth while butterflies flitted about his stomach. "I'm not sure. I hope so, but there is only one way to find out. Can someone please retrieve the cloth for me?"

Henrick glowered at Everson before stomping over to the stump. Hesitating for a moment, he bent over and gripped the cloth. With obvious effort, he grunted and lifted it, the free ends sagging heartily, as if they were soaking wet. He turned around and shook his head.

"It feels as if it's now made of lead." Henrick's tone carried a sense of awe.

He let it drop and the cloth thumped the gravel hard enough to stir up a cloud of dust.

A wide smile spread across Everson's face. He had done it. With his theory proven, anyone possessing his new invention and knowledge of runes could perform magic. Anyone.

13

WARDENS

C assilyn emerged from the carriage, stepped on the gravel road, and stared at the lonely building before her. Although not as tall, the Fallbrandt Academy of Magic and Engineering was longer than her father's castle in Kantar. Blocky and consisting of numerous inter-connected buildings, there was a sense of age to the academy – as if the building itself had absorbed centuries of knowledge. Her focus shifted up, toward the daunting tower behind the school – a tall, rectangular monolith that thrust toward the sky. *Odd*, she thought, *there aren't any windows.*

Squinting in the late morning sun, Brandt climbed out of the carriage and stood beside her. As he gazed upon the building, he sent thoughts toward her. *Why would anyone build something like this in the middle of nowhere?*

Perhaps they desired less distraction. Cassie felt the solitude of the valley, the buildings before her signs of mankind surrounded by nature. She turned toward the south and saw the distant Torreco Academy of Combat and Tactics, a building they had passed ten minutes earlier. Clearly of newer construction, the combat academy stood two miles south of the school of magic and engineering. In between the two institutions was an open lawn, interrupted by a tree-lined road down the middle.

76

South of the field, the road cut through a mile of thick forest before entering the town of Fallbrandt. Nestled beside a lake of the same name, Cassie had found Fallbrandt to be a modest place compared to Kantar, lacking the bustling streets and busy harbor of her home city. Even worse was Sarville. A full day's ride south of Fallbrandt, Sarville was a minor village beside the Alitus River, consisting of two dozen buildings and little else. During their journey through the Greenway Valley, she had seen no other hints of civilization.

She then stared at the tall mountains that defined the surrounding horizon. Despite it being the heart of summer, snow still clung so the north side of the higher peaks. She wondered how cold it must be up at that height. Even on the valley floor, the mid-summer sun felt comfortable. A cool mountain breeze and the lack of humidity certainly helped.

Brandt spoke aloud, interrupting her musing. "We should grab our stuff so the driver can head back."

Cassie joined him at the back of the carriage, where he opened a compartment and handed her a pack. She took it with a frown, recalling the items she had been forced to leave behind.

You'll have no time for dressing up or playing games, her mother had told her. *Bring only the items you need and make them fit in this pack.* The woman then handed the pack to Cassie, who had stared at it and wondered how anyone could fit the things needed into such a small space.

A sigh slipped out as Cassie recalled all the wonderful shoes she had left behind…and her dresses, her jewelry, her books, her figurines, her bed…

Brandt circled to the front of the wagon and waved at the driver. "Thanks, Vilroy. Have a good trip back to Kantar."

"Very well, Prince Brandt." The man tipped his cap. "May Issal watch over you and Princess Cassilyn."

With a snap of the reins, the carriage lurched into motion, following the workhorses as they circled around and headed down the south-bound road to Fallbrandt. A rune on the rear of the carriage began to glow the bright red of Chaos, pulsing in the sunlight before fading.

When did you draw that rune? Cassie asked in her head.

Before we left The Quiet Woman this morning.

Brandt began to laugh when the carriage lifted off the ground, eliciting a cry of surprise from Vilroy. It bounced back down, wobbled and floated back up as Vilroy screamed. Spooked by the man's screams and the odd behavior of their load, the horses burst into a gallop. The man pulled the reins and wailed for them to stop, but they fled in terror as the carriage raced down the road behind them, bobbing up into the air again and again.

In spite of herself, Cassie laughed, joining Brandt as the carriage quickly faded into the distance. The laughter then subsided, and Brandt finally clapped her on the shoulder.

"Come on," he turned and headed toward the academy.

Cassie followed him up the stairs and paused while he opened one of the oversized doors. A creak came from the hinges as he moved aside and waved her through.

The hall inside was spacious, empty, and quiet. Light from high windows lit the room, revealing a ceiling three stories above, held up by two rows of stone columns. Doors lined the walls to the left and right on all three levels, the top two visible past railing-lined terraces.

The distant tapping of heels on the tiled floor arose, the sound growing louder until a man emerged from a corridor at the far end of the room. He strode toward them with an air of confidence, dressed in black boots, gray trousers and tunic, and a silver-paneled coat. The man was tall, thin, and middle-aged with groomed brown hair and a trimmed beard to match.

He stopped two strides from them and shared a squinty-eyed smile. "Brandt and Cassilyn, right on time. Welcome."

Cassie frowned, unused to strangers addressing her in such a relaxed manner and without using her title.

"Come along. I will walk you to the Ward so you can get started."

He turned and began walking across the room. Cassie sent, *Who is this guy?*

Brandt shrugged and moved to follow. *Let's find out.* "You seem to know our names, but we don't know who you are."

"Oh, yes. Sorry about that," the man said over his shoulder as he continued across the hall, "My name is Abraham Ackerson. I'm Headmaster of the school."

Brandt glanced at Cassie and shrugged again. "Where is everyone?"

Ackerson paused for a moment as they caught up. "The school session ended yesterday. The students are now away, either graduated or back home for the summer. They return in six weeks."

Cassie's brow furrowed. "Why are we here, then? Shouldn't we have come later, when school is about to begin?"

Ackerson chuckled. "Not you two. Your work begins now. We have a special session planned for you and the other new recruits."

They entered a windowless corridor, lit by sporadically spaced glowing floor tiles, their blue light reminding Cassie of Glowridge Pass. Before their trip from Kantar, she had known about the legendary glowstone formations that lit the pass, but seeing it was an entirely different thing – beautiful and eerie at the same time.

At the second intersection, Ackerson turned right and led them down a corridor that ended with a set of black doors. The plaque above the doors read *Forbidden*. Cassie caught Brandt staring at the plaque and smiled. *I could think of no word they could have put there that would be more enticing to you*, she sent to him.

Brandt chuckled as Ackerson reached the door. *You know me too well, sister.*

The heavy doors opened out to a shadow-covered courtyard. The teens stopped to stare.

An ominous structure loomed before them, huge and imposing – a building that seemed threatening by its mere presence. While there was a merlon-lined terrace three stories up, the top of the tower stood much higher – twelve stories or more. The building was hundreds of feet wide and seemed just as deep. Its lack of windows added to the menacing nature, an oddity that conveyed a sense of danger and dark secrets.

Ackerson pointed toward the tower. "Amazing, isn't it?"

"What...what is it?" Cassie asked.

The man grinned. "This is the Arcane Ward...your new home."

Cassie looked at Brandt, their eyes meeting for a moment, but their thoughts remained unsaid – verbally or telepathically. Somehow, Cassie knew that their days of childish pranks were over. Whatever it meant, life in the Ward was sure to be of a more serious nature.

Ackerson began crossing the courtyard, his heels tapping on the cobblestones and echoing from the surrounding walls. To the left, there was a three-story wall with a black gate and a guard posted outside. The wall ran behind the school and connected to the Ward. Cassie turned to the right and found a large building a few hundred feet away with a road that ran between it and the Ward.

As they neared the tower, Ackerson nodded to the two armed guards who hovered beside two pairs of black wooden doors.

"Hello, Lyla, Craigler. We have two new recruits," he said. "Note their faces. They belong in the Ward."

"Very well, Headmaster," the woman on the right said before the male guard added. "Have a good day."

Ackerson opened a door and led Cassie and Brandt inside.

Similar to the academy, the windowless interior was lit by pale blue tiles. Heavy beams overhead glowed blue, offering additional light. Ackerson led them directly to a stairwell where every third step glowed. Two flights up the trio climbed without anyone saying a word. They then entered a long corridor that turned at both ends. Ackerson stopped at a door, opened it, and stepped aside to wave them through.

Inside, three men and a woman were seated around a long table made of dark, polished wood. On the other side of the room, a desk and shelves lined with books waited, while dark curtains covered the wall opposite the door. Thin strips of light shone between gaps where the curtains met. *At least there are windows* somewhere *in this place,* Cassie thought.

One of the men at the table stood, and Cassie smiled. Standing slightly taller than she and matching Brandt in height, a familiar man with disheveled brown hair and rectangular spectacles rounded the table.

"Cassilyn. Brandt. It is good to see you." He flashed a goofy grin while wrapping his arms about Cassie with a hug.

"Uncle Benny," Cassie grunted as he squeezed her. "We are happy to see you, too."

Brandt smiled as he thumped Benny on the back. "I thought we might see you while we were here, but this place – this Arcane Ward – seems…unlike you."

Benny nodded. "Yes. Its ominous appearance can be off-putting. In truth, that is quite intentional." He smiled and rocked his shoulders. "We *do* have secrets to keep."

Another familiar voice came from someone at the table. "You two have grown."

Cassie smiled at the man. "That tends to happen during one's teens."

A sardonic smile spread across his face, twisting his thin black goatee. "It *has* been a few years, hasn't it?"

"Yes, Delvin. Five years, to be exact."

"Well, your father and these jokers have kept me busy. Time moves swiftly when one is tasked with saving the world."

Ackerson interjected. "Enough small talk for now." He moved to the table and pulled out a chair. "Cassilyn. Brandt. Please, sit. We have things to tell you and little time remains before your training begins."

Without a word, Cassie and Brandt approached the table to sit between Benny and Ackerson. The man at the far end of the table – with long graying hair tied into a tail and dark eyes – leaned forward.

"You have met Headmaster Ackerson, and it appears that you already know Master Hedgewick and our resident miscreant, Delvin Garber. My name is Elias Firellus. Along with the other three, I run the Arcane Ward and am a member of the organization behind it."

Elias gestured toward the woman at the table. "This is Master Salina Alridge. She will be your Arcane Arts instructor."

The woman's dark eyes drew Cassie's attention – eyes that conveyed an unspoken challenge. Cassie had to admit that the woman was pretty, with long, lustrous black hair that framed her mocha-colored face. When Cassie glanced toward her brother, she found him leering at the woman's partially exposed chest. Cassie nudged him, eliciting a grunt.

Ouch, he sent. *What was that for?*

Get ahold of yourself, she replied. *Listen because this seems important.*

Elias continued, "I suspect that your father has told you little of what occurs inside the Ward, or what role you might play in the future."

Brandt shook his head. "In truth, we know very little of this place."

Benny spoke, drawing everyone's attention. "The Arcane Ward was originally intended to be a haven where magic could be practiced in secret. It was to be a safe place for arcanists to live and would help us control who was exposed to certain dangerous knowledge."

"Originally?" Cassie asked.

"Yes," Benny replied. "Five years ago, things changed as we recognized the need for something that had never existed prior to then. Since the Ward was almost finished at that time, we secretly opted to alter its purpose. While some arcanists do live here, they are now part of something else…something far more significant."

"ICON?" Brandt guessed.

"Precisely." Elias responded. "This is the headquarters for our operations. The Ward is where we train our wardens, and it is where they live when not in the field. Here, we also develop new weapons and tools that help protect our people and combat our enemies. This will be your home for a while, at least until one of you is sent on a mission."

Cassie turned toward Brandt. "One of us?"

Elias nodded, his expression grim. "Among other things, ICON is an organization of secrets. Each piece of information holds value, and the higher the value, the more important it is to keep the secret held tight, limiting the knowledge to as few people as possible. You two possess exceptional abilities – unique and priceless. Other than your parents and the people in this room, your telepathic connection will remain unknown to others. If our enemies become aware of it, they could counter it with false information or remove it by killing one of you." Cassie gasped at the thought. "Worse yet, they might attempt to capture you and use your abilities for their own purposes."

Brandt shook his head. "We would never let them do that. My sister and I stand for the people of Kantaria and Issalia. Nobody could ever make us betray them."

Elias' grim expression softened. "That is commendable and should be the perspective of every Warden we recruit. However, torture can change a person. Over time, and with enough pain, your opinion on the subject may be swayed. That is something we must avoid. As long as one of you is out of harm's way, we retain a level of safety. As long as one of you remains here, he or she can communicate with the other, offering us the ability to access and convey information immediately, regardless of distance."

Concerned, Cassie said, "So, we are merely tools to you? Do our lives not matter?"

"We are *all* tools, Cassilyn," Benny said. "We each offer skills that we utilize to ensure a better world. Within ICON, those skills are honed, polished, and perfected until one of you equals a hundred of our enemy. Your telepathic connection is just a piece of the puzzle. In addition, you both can access Order and Chaos, perhaps to an extent that we have never before seen. Your parents remain among the most powerful magic users ever recorded, and we have discovered that magic abilities are inherently genetic.

"If you were born into another family, perhaps you could just quietly live a simple life. You could marry a blacksmith and have children. Your days could be spent working in a bakery and then coming home to your family." He leaned forward. "I know you two well enough to confidently say that you would hate such a life." Benny shook his head. "No, you two have always pushed against the limitations your parents established, never happy with taking the easy path. You two have ambition. You have a thirst for adventure, for intrigue, for challenge. Brock and Ashland know it. That's why they sent you here. You two were meant to be wardens."

14

CHALLENGE

Brandt peered down the hallway, his eyes meeting Cassie's for a moment. Her position mirrored his as he stood with one hand on the door to his new room, two doors down from hers. Cassie gave him a nod, opened her door, and slipped inside. With a sigh, Brandt did the same.

Inside, he found a big man lounging on a sofa. A frown twisted the man's stubble-covered face, and the dark brows beneath his long blond hair furrowed.

"Who are you?"

"You must be Wyck. I'm Brandt – your new roommate."

Wyck sat up, the thick muscles of his exposed arms noticeable as he pushed himself upright. "I didn't ask for a roommate," he grumbled.

The man's tone put Brandt on edge. "I didn't ask to share an apartment with an overgrown knucklehead, but I guess I got stuck with the short straw."

The grimace on Wyck's face deepened and he stood. Brandt found himself staring up at a man who stood well over six-feet tall.

"Come here, and I'll show you a few knuckles."

Unused to others challenging him, Brandt stared at the man and tried to decide how to best respond. A fight would go poorly, and the man might even kill him. With Brandt only knowing the Illuminate and Reduce Gravity runes, magic would be of little use. There was only one path to take – a path Brandt detested.

"I'm sorry," Brandt said with a sigh. "I've been traveling for the past week and just arrived this morning. I'm tired and grumpy. I shouldn't take it out on you."

Wyck stared at him for a moment before replying. "I would still prefer to live alone."

"You'll have to take that up with Elias. He told me to take this room…said it would be good for me."

"Wonderful," Wyck grumbled. "Now I get to care for a whelp, like some sort of nursemaid."

"I'm actually seventeen, just turned last week."

Wyck snorted. "It's even worse than I thought. Please tell me that you don't need me to help you dress each morning."

"You're hilarious."

Wyck grinned. "I've always thought so."

Brandt restrained his retort as he stared at his massive roommate.

"Your room is the one on the left." Wyck pointed across the apartment, toward two open doors. "I get the window."

The mention of a window drew Brandt's attention toward the light coming through the curtains across the room. Curious, he walked toward them and pulled the drapes aside to reveal a pair of glass-paned doors and a balcony outside them. Beyond the balcony was an open indoor space, lit by a glass ceiling high above.

"The Atrium," Wyck said. "Impressive, isn't it?"

"Yes." Brandt turned to find Wyck again on the sofa. "I've never heard of a building designed like this. What was the intent?"

Wyck shrugged. "I never really thought about it. If you care so much, you figure it out."

Again, Brandt stared at the man with a grimace. As a prince, he was unused to others treating him as if…he was unimportant.

A bell rang from the Atrium, the peal echoing throughout the cavernous space. "What's the bell about?"

Wyck stood, grinning. "That means it's time for lunch." He started toward the exit. "Let's go eat."

—+ ⏀ +—

When they entered the dining hall, Wyck introduced Brandt to those seated at their table while Cassie's roommate, Rena, did the same for her. Brandt did his best to remember the names, able to recall seven out of twelve. A telepathic exchange with Cassie brought the number up to eleven, leaving just one name a mystery – a quiet girl with dark hair who sat at the far end of the table, periodically pushing her spectacles up in between bites.

The dining hall was larger than Brandt's father's dining hall in Kantar. Six long tables occupied the space, each able to seat sixteen people. Half of the tables remained unoccupied. Brandt sat beside his sister during the meal, eating in quiet. Wyck sat on the other side of Brandt, boasting about this and that to a quiet man named Thiron and a redheaded teen named Jonah. Nobody appeared younger than Brandt and his sister.

Halfway into the meal, a girl entered the room, drawing Brandt's attention. With long blond hair and blue eyes that surveyed the room while she walked toward her seat, her tight jerkin and breeches revealed an extremely fit physique, her bare arms toned and muscular. He stared at her until an odd whirring sound redirected his attention.

A boy with dark hair entered the room, the whirring sound coming from him in bursts that matched each step. An odd type of armor encased his legs, the metal bands glinting in the sunlight streaming through the windows that faced the Atrium. Brandt stared at the mechanical legs as the boy walked past and claimed the last open seat, across from the blond girl who had preceded him.

"Hello, Everson. Hi, Quinn," Jonah said to the newcomers.

The blond girl gave him a silent nod. When her eyes met Brandt's, he found himself glued to her gaze, unable to turn away.

"Hello. I'm Quinn," she said before nodding toward the dark-haired boy seated across the table. "That's my brother, Everson."

Brandt smiled his best smile. "I'm Brandt. I just arrived here."

"Don't you think she knows you just arrived?" Wyck asked.

The smile fell away from Brandt's face.

"Since my brother neglected to introduce me as well, my name is Cassilyn. You can call me Cassie," Cassie said.

"Hi, Cassie." Quinn smiled. "Hey, Ev. We are no longer the only siblings here."

The boy with the metal legs gave Brandt and Cassie a shaky grin as he slid his chair in.

The small talk among the group continued throughout the meal until Master Alridge entered the room. Brandt found himself distracted by her beauty and the way she filled her tight breeches and purple tunic, despite the woman being as old as his parents. His gaze drifted and he found himself staring at the blond girl across the table. He found her face more handsome than pretty, despite the bruise to her cheek. Her blue eyes held an ever-present hardness, as if challenging anyone who dared to look at them. He found himself drawn to that challenge and wondered why she was at the Ward – wondered what attributes she possessed that enticed ICON to draw her into the fold.

When Master Alridge finished speaking, turned, and departed, the others began gathering their empty plates and rising to their feet.

Cassie nudged him. "You heard her. Hurry up."

"What?" he asked as he tried to recall the words Master Alridge had said.

Cassie rolled her eyes. "Weren't you listening? She said that we are to be in the briefing room in five minutes."

"Who?"

Cassie glared at him. "All new recruits, which includes you and me."

Brandt stood and turned to leave.

"You forgot your plate," Jonah said.

"I'm finished eating." Brandt's brow furrowed. "Why do I need my plate?"

"You can't leave your plate there. You have to bring it to the kitchen."

"That's a job for the servants."

The comment sent a round a laughter throughout the room, one that touched everyone but Brandt and Cassie.

Jonah shook his head, smiling. "Good joke...servants."

After a moment of sulking, Brandt followed Jonah, the tall Tantarri girl, and a portly boy named Henrick through the door while a handful of others trailed behind him. They went down a flight of stairs, dropped their plates off in the scullery, and headed upstairs before entering a room three doors from the dining hall.

The room was as long as the dining hall, with a wall of windows that faced the Atrium. In the center of the room were six tables, arranged in the shape of a U. The wall at the far end of the room was solid black. Master Alridge stood before that wall, tapping the nails of her fingers on the end of a table while she waited for her students.

"Everyone, please sit," she said.

Brandt found a chair at one end of the U, and Cassie sat beside him. When everyone was settled, and the room had quieted, Master Alridge addressed them.

"While I do not normally spend much time in the Ward, the academy is on summer break and the students are away, which affords me time to contribute here. Over the next six weeks, you will learn more about Chaos than most academy students learn during their three-year tenure."

A student's hand raised into the air and Alridge said, "Yes, Jonah."

"Some of us already know how to use Chaos."

"Yes. Some can, but most of you will never be able to use it," she said. "What's your point?"

Jonah asked, "What will we learn?"

"Hmm. Where do I even begin?" She turned around, pulled a chunk of glowstone from her pocket, and began drawing on the black wall. Once finished, she moved back and pointed toward the rune she had sketched. "Who can tell me what this rune means?"

Silence.

"That's what I thought." She turned and traced another one. "How about this one?"

Silence.

"Now that we've established that you have much to learn, understanding and memorizing every known rune and how to apply it will be our first focus. After that, we will work on how to apply permanent augmentations."

"Enchanting?" Everson asked as he leaned forward, the eagerness in his voice matching his expression.

"Yes, although we call it Infusion...and I must warn you, it is among our most closely guarded secrets. The mere existence of the ability is not something we discuss outside this building. If the ability got into the wrong hands and was used without regard, the consequences could be devastating."

Brandt considered what she said. "Did you say that some of the people here cannot use Chaos?"

Master Alridge nodded. "Yes. In fact, only three of the wardens in this room have the ability."

With a questioning glance toward his sister, Brandt asked. "Why teach it to the others, then? Why risk the secret of Infusion to additional exposure?"

"Good question." She began to walk around the room as she spoke, clasping her hands behind her back as Brandt had seen his father do often. "Infusion can do wonderful things. A permanent augmentation, when intelligently combined with science, can yield amazing results. Within the Ward, a controlled environment filled only with trusted personnel, we can and will use Infusion to our advantage."

The blond girl raised her hand, the girl with the challenging eyes. *What was her name again?*

"Yes, Quinn?"

That's it! Her name is Quinn, He thought.

Quiet. This is interesting, Cassie sent to him.

Brandt blinked at her response. He hadn't meant for her to hear that thought.

Quinn said, "I understand why my brother and the other engineers need to know this, but why should I learn it?" She gestured toward the Tantarri girl beside her and the imposing teen beyond. "Why Chuli, or Bilchard?"

"Well, you three are being trained for combat, whether as a wildcat, espion, or ranger. There will be times when Chaos augmentations will help you in tight situations – whether applied directly to your person or to a device that has received a permanent augmentation. Understanding these things will help you anticipate the result and will assist your decision-making when your life is on the line."

Brandt found himself again staring into Quinn's eyes, the look within them firm…resolute.

"Now that we are through the introduction, let's get started."

Master Alridge again moved to the black wall and began drawing a rune. "We have little time, and you have much to learn."

15

PRINCE

With his right arm extended, Broland Talenz held his longsword with the point toward his imaginary enemy, the blade unwavering until he lowered it, spun and whipped it around with an upswing. Sweat beaded on his forehead and tracked down his temple. The sunlight streaming through the high windows of the circular room created bright rectangular beams filled with specks of swirling dust. Shifting from one stance to another, he spun through one such beam and his sword sent a flash of reflected light streaking across the wall. In his mind, he pictured an imaginary enemy and countered a pretend strike before flowing into the next form. In times past, he would have been performing these steps with a wooden weapon against an actual dueling partner. That person was no longer at the castle, and the vacancy left Broland alone in more ways than one. The thought rekindled memories of the week prior.

Brandt and Cassilyn stood beside a waiting carriage. On the ground beside them was a trunk filled with the possessions that would join them on their journey. Broland's father hugged the twins and told them he was proud of them. His mother's tearful goodbye left Broland uncomfortable, and he found himself looking at the carriage wheels rather than his family. When his parents had finished their farewells, Broland hugged Cassie and wished her well before clasping his brother's arm and giving him a nod. After a close brotherly bond during their younger years, their relationship had become a rivalry as the two boys aged. Being a year older had given Broland an edge over Brandt until recently. Over the past two years, their interactions, whether dueling or otherwise, had become tainted by an unspoken bitterness.

When the siblings climbed into the carriage and the porters had loaded the trunk in the back, the driver coaxed the horses into motion, and the carriage rolled toward the citadel gate. Brock put his arm about Ashland, the two watching their children depart without knowing when they might see them again. Ashland wiped her eyes dry and put her head on Brock's shoulder. Broland had anticipated his mother crying during Brandt and Cassie departure.

When the carriage rolled through the gate and disappeared, Broland stewed about his sibling's departure. Rather than feeling sad, the acrid taste of jealousy twisted Broland's mouth when he found himself wishing he had their independence. His role of heir prince left little room for the freedom he so desired. Neither Brandt nor Cassie understood what it was like to be shackled in that manner.

With a sigh, Broland lowered his sword and shook the memory from his head.

"I am encouraged to see you practicing, even if you are without a sparring partner."

Broland turned to find Wharton standing in the doorway. "Sword practice is part of my daily routine. Besides, I have worked for years to get to this point, and I would hate to lose what I have trained so hard to attain."

A grin crossed Wharton's face. "Good response, my Prince."

"I'm glad you approve."

Wharton shifted aside, gesturing toward the door. "I was sent to retrieve you. Your father requested your presence."

Broland slid the sword into the scabbard at his hip. He had been wearing it often for the past year, trying to get used to having a weapon at his side. Moving past Wharton, he exited the sparring room and walked down a long corridor with the captain of the guard trailing him. At the far end, he went through a doorway, ran up a flight of stairs, and rounded a corner that connected to another corridor.

"Your father is in his office." Wharton said from behind.

Broland approached the door and knocked.

"Come in," Brock's voice called from inside.

When he opened the door, Broland found General Budakis seated in a chair that faced the king's desk. From behind the desk, Brock nodded to Broland as he entered.

"Thank you for joining us, Son."

"Yes, Father."

Wharton stepped inside and closed the door. "I found him in the sparring room, practicing his forms."

Brock gave Broland a nod, his eyes focused on him. "I am glad that you remain serious about your training."

"Yes. However, I now lack a sparring partner."

"That is part of why I called you here." The king sat back in his chair. "When I decided to send your brother and sister to Fallbrandt, I realized you would be losing not only a sparring partner, but also the only real peers you have in the castle.

"I took the opportunity to have a few private discussions with the other royals before they departed Kantar following Libra Te. It turns out that Chadwick's cousin, Baron Rhone of Hipoint, has an adopted son who is your age and is apparently quite skilled with the sword and shield.

"Baron Rhone agreed to send Kony to live here for a year, perhaps longer. He will train with you as your new sparring partner. I ask that you do your best to get along with him. I promised Rhone that Kony would gain valuable experience from his stay at the capital. After all, Kantar is the largest city in the Kingdom, while Hipoint just a seaside village built on a cliffside."

Broland considered the idea and found himself hopeful. Having someone his age around would be even more welcome than having a sparring partner. "I will do my best, Father."

"Good," Brock said with a slow nod.

"You said there was more than one reason you called me here."

"Yes." Brock gestured toward Budakis.

The man looked up at Broland. "With the Empire looming as a threat and their borders running to Yarth, we have decided to reinstate the old Holy Army garrison at Hipoint. It will require some rebuilding, but having a foothold there will discourage them from expanding toward Wayport. The village of Hipoint has no wall and is not particu-larly defensible, but the garrison is another story. If we also position catapults atop the cliffside, we can discourage naval attacks with the height advantage providing extended launch range. Two full ranks of soldiers are already in route to the garrison."

Broland's brow furrowed. "I understand. May I ask why you are explaining this to me?"

Brock stood. "If anything should happen to me, you must be aware of the political situation and our military strategy. Addressing these types of issues would become your job, and the lives of our citizens would be in your hands."

The king circled the desk and stood before Broland, locking eyes with him. "You have always been the responsible one when compared to Brandt and Cassie. Your mother and I saw this, yet we encouraged you to enjoy your youth because it will only come once. I'll not tell you that you must stop enjoying life, but you are now an adult and you must embrace your obligations. Things will change for you, just as they have changed for your brother and sister. We must be ready for anything that might occur."

Following his guards, Lorna and Burke, Broland emerged from the steam carriage and squinted at the brightness of the afternoon sun. Workers milled about the docks below, busy as they loaded and unloaded wagons that ran from the city to the warehouses along the shoreline. Carts ran up and down the three major piers, along with sailors and passengers who had recently docked or were preparing to depart. Two ships were docked on the north and center pier, while a single vessel was moored at the south pier. With his hand shading his eyes from the sun, Broland searched for the teen he was to greet, but sunlight mixing with the milky sea spray over the harbor made it diffi-cult to discern one person from another.

A young man with black hair, a sword at his hip, and a pack over his shoulder emerged from between two warehouses. He was tall and broad-shouldered, dressed well enough to belong in Upper Kantar without appearing as if he were headed to a formal dinner. As the teen drew nearer, it became clear that he had the muscular build, yet lacked the bulk that might negate his flexibility or quickness. Above his amber eyes and dark eyebrows, a rune marked his forehead – the rune of Order.

The teen called out as he approached the carriage. "Are you here to bring me to the citadel?"

Broland replied, "That depends on your name."

"I'm Kony Kearns," he said with a smile. "Are you my escort?"

"I suppose I am. Do you have additional items that need to be loaded into the carriage?"

"No." He swung the pack over his shoulder and held it toward Broland. "This is it. Do you mind loading it for me?"

Kony shoved the bag into Broland's hands, nodded toward the two guards, and climbed into the steam carriage. With an arched brow, Broland turned toward the guards. Lorna chuckled while Burke stepped forward, took the pack, and stuffed it into an external storage compartment.

Broland climbed onto the step, ducked into the carriage, and sat on the bench opposite from Kony. The two guards climbed inside with Lorna sitting beside Broland and Burke beside Kony. The driver, standing behind Kony's seat with his head sticking up over the boiler at the front, opened the firebox door and dumped a bucket of coal into it. The man opened the flue and spun a crank that sent a whistle from the steam engine. Moments later, he pushed a lever forward and the machine began to rotate. Once it faced the road that lead back to the city, he pushed the other lever forward and it lurched into motion, puffing steam from the stack at top. The white exhaust mixed with the black smoke of the fire that billowed from the other pipe.

Knowing the rarity of steam carriages, Broland examined Kony throughout this process, curious to see his reaction. He found himself disappointed when the newcomer acted as if it were nothing of note. Kony just stared at the passing palm trees, their green fronds swaying in the breeze.

Kony leaned forward, his eyes narrowed as he pointed out the window. "I assume that's Southgate Bridge?"

Broland peered to the south and found the bridge coming into view as the carriage crested the hill that led down to the docks. Shaped like a shallow arch, a quarter mile in length, the blue stone bridge was an engineering marvel.

"Yes. That bridge crosses the Alitus River, with a two-hundred-foot drop."

"I heard that magic was used to build it."

Broland nodded. "Yes. At least, that is what scholars believe. Since the records were destroyed centuries ago, we can only guess."

The carriage rolled on, the wheels rumbling as it approached the city gate.

"Have you been to Kantar before?" Broland asked.

"No. I haven't been west of Wayport. My aunt is Duchess Illiri, and she has had me at the castle a number of times."

"So, you are important?"

"That depends on your definition. I live in Hipoint Manor. I know important people. I'm related to important people. In fact, I was brought here as a companion for Prince Broland."

Lorna covered her mouth and turned away from Kony, attempting to hide her grin. Somehow, Broland buried his urge to smile and remained stoic. When his glance landed on Kony's scabbard, a longsword much like his own, he altered the course of the conversation.

"Are you good with a blade?"

Kony replied, "I don't like to sound like a braggart, but there are few who can best me. None in Hipoint nor anyone at my aunt's court."

"For not wishing to sound like a braggart," Lorna noted, "You did an excellent job of doing so."

Kony turned toward her and frowned. "Aren't you a guard?"

Her eyes narrowed. "Members of the king's guard are not just guards. Only the best and most trustworthy are offered such a position."

"They sent the king's guard to the docks just for me? I do feel special now." Kony said.

Lorna rolled her eyes and turned toward the window. The carriage slowed for the thickening traffic when they entered the city. People gave way to the noisy steam carriage as it rolled up Center Street. They passed inns, shops, carts filled with produce, a street musician plucking a lute, and a baker with two baskets of bread. Foot traffic included city guards, merchants, sailors, officials, shoppers, and beggars. An occasional horse or horse-drawn carriage slid past them, but those were few compared to the people on foot. All the while, they rode uphill, through Lower Kantar, until they rolled past another gate.

While the traffic volume remained, the road widened and created the illusion of it being less busy. The buildings that lined the street were more impressive than those in Lower Kantar, often three stories tall and well maintained. Here, rich marble or alabaster pillars replaced the rough stone or wooden posts in the lower portion of the city. The storefronts displayed fine fabrics, well-crafted weapons, jewelry, and works of art.

Kony leaned out the window and gaped, commenting. "This area of the city is much nicer than the rest."

"Upper Kantar," Broland noted. "This is where the wealthier merchants and minor aristocrats live."

They crossed a small plaza encircled by carts selling handcrafted wares, passed a fountain, and headed through another gate. Broland waved to the guards on duty as the steam carriage – painted in the black, red, and gold of Kantar and marked on the side with the king's sigil – rolled past.

They crossed the edge of the open square that lay before the palace. Kony stared at the towering black sculpture at the center, featuring a giant dog and a thin man, pointing toward the horizon.

"What's the sculpture about?"

"It represents the hero within each of us. The intent is to inspire the people of Kantaria to be the best person they can be."

Broland had heard the story from his father numerous times, along with the stories of the dog and man that the sculpture was meant to represent. There was a time when Broland was young that he had a giant imaginary dog named Wraith, inspired by his father's stories. She would follow him through the castle and often hide from him, only to pounce when young Broland found her. A smile crossed Broland's face at the memory.

The statue faded from view as the carriage rounded the building and entered a courtyard. A cobblestone loop encircled an ancient oak. A flower-filled garden filled the space between the drive and the western wall. When the carriage stopped, Burke opened the door and climbed out with Lorna a step behind. Broland gestured for Kony to exit and then climbed out behind him.

As he turned from the steam carriage, Broland found Burtles and two porters waiting. The porters ran to the wagon and opened the storage compartment to collect Kony's belongings. Burtles shuffled forward and gave a shallow bow.

"Welcome back, my Prince," Burtles intoned before turning toward Kony. "Welcome, Master Kearns. I have prepared a room for you on the fourth floor. If you please, follow me."

The silver-haired man turned and walked toward the palace door, moving in his stiff, formal manner.

Kony turned toward Broland with a pained look on his face. "Prince Broland?"

Broland smirked. "That's me."

"Oh, no," Kony cringed. "I've made a complete fool of myself."

"Well, not a *complete* fool. You made a valiant effort, and you display serious potential. However, you have work to do before you achieve full fool status." Broland grinned at his own humor. "If you apply yourself, I'm sure you'll get there. Now, come along. Burtles despises it when people dally."

16

AN ANGRY PIG

Quinn held the Impending Thunder pose, balancing on one foot, her core tight, her form perfect. Nalah, Wyck, Thiron, Chuli, Kirk, and Bilchard also maintained their forms as instructed, but the new boy didn't fully extend his leg, and he held his arm in the wrong position. While Quinn hadn't yet interacted with Brandt or his sister, she had discovered that they were Kantarian royalty. Other than a slight arrogance, she hadn't discovered anything royal about either of them. She stared at Brandt as his leg trembled, trying to decide what she thought of him.

With his athletic build, short brown hair, and intense green eyes, she had to admit that she found him attractive. However, dressed in a black-padded sparring vest and gray breeches like Quinn and the others, he didn't appear very princely.

Kwai-Lan moved to the next pose, and the students mirrored his action without thought – all but Brandt, who wobbled and lost his balance.

"You must maintain balance, Brandt." Kwai-Lan said without affecting his pose. "Focus on your core. The position of your arms will act as a counterweight to your leg."

"Why are we doing this? I already know how to fight."

Kwai-Lan frowned, his thin black mustache bending with his mouth. "No. You know how to brawl. This is Singa Chi."

"Well, I think it's a waste of time. For three days, you've had us posing as if we were performing a dance. When do we fight?"

Kwai-Lan lowered his leg to stand, his face a grimace. He strode up to Brandt while the others maintained their poses. Although the Singa Chi master stood two inches shorter than Brandt and a full foot shorter than Bilchard, the man's presence loomed much larger than his stature. Kwai-Lan's compact build matched Quinn in height and consisted of nothing but muscle – toned, and lean.

Despite the way Brandt set his jaw, he backed a step when Kwai-Lan drew close.

"You think you know all there is to know about fighting?" Kwai-Lan asked.

"I was trained by the captain of my father's elite guard, a trained military man with combat experience. He told me I had learned all he had to offer. He's much bigger than you, and I'm sure he could beat you soundly." Brandt glared at the man with challenge in his eyes.

Kwai-Lan's eyes narrowed. "I see. Since you are so sure of yourself, and you seem to think that size and strength are so important, I'm sure you won't mind sparring against Quinn."

Quinn blinked and turned toward Brandt, still holding her pose. Their eyes met.

"You want me to fight…a girl?"

Kwai-Lan arched a brow. "Are you afraid you might lose?"

Brandt grimaced. "No."

"Very well." Kwai-Lan turned toward the students. "Relax, everyone. It appears we have ourselves a little diversion today. Brandt and Quinn have agreed to provide our instruction."

"I have?" Quinn said.

"I believe you are perfect for this particular lesson, Quinn. In fact, I would like to see you two spar on the platform." The man pointed up toward the lowest crossbeam of the Jungle, standing ten feet above the Atrium floor.

Quinn nodded. "Fine."

Brandt stared up at the platform, the arrogance absent from his expression.

"Are you having doubts, Mister Talenz?" Kwai-Lan asked.

"No." Brandt shook his head. "Of course, not. Let's do it."

Without a word, Quinn gripped the nearest rope and began to scale it hand over hand. When she cleared the top of the beam that led to the platform, she swung her body, placed a foot upon it, and dismounted before scrambling across the beam. There she stood on the platform with hands on hips and staring down at her opponent. Brandt set his jaw in determination and climbed up to join her, the action causing little apparent effort. *He's strong for his size*, Quinn thought, *and outweighs me by twenty or thirty pounds*. She backed up, giving him space. A glance down confirmed her position a foot from the end of the platform, with two feet to either side of her and a length of nine feet before her. Brandt stood on the other end, appraising her. *Does he see me as a girl or an enemy?* she wondered. *I guess I'm both.*

Kwai-Lan called out from below as the other students gathered behind him to watch. "You lose if you give up, have a major bone broken, get knocked out, or fall from the platform." Quinn and Brandt both nodded and the man called out, "Begin."

Quinn stepped forward, falling into the Nitor Bellum pose, balanced, yet ready to react. Brandt eased himself forward with his left foot and left hand in the lead, like a brawler. Without moving, Quinn held herself still and calm, waiting for him to close the gap.

His left fist flashed toward her face but missed the mark when Quinn jerked her head to the side with a slight twist of her body. A right punch followed, but he missed when her forearm smashed into his and knocked it aside. He had moved too close and left himself open by overextending. Quinn's open hand lashed out and chopped him in the throat. His eyes bulged, and he lifted a foot to take a retreating step. Quinn's sweeping kick connected with the back of his opposite knee, taking the leg from beneath him. His back landed on the platform with a thud, his momentum taking him over the edge to fall to the floor below where he bounced off the magically modified stone before settling on his side.

Quinn stood at the edge of the platform as Brandt squirmed below, trying to breathe. When a healer ran over and knelt beside him, Quinn placed her hands on the platform edge, flipped her legs high overhead, and vaulted toward the floor below. She bent her knees with the landing before standing over her fallen opponent. The healer stepped away, and Brandt looked up at Quinn.

"Sorry, but you lose," Quinn said.

He rolled over and scrambled to his feet, his face a thundercloud. With his chest thrust out, he moved close to Quinn and sneered. "That was cheap. We were sparring, and you hit my throat."

Quinn's eyes narrowed, and she remained still despite him invading her space. "I fail to recall any rule against such a move. Now, I suggest you back away before I beat you again...much worse."

Brandt glared at her for a moment before backing away.

Kwai-Lan clapped his hand on Brandt's shoulder. "She is correct, Brandt. Maybe you understand better now. You must learn discipline and maintain balance. Think, focus, react. These tools supersede brawn for those properly trained. You are a warden, now. We aren't here to teach you how to fight for sport. This struggle is much greater. If you find yourself in the field, you will be fighting for your life. There are no rules...only the living and the dead. Which would you rather be?"

The Singa Chi master turned and strolled toward the exit while Brandt stared in his direction. Quinn understood. She had gone through a similar experience with Kwai-Lan when she had first arrived at the Ward. Being fast, strong, and relentless had given Quinn an edge against her fellow female cadets at the combat academy. After arriving at the Ward, she quickly discovered that the hand fighting taught at the academy was only a pale imitation of Singa Chi. The art, combined with her training, were changing her into something more than a mere fighter. She knew she could now defeat opponents who presented a physical mismatch. Her skill had surpassed that of Nalah, despite the girl's extra year of practice. It left Quinn wondering when her first mission would come.

Quinn gathered herself as she stared at the door. The corridor was quiet – nobody in sight and nothing of note other than the glowing tiles below and illuminated beams above. She took a deep breath and lifted her fist to knock when the door swung open.

"Hi, Doll," Wyck grinned. "I see you've finally given in to your desires and have come for a taste of what Wyck has to offer."

Quinn's mouth twisted before she responded. "Sorry, but I don't have the stomach for that particular dish."

His grin widened. "I do love dueling with you."

"You mean you enjoy losing." She peeked past him and into the apartment. "Is Brandt here?"

"Oh, so you'd rather have a run at the little stuck-up prince?" He moved aside and waved her in. "Come in. You can join him in his pouting."

Quinn entered the room to find Brandt lying on the sofa. When he saw her, he sat up and swung his feet to the floor.

"Quinn," Brandt said.

"You must admit, he is observant." Wyck said from behind her. "You didn't even have to sit on his lap and give him a tickle for him to notice you."

Rolling her eyes, she turned toward Wyck. "Weren't you about to leave?"

He chuckled. "Yes. I'm joining Thiron for a few mugs of ale. Care to join us?"

She shook her head. "No, thanks. I've heard your stories. You two go on and compare conquests."

He shrugged, "Suit yourself."

When the door shut, she turned toward Brandt and found him staring at her from the sofa. Clinging to her resolve, Quinn crossed the room and sat in the chair across the Ratio Bellicus table from him.

"I...I wanted to apologize," she said. "Kwai-Lan teaches us to be quick, efficient, and ruthless when we fight. You left yourself open, so I responded as I was trained."

Brandt's grimace deepened, his eyes narrowing as he stared at her. The intensity she had noticed before was again present, lingering, until he looked away and sighed.

"Don't worry about it. Kwai-Lan wanted to prove a point – a point well made. I can sometimes be...over confident."

Quinn snorted. "Among other things."

"What's that supposed to mean?"

"You act like you're waiting for others to do everything for you, to bow down and treat you like you're exceptional." She pointed toward the door. "Out there, you might be someone important, but in the Ward, you are no different than the rest of us. You're training to be a warden, now. I suggest you forget your title and focus on learning everything you can as quickly as possible."

Brandt sat back and smiled. "You sound like my father."

"Smart man."

He chuckled. "Some would say so. Most people, in fact."

"So, you're not...angry with me?"

"No." Brandt shook his head. "You're fast. One moment, I was trying to punch you and the next...I was on the floor choking for air."

"Fast and efficient. Balanced and focused. That is how Kwai-Lan trains us."

"Well, you appear to be a good student."

She snorted in response. "Don't think I was always that way. We all take our lumps as we learn our lessons. Some require more beatings than others do. I'm here to recommend that you limit yours as much as possible."

His eyes narrowed. "Why all this concern?"

Quinn looked toward the window. "When I first got to the combat academy, it seemed as if everyone stood against me. In many ways, it was my fault. I have a tendency to push others away and try to do everything on my own. My father has often said that I'm more stubborn than an angry pig." She turned toward him, the pair locking eyes. "I see some of that in you. While they're not horrible traits, I prefer not to watch things be more difficult for you than necessary."

Brandt leaned forward. "Thank you."

She lowered her eyes, her gaze falling on the game board. "Do you play?"

"Ratio Bellicus? Yes. In fact, I was the best in the citadel by the time I left."

"Really? You sound pretty sure of your skill."

"Perhaps you would like to find out for yourself?"

Quinn smiled. "I thought you'd never ask."

17

MAGIC

C assie gripped the ladder rungs and glanced down at Everson, who was the last person to make the climb. He moved carefully, his odd mechanical legs whirring as he slowly worked his way up the ladder. When she looked back up, her brother stepped off the ladder and faded from view. The bright sunlit sky waited above, beckoning her. She resumed her climb and surfaced into daylight.

Wind blew her hair into her face as she stood on the rooftop, but the wind was welcome with it being the heart of summer and the midday sun making its presence known even in the high altitude of the valley. Similar to her fellow wardens-in-training, Cassie felt herself drawn toward the half-wall that encircled the Ward rooftop. She found a spot between Jonah and Brandt and rested her arms upon the wall as she stared out at the vista before her.

The valley stretched out to the south – the grassy fields of the lawn split by a brown strip of road lined by trees. At the far end of the lawn was the combat academy, nestled beside the forest that lay between it and Fallbrandt. In the distance, she could see a smattering of rooftops beside the lake that shared the same name as the city. To the east and west, tall, pointed peaks enveloped the valley and made Cassie think of giant teeth, as if the academies were in the mouth of some unimaginably gigantic monster. Gray rock, with patches of snow still on the north face, covered the mountaintops before giving way to the greens of trees at lower elevations. The scene was one of tranquil beauty. Something to cherish. With a sigh, Cassie turned her attention to the building complex below.

The Fallbrandt Academy of Magic and Engineering sprawled out in all directions. The domed roof of the Academy Temple and the glass panels of the Arena reflected sunlight, causing her to squint when she looked in their direction. Other portions of the building extended in all directions like a spider's legs.

"Yes, the view is wonderful," Master Alridge called out, drawing everyone's attention. Cassie turned to find the woman and Everson standing a dozen strides away, beside an oddly designed catapult. "You may spend more time gazing at the view after we complete our lesson. For now, come over and gather around so you can see better."

Cassie scanned the rooftop as she and the others gathered around the Chaos Theory instructor. The middle of the building was capped by a low-angled pyramid of glass windows, which she recognized as the ceiling of the Atrium. Surrounding it was a walkway twenty feet across, and a low wall at the outer edge of the roof. *I'd hate to fall from this height,* she thought to her brother.

His voice rang back in her head, *I wonder what it would be like to jump from up here while charged with a Reduce Gravity augmentation.*

She imagined falling from twelve stories up. Even if she were charged with the augmentation and needn't fear dying from the fall, the thought gave her a shiver and sent her stomach aflutter.

The students gathered in a circle, leaving Alridge and the catapult at the center.

"The siege engine behind me was designed by Master Hedgewick. Rather than possessing a single launch arm, intended for a heavy projectile, this one can rapidly fire up to four smaller objects. The concept enables us to take advantage of certain augmentations in a combination of science and magic."

Using both hands, the woman lifted a wooden disk, a foot in diameter. "This disk is marked with the Heat rune we discussed in this morning's session." She gestured toward a stack of disks that rested beside the machine. "As are each of these.

"We use the disks as a means for you to train your abilities. At the same time, by periodically sending fireballs off this rooftop, it reinforces the image of the Ward. Others see it as an imposing building where arcanists practice dangerous magic." She smiled. "While fear mongering can cause many problems, in this case, it encourages others to stay away from the Ward and allows us to maintain the secrecy of its true purpose."

She held the disk out toward the nearest student. "Everson, would you care to show us the modifications you made to this machine?"

Everson accepted the disk, grunting at the weight as he held it in both hands. He moved closer to the catapult and gripped a lever while holding the disk against his stomach. "I have used Chaos Conduction to modify the reloading mechanism. Behold…"

When Everson pushed the lever down, a whirring sound emerged, accompanied by a series of clicks. The four launch arms slowly lowered before clicking into place. He then lifted the lever and the whirring stopped.

"Ivy, will you please grab a disk and join Everson?" Alridge asked, receiving a silent nod from the quiet girl.

Ivy shifted over to the stack, picked up a disk with a grunt, and settled beside Everson.

Alridge said, "Be sure to have the rune side of the disks facing this direction when you load the launch basket. Once loaded, I need each of you to stand ready at the release lever."

The two students each placed a disk into an oddly shaped catapult launch bucket, designed to hold the disk upright…like a coin on edge.

"Jonah, Cassie, Brandt…which of you wants to go first?"

Cassie stepped forward before her brother could react.

"Very well, Cassie." Master Alridge said. "You likely guessed that I wish you to perform a Chaos augmentation. However, a fully powered Heat augmentation creates an intense fire, hot enough to burn one of these wooden disks in a mere second or two. Instead, I want you to try something new. Once you have gathered the Chaos energy, release only a portion of it into one rune before moving on to the other. This will create a lesser augmentation in each, while allowing for multiple applications."

Cassie nodded and closed her eyes, preparing to access Chaos.

In the beginning, extreme fear or anger were required to feel Chaos, to gather it and channel it into a rune. With each subsequent attempt, the process had grown easier. Now, a year after her first successful augmentation, it took her mere moments to access the power.

She sensed the raw and angry power of Chaos surrounding her, a tempest of energy that was invisible to the naked eye, but was always there. Opening herself up, she drew it in as simply as taking a breath. By the time she opened her eyes again, it seemed like she might melt from the fury of Chaos raging inside her.

Focusing on the first rune, she allowed the Chaos to flow out and then urgently cut off the flow, feeling as though she were trying to hold back a herd of horses. She found herself sweating, shaking, and dizzy from the pressure building inside her. The first rune glowed and Alridge commanded, "Everson, launch!" He pulled the lever and launched the disk while Cassie focused on the second rune. She removed the block and allowed the remaining energy to flow out. The rune on the disk began to glow and Alridge called out, "Ivy, launch!" The girl pulled the lever and the launch arm sprang forward.

Breathing heavily from the effort, Cassie felt relieved to be free of the power as the anticipated wave of exhaustion hit her, causing her to stagger. She gazed toward the east and found a distant fireball, thousands of feet away, burn out. The second fireball chased it until, it too, snuffed to a puff of smoke and ash.

Alridge clapped her hand on Cassie's shoulder. "Very good, Cassilyn. You were able to perform a two-part partial augmentation on your first attempt. Very good, indeed."

Cassie stopped before the closed door and turned toward her brother. "This is where she said we were to be, right?"

"Yeah," Brandt said.

She gripped the knob and opened the door. The room was dark, save for the light coming through an open door on the opposite wall. Beyond the door was the Atrium floor and warriors training with wooden sparring weapons. They were going through stances, similar to the training she had seen soldiers performing at the Kantar Citadel.

Among seven fighters training on the floor, she had only met Quinn, Chuli, Bilchard, and Wyck.

"You resemble your parents."

Cassie jumped, startled by the voice. She turned and found a man sitting in the shadows. Dressed in a purple-paneled black coat and possessing dark skin and short, dark curls, he blended well with the shadows.

The man stood and bowed his head. "My name is Jestin Wykatt. I've known your parents since they were your age...or close to it. I'm an ecclesiast instructor at the academy, and I'm here to assist in your development."

Brandt's brow furrowed. "Just the two of us?"

"Order is not like Chaos. Order is an internal magic with limited application. The others have mastered the ability to heal. What else they may someday achieve depends on their individual abilities."

"And us?" Brandt asked.

"Your parents are two of the strongest ecclesiasts of my generation. We have found that genetics often dictate one's capacity for magic. Although your untapped potential is undetermined, we suspect it will reach a significant level." His voice lowered, "I know your secret, and I have been among the very few who are aware that your parents possess the same ability."

Brandt's voice rang in her head. *I think he means telepathy.*

Of course he does. I'm not stupid.

"I assume your parents have outlined some of the abilities that manifest through Order?"

"Yes," Cassie replied. "We understand that meditation helps us tap into our talents. We know that healing, prophecy, and telepathy are possible through the use of Order."

"Good. That's a start." Jestin gestured toward the two open chairs as he reclaimed his seat. "Please, sit."

"You said that you know our parents?" Brandt asked.

"Yes. I was there with them during the Battle at the Brink."

Cassie glanced toward her brother as he addressed the man. "They won't talk much about the war or that battle. What can you tell us?"

Jestin stared into space while he spoke. "They were young...we all were. None of us understood what we were to face...none except perhaps your father. There was something about him. Even Budakis saw it."

The man's gaze found the floor. "While many died, far more would have if not for your parents, Master Hedgewick, Master Nindlerod, and a few others."

"Benny?" Disbelief was thick in Cassie's tone.

"Nindlerod?" Brandt's voice was incredulous. "The old man we saw when we first arrived?"

Jestin chuckled. "Yes. Sometimes, the mind is mightier than the sword...and both men possess extremely mighty minds."

Brandt huffed. "How is that possible?"

"Did your parents ever tell you what drove The Horde? How those mindless monsters were controlled?"

Brandt shook his head. "No."

"Among them were two arcanists, men who used their abilities to guide the Chaos that was bound inside the banshees."

Cassie leaned forward "How can Chaos be bound in someone?"

Jestin shook his head. "That is a secret for another day. You'll find out soon enough. Regardless, the enemy arcanists were the key to winning the war. Brock figured it out as did Nindlerod. The old man killed one of those men, and the monsters under his control scattered. As for what happened to the other arcanist, you must ask Master Firellus, for that is his story to tell.

"Enough of the past. I'm here to help secure the future. There is more to Order than you know and more to your abilities than what has manifested thus far.

"Divining, or determining the inherent skills a person possesses, is among the easiest abilities to perform. Healing, prophecy, and telepathy are other well-known abilities, but none are what we would consider common. And then, there are other skills that remain a mystery.

"For instance, your father once told me of a Tantarri elder who possessed the ability to enter the dreams of others, to implant images or relay messages, regardless of distance. He also described this man sharing prophetic visions with Brock in such a way that your father was able to experience the same vision as the elder. Unfortunately, we have yet to discover how to access such abilities."

The man sat forward, put his elbows on his knees, and looked Cassie in the eye. "I understand that you have been able to heal. Tell me about the experience."

Cassie bit her lip and recalled the memory. "First, I found my own center – my source of Order. With my hand on my brother, I sensed another life force, cool and pale blue, like my own. I also sensed…a wrongness that appeared like tiny red symbols, swirling about. I willed his life force to smother the wrongness. The symbols began to unwind, as if I were pulling the threads of their existence until they unraveled, and then…it was gone. When I opened my eyes, he was healed."

"Thank you, Cassie." Jestin turned toward Brandt. "What about you?"

Brandt frowned. "I…haven't been able to make it work."

"Don't worry about that. It will come. Healing is difficult to perform. You'll keep trying until you succeed."

What if it never works for me? Brandt said in Cassie's head.

It will. I know it.

Jestin sat back, eyeing the twins. "If you two are through talking behind my back, we can get started."

Cassie's eyes widened in surprise. She was unused to others being aware of their conversations.

"It all begins with meditation," Jestin said. "Close your eyes and find your center."

Shouting from the Atrium captured Cassie's attention. She saw people pairing up as Wyck and Bilchard took their wooden training weapons to a ring at the center.

"Can we close the door? The fighting is bound to be distracting."

Jestin shook his head. "The noise is a necessary distraction. You must be able to seek your center under any conditions, regardless of distractions. In addition, you cannot practice healing without patients." He pointed toward the open door. "Injuries happen while sparring and that is why you're here.

"Now, close your eyes and relax."

Doing as she was told, Cassie shut her eyes and listened to his soothing voice, which somehow sounded distant

"Seek the cool blue rune of Order at your center and embrace it…

embrace the calm...embrace the serenity. Allow the calm peace to surround you, to envelope you completely."

In her mind's eye, Cassie saw the pale blue aura of Order and held it close. As her consciousness floated in the ether, she was connected with...everything. It felt *so* right. A flash of red appeared in the periphery, accompanied by a cry of pain.

"It appears that our first patient is ready." Jestin's voice pulled her back to reality "Who wants to go first?"

Cassie circled the stables and strolled onto the training field. A three-story tall wall surrounded the area, a mile wide and twice the length. The wall was made of gray stone, the same as the walls of the Ward itself. Cassie knew that the magic academy stood just beyond the wall, but other than the temple dome to the west, she couldn't see any sign of the school.

An archery range stood along the western wall, backed by a stack of hay bales. In the center was the horse track – a loop with ditches dug across it and fences blocking it. Despite having ridden her entire life, her attempt to ride a horse on the track had proven painful. She vowed to do better next time. The thought of her fall brought images of her brother landing in the muck and brought a grin to her face. He didn't notice, instead looking ahead as he and their fellow trainees circled the track. Cassie followed Brandt's gaze and found both Quinn and Master Alridge in his line of sight. She found herself wondering which female had drawn his attention. Unable to resist, she decided to mess with him to gauge his response.

Careful, brother, she sent. *You may want to watch where you step rather than watching that girl walk. If not, you may end up in the muck again.*

You're hilarious, he turned toward her. *Was it that obvious?*

She remained unsure of which he had been staring toward – the athletic blond girl or the curvaceous instructor. *No. I was just messing with you.*

He didn't reply, but he did appear relieved.

Master Alridge stopped and turned toward the group who had trailed behind her. Knee-high grass surrounded them, spreading out in all directions. Scattered trees dotted the area and a dirt road encircled it, running along the walled perimeter. When everyone had stopped and was looking in her direction, the Arcane Arts instructor addressed them.

"As you know, we use this field to test the skills of our wardens and to execute certain augmentations that might otherwise cause damage. I shudder to think what destruction a shockwave rune charged inside the building might yield."

"Are we going to see a shockwave rune today?" Everson asked with undisguised eagerness in his voice.

Alridge shook her head. "No. For that one, we will actually move beyond the back wall. Depending on the strength of the caster, it might carry farther than anticipated. I would have much explaining to do if a section of the wall falls under my watch." She shifted toward an area where the grass was sparse, growing in scattered tufts amid bare earth. Pointing toward it with the stick she held in her hand, the woman said, "Cassie. Come here and draw a Cold rune in the dirt."

Cassie moved forward, nodding as she accepted the short stick from the woman. She then squatted and recalled the rune, drawing a version that was three feet across and half the width. When she was finished, Cassie stood and looked toward Alridge in anticipation. The woman nodded her approval and turned toward the others.

"Witness what happens when this rune is applied in the open air, particularly on a humid summer day." Master Alridge's dark eyes settled on Cassie. "Go on, Cassie. Charge it."

With a nod, Cassie closed her eyes. She felt the sun beating down on her, particularly warm today with a stickiness that left her wishing for a breeze. Beyond the heat of the sun, she sensed the now-familiar energy of Chaos. Cassie opened herself to it and pulled the power toward her, the power gathering in a rush that filled her until she thought she might burst. She opened her eyes and stared at the symbol drawn in the dirt before releasing the energy into the rune, which glowed with a bright crimson light. As it began to pulse and fade, Alridge spoke again.

"I suggest that everyone back away."

The ground around the rune turned to white frost, the ground crackling as it spread out from the core. A wave of cold air flared outward, forcing Cassie backward as she scrambled from the expanding ring of ice. A cloud emerged above the rune, spreading in a living, rolling wall of fog, thick and white. In an instant, the fog obscured the sun and made it appear as a small ball of light within the gloom. Water droplets coated her hair, her skin. She turned and discovered that the others were now shadows encased in milky white mist – silhouettes without definition.

I can't see, she sent.

Me neither, Brandt replied.

"Follow my voice," Alridge called out from somewhere to Cassie's left. "Keep moving, but slowly. No need to rush. Other than tripping over each other, you are at no risk of harm. Keep moving, and you will eventually move beyond the fog."

The shapes before Cassie began to sharpen as the fog thinned, and gave way to sunlight. Everson walked before her, his legs whirring with each step. Beyond him, she found Quinn and Chuli. To her right, Brandt emerged with Jonah beside him, Henrick and Ivy to his other side.

After wading through the murk for a number of minutes, the wispy outer edges of the fog fell away. The students gathered around Master Alridge with everyone staring toward Cassie, since she was the last person out. Their mouths gaped in wonder, gazes sweeping from the ground to the sky. She turned and saw what had drawn their attention.

Over half of the training yard was covered in thick fog, a wall that stood as high as the Ward rooftop, perhaps higher. The white mass roiled and churned, the mist inside seeming alive. The monstrosity – a thing that Cassie had created herself – was at least a half-mile in diameter. She suddenly understood that Chaos could do more than she had ever imagined.

"Impressive, Cassilyn."

Cassie turned toward the Arcane Arts instructor. "Why do you say that?"

"How old are you?"

"I am in my seventeenth summer."

"As I thought." Alridge turned toward the towering fog bank. "I have only seen a few who could generate a fog of this magnitude…and you still have a year or two before you reach your full potential."

18

THIEF

With a sidelong glance, Quinn found Delvin lit by the pale blue light of the corridor beams. He nodded toward the door and gave her an expectant stare. Words were not required to guess at what he intended. She reached toward the small of her back and withdrew the sheath he now made her carry. From it, she removed two bent needles and a narrow dagger.

With barely a rustle, she began working on the lock. One needle slipped in, turning, bending to the pressure applied until she felt a click. The other needle followed, the procedure and result the same. She inserted the dagger and twisted it while also twisting the knob. When the door opened, she flashed Delvin a grin. He put his finger to his lips and waved her forward.

Slipping inside with Delvin on her heels, Quinn crouched beside the door as he quietly closed it, the pale blue light from the hallway fading to blackness. Surrounded by darkness, Quinn listened.

Her breathing was slow, drawn out, stifled…as was Delvin's. More distant was a wheezing breath, trailed by a snore. She covered her mouth to hide her smile, despite the darkness. Delvin gripped her wrist and tugged her forward.

Without a sound, Quinn crept across the room, an apartment

similar to her own. Open curtains to the balcony allowed starlight to filter into the room and outlined their surroundings. A glance to the side revealed the bedroom door standing open, another snore coming from within.

Delvin slinked around her and approached the Ratio Bellicus table in the sitting area. After rearranging the pieces a bit, he picked one off the board and held it toward Quinn. She accepted it with a grimace, wishing she could tell him what she thought of his methods. He waved her away and refocused on the board.

Quinn turned and pressed her lips together as she stared toward the open door. Another snore came from inside, prompting her forward. Moving with silent footsteps, careful, even, balanced on the balls of her feet – as Delvin had taught her – she entered the bedroom to find a man sleeping alone on the bed. A noisy snore, louder than the others, almost forced out a guffaw, but Quinn restrained herself and remained silent as she eased toward the bed. She reached out and was about to put the game piece she held on the nightstand, but she saw another opportunity.

The man's hand lay open on the bed, well within reach. With careful precision, she reached out and gently placed the game piece into his palm. When she let go, he stirred, gripping the game piece as he moved his hand to his chest. Quinn nearly snorted in laughter, her eyes bulging as she waited for him to wake. When he snored again, she released her breath and relaxed.

She snuck out of the bedroom and found Delvin waiting by the door. When he saw her, he opened it, waved her through, and closed the door behind him.

"I thought for sure he was going to wake," Quinn whispered.

Delvin held his finger to his lip and waved her to follow as he headed down the hallway.

"While sneaking is sometimes necessary, the best infiltration – be it thieving or reconnaissance – occurs right beneath the nose of your adversary," Delvin explained as he stirred his tea. "You have skill,

Quinn. More importantly, you have a fearless nature...and that is something that cannot be taught."

"I wouldn't say fearless. I have been scared many times, even tonight."

"Yes. However, bravery is not the absence of fear, but rather moving forward despite your fear." Delvin took another sip of tea. "Now, back to my point. True espionage comes when you are in plain sight."

"I know. Personas."

Quinn took a sip of her tea and pinched her face, thinking that it could use some lemon but lacked the option since Delvin's apartment was not well stocked. The man spent less than half his time at the Ward and tended to avoid food that might spoil, such as produce.

"Exactly," he said. "Your personas must be perfect, impenetrable, and you must be able to assume them as simply as changing your smallclothes."

She gave him a sideways glance with one arched brow. "Now, you're talking about my smallclothes?"

Unaffected, he grinned. "Does that bother you?"

Quinn shrugged. "Not really. My sensibilities are not quite so sensitive."

Delvin gave a slow nod. "Good. You might be subjected to impolite comments while you are on a mission – some far worse than merely impolite. Regardless of how inappropriate or disgusting the comment, you must remain in character. Always consider how your persona should react, not how Quinn would react."

He sat back in his chair and took a long sip of tea. He swallowed, his eyes narrowing as he stared at her. Quinn refused to look away, despite the discomfort of the scrutiny. She could only guess at what might be going through the man's mind. Past attempts at predicting Delvin had only rendered frustration, so she preferred to focus her efforts elsewhere.

Finally, he broke the long moment of silence. "I must leave again."

"Already? You returned only a few weeks back."

"True," he nodded. "Yet, the world does not sit still nor does it wait upon our demands. Instead, we must adjust our plans to fit reality and make the most of what is offered."

Quinn's mouth twisted, her brow furrowed. "What does that mean?"

"It means that I am leaving again, and I have a new persona for you to develop while I am away."

"How long will you be gone?"

Delvin shrugged. "Weeks. Two or three…four at most."

"I won't bother asking where or why. I know your response." Her voice took on a nasal tone. "You'll be told if you need to know."

He smiled. "I find it refreshing to have a pupil who is willing to learn…and to accept the limitations that bind her."

"Speaking of which, what about this new…"

The door burst open, interrupting Quinn. She and Delvin turned toward it with a start and found a man dressed in black. With his long hair wild and frazzled, Elias' face was red with fury. He hobbled into the room, leaning into the cane he held in his left hand. When his right hand swung around, it smacked the table between Quinn and Delvin. The hand pulled away, leaving a wobbling Ratio Bellicus unit behind. Of course, the game piece was that of a thief.

"I told you to stay out of my room!" Elias bellowed.

"Yes, I recall that conversation," Delvin said calmly. "What makes you think I was in your room?"

"I found that game piece – a thief turned assassin – in my hand when I woke. I checked my game board and discovered it rearranged, as if it were in the middle of a highly contested match."

Delvin glanced at Quinn with a grimace. "I still don't understand the connection."

Quinn stifled her desire to laugh, her face remaining stoic as she listened to Delvin's responses – non-incriminating, yet, without a lie of denial.

"Nobody else would dare break into my room like that. None would find humor in such a childish prank. I am not sure if any of them could pull it off anyway."

Delvin tilted his head. "So, you believe I broke into your room and messed with your game pieces because you can't think of anyone else who would or could do such a thing? Is this how you assign guilt to somebody?"

The arcane master's face grew even redder until Quinn feared his head might explode. Finally, he huffed, spun around, and hobbled from the room, using the slam of the door as his final expression of frustration.

"That went well," Delvin grinned at Quinn as he lifted his teacup to his lips. "Don't you think?"

19

THE ASPEN INN

Hastily raising his shield, Broland blocked Kony's practice sword, the impact sending a jolt through his shoulder and causing him to wince. He spun with the blow to create space and to provide him time to regroup. After two heavy breaths, Broland advanced with his sword extended before him. A feint forced Kony to react and lift his shield. Broland thrust again while dropping low, Kony's blade harmlessly sweeping over his head. Broland's blade struck nothing but air as his opponent twisted. A reverse of Kony's sweep had Broland lifting his blade for an urgent block, the force of which knocked him off balance. He rolled backward and rose to his feet in one smooth movement.

The two opponents stared across the sparring room, measuring each other. Broland found Kony to be as quick as Brandt, but stronger. Fighting against another longsword required different tactics than when he had dueled with Brandt and his quarterstaff. The differences were enough that Broland had lost every match for the past two weeks. That, along with Kony's skill with a blade. Still, Broland believed that he was closing the gap.

Broland moved forward before lunging with a quick thrust. He pulled away when Kony countered and then drove toward him with repeated swipes. When Broland felt his back nearing the wall, he raised his shield, blocked a blow, and dove to the opposite side of Kony's sword. A roll and a scramble to his feet had Broland back in the center of the room.

"You two fight like you're courting one another, like a pair of jacka-roos, strutting about." Lorna's voice came from the doorway. "Just get on with it."

A grimace crossed Broland's face. He hoped it appeared like deter-mination and not a reaction from the guard's comment. With a quick step, he crossed the gap and swung. Kony's sword blocked the strike and Broland swung again, their repeated strikes sending a staccato of *clacks* off the circular chamber walls. After nine or ten swings, Broland thrust his shield toward Kony's blade and swung his sword beneath it. Again, Kony twisted and Broland missed. The move cost him the match when Kony thrust his shield into Broland's head. The *clang* of the shield striking Broland's helmet sent him stumbling to his knees and left a ringing in his ears. When he leaned forward and spat blood, the room tilted and forced him to place one hand on the floor to remain upright.

"Match," he said aloud, the taste of the word worse than the metallic tinge of blood in his mouth.

Kony removed his helmet and wiped his damp hair from his fore-head. "You did well. This was our longest bout yet."

Broland turned toward Kony, and he put one foot beneath himself. "That offers little solace. Dead is dead, and that is what I would be if this were a real fight."

He stood and stumbled as the room tilted again. His head throbbed to the rhythm of his heartbeat. An itch on his forehead caused him to wipe his arm across it. When he looked down, he found a crimson streak across the bracer on his forearm.

"You should get that healed," Lorna said as she stepped into the room.

"Thanks. I don't know what I would do without you," Broland grumbled.

She smirked. "You idiots need us women around. If not, you'd all either kill each other or drink yourself into a stupor."

Broland snorted. "I've heard a few stories about you. Don't pretend you don't throw down ale like the other guards."

Lorna shrugged. "Never said I didn't. Unlike most of the men, I know how to handle it and when to stop."

Broland turned toward Kony. "You go on and get cleaned up. I'll meet you for lunch after I get myself healed."

"You might want to clean up some of that blood as well." Kony said as he left the room.

Broland turned to the guard. "Let's go upstairs and see if my mother or father can heal me."

"You don't want to go down to the temple?"

Broland shook his head and walked into the corridor. "No. Last time I went down there, Master Beldon scolded me for not visiting the temple more often. He wants me to pray there to get closer to Issal, as if god cannot hear me anywhere else."

Lorna grunted. "I'm not so sure Issal is listening to our problems anyway. I suspect that god has bigger issues than our petty concerns."

A grin crossed Broland's face and he clapped her on the shoulder. "I always did like you, Lorna. You're not horrible company...for a girl."

Broland led her upstairs, and he found Nels pacing the fifth-floor hallway. He waved to the man before knocking on the door to his parents' room.

Ashland's voice came from inside. "Come in."

Opening the door and stepping in, he glanced back to find Lorna leaning against the corridor wall. He closed it, leaving both guards outside the room.

His mother was seated at the sofa, across from his grandmother, Ashley.

As he crossed the room, Broland wiped his forehead and found his fingertips covered in blood.

"Did you fall or were you sparring again?" Ashland asked.

"Sparring."

"How bad is it?" he could hear the concern in her voice.

Broland stopped beside the Ratio Bellicus table and said, "Hello, Grandmother,"

The woman eyed him with a critical glare before shaking her head. "You boys and your fighting."

"We weren't fighting, Grandma. We were training." He turned

toward his mother. "Nothing broken. Just bruises, cuts, and a throbbing headache."

"Come here."

He bent over, and she placed her palm against his forehead. The warmth of her hand was soon offset by a chill that wracked his body and left him gasping. Already hungry from the morning's exercise, Broland's stomach rumbled loudly when the healing left him ravenous.

"There," his mother smiled. "There is a cloth and bowl of water on the vanity. Get yourself cleaned up and then you can grab some food. Burtles was in here not twenty minutes ago to inform us that lunch was ready."

Broland walked past her to her vanity and found a cream-colored cloth between her hairbrush and a shallow bowl of water. He dipped the cloth in the water and eyed himself in the mirror as he wiped the blood from his forehead, temple, cheek, and forearm. When finished, he walked past his mother and grandmother.

"Thank you, Mother." He said as he headed toward the door.

When he stepped outside, he found Lorna and Nels in a quiet conversation. Lorna patted Nels on the shoulder and shifted closer to Broland.

"That was quick," she noted.

"Thank, Issal. I'm starving."

"I'm sure."

He ran down the stairs with her a step behind, neither one stopping until they reached the third floor. When Broland entered the informal dining room, he found both of his grandfathers, his grandmother Sally, and General Budakis in conversation with Kony.

"Hello, everyone. Sorry I'm late."

A smattering of hellos came in reply as Broland circled the table, eyeing the food waiting there. A ham, a bowl of potatoes, steamed green beans, and a basket of bread sat at the center, the smell making his mouth water and his stomach aching to be sated. He claimed an open chair between Kony and his grandfather Milan while a steward circled behind him and filled his glass with milk. The moment the man moved away, Broland began loading his plate with food.

The others had already finished eating, save for Kony, who was in mid-meal. While Broland began stuffing his mouth, General Budakis stood, his arm shaking violently as he leaned on his cane.

"I must be going. I have field reports to go over."

"Bye, Gunther," the group replied.

The man gave them a nod, and he proceeded to limp toward the door.

Milan wiped his mouth with his napkin and turned toward Sally. "Shall we?"

"Yes, dear."

"Where are you two off to?" Landon asked.

"I promised Sally a walk to the beach south of the harbor," Milan replied.

Sally stood and took Milan's arm and gave him a glowing smile. "We must keep the romance alive. Right, dear?"

Milan chuckled. "I must work at it, yes. But when it comes to you, a mere smile and I melt."

She gave him a kiss and patted his cheek. "Very good. Careful or you may get more in return than you expect."

Broland found himself blushing at the older couple's exchange. His grandfather Landon stood and patted his stomach. "Now that I'm fed, I think I'll go find Ashley and see if she would enjoy a walk as well."

"You may join us if you wish," Sally added.

The man smiled. "We may take you up on that offer."

Broland looked toward Landon, swallowing before speaking. "Grandmother is in my parent's chamber, having tea with my mother."

"Thank you, Broland," Landon smiled. "You just saved me time in hunting her down. This place is expansive, and she moves around more than one might expect."

His grandparents left the room, leaving Broland and Kony alone. Kony put his fork down, his plate almost empty.

"I've been here for two weeks, but I haven't seen any...girls. What do you do for fun?"

Broland stopped chewing and swallowed. "You won't find many for girls in the citadel...a few maids, one kitchen helper, and another down in the laundry room. None are...suitable."

"What about the local taverns?"

A grimace crossed Broland's face. "I wouldn't know."

"What do you mean?"

"I have never been to one."

"You have never been to a tavern?"

"No." Broland shook his head. "I'm not exactly allowed to roam freely."

"This has to be corrected."

"What am I supposed to do?"

Kony leaned back. "Sneak out."

Broland considered the idea. "My brother and sister used to do that. When caught, they would get in trouble, but at least they were able to pull it off first."

"So, why not you as well?"

"Isn't it…irresponsible?"

Kony snorted. "Life is short. You can't *always* be responsible. You need to catch a star and ride it now and then."

"What if you crash and burn?"

"There are no guarantees…even here, locked up in this castle."

Broland recalled the antics of his siblings, the stress they put on his father, the worry they gave his mother. Still, they had been able to experience things that eluded him and would continue to do so unless he took a chance.

"All right. I'm in."

Kony flashed his perfect white teeth. "Great. Let's think up a plan, and we'll slip away tonight. If things go well, we'll be back in our beds before sunup, and no one will be the wiser."

—✧—

The evening was cool and shadowy fog filled the courtyard – evidence of the marine layer that had rolled in once the sun had set. Broland emerged from beneath the trees and snuck toward the waiting carriage with Kony a step behind him. The sound of distant waves crashing helped to mask their footsteps, but Broland wasn't overly concerned. He suspected that the driver was dozing in the seat as he waited for his passenger.

Sitting behind the carriage, Broland eased himself beneath it while Kony did the same. The moment they had settled, the castle side door opened and blue light illuminated the swirling mist. The guard escorting Guildmaster Gilmore and his wife held the glowlamp up as he walked them to the carriage. When the man stopped to open the door, his feet were mere inches from Broland's face. The other two pairs of feet disappeared as the couple climbed in, rocking the carriage. Two thumps sounded when the guard notified the driver that his passengers were loaded. The guard then turned and walked toward the building.

Broland hooked his heels to the front axle and gripped the rear axle. A glance to his right confirmed that Kony had done the same. The driver shouted to his team, and Broland lifted himself off the ground just before the carriage lurched into motion.

The bouncing of the wheels on the cobblestones shook Broland, causing his teeth to chatter. He clamped his mouth shut and held on tight as the carriage headed toward the castle gate. When it slowed and a guard approached from either side, Broland found himself straining to remain aloft. The guards gave the carriage a brief inspection and two thumps, sending them on their way.

Across the plaza and circling the fountain, the wagon headed toward the heart of Upper Kantar. Broland gasped as he struggled to hold himself up, his muscles protesting. The carriage turned at the second intersection and Kony let go, his body sliding past Broland before he also let himself drop.

"Oof," came from his lips as the impact drove air from his lungs.

He sat up and saw the carriage drawing away from him, passing a brightly lit glowlamp, before fading into the fog. As Broland stood, he turned and found Kony stretching his muscled arms.

"I was beginning to cramp up," Kony said.

Broland snorted. "Same here." He patted his rear clean and walked toward his friend. "Where to now?"

"This is still Upper Kantar, right?"

"Yes."

"We go farther down Center Street, then." Kony turned and began walking toward the intersection.

Broland hurried to catch him. "Why?"

"Three reasons," Kony began as the turned the corner and headed toward the gate. "First, if anyone might recognize you, it would be the citizens of Upper Kantar. You don't need that, so Lower Kantar is the place to go.

"Second, we are out for fun. If it were about wine and quiet conversation, Upper Kantar would be suitable. In this case, it is not.

"Third, we have only two silvers between us. That won't go far up here, but it should be more than enough in the lower part of the city."

They soon passed beneath the gate and entered Lower Kantar. The street narrowed and a string of glowlamps shone in the fog, leading toward Southgate. A ruckus came from a building on the right. Above the door was a sign with a tree carved into it.

"Do you know this place?" Kony asked.

"The Aspen Inn. The guards say the taproom is not as seedy as some others, and it is quite popular."

"Perfect. Let's go in." Kony stepped through the door and led Broland into the tavern.

As they entered, the volume of chatter increased threefold. Glowlamps lit the space, and a fire burned in an arched hearth at the far end of the room. An old man marked by a Musicus rune strummed a lute in one corner, the crowd seemingly ignoring him. Most of the tables were full, occupied mainly by men. A cluster of standing patrons encircled a table in the back. Half the heads in the building turned toward the table when a loud cheer rose up. Kony leaned close while Broland stared in that direction.

"Dice," Kony said. "It must have been a good throw."

Waving his hand for Broland to follow, Kony weaved his way past a cluster of patrons, leaned against the bar, and waved to the barkeep – a pudgy, balding man with a gray-peppered mustache. The man plopped a mug atop the bar and waddled over. Beads of sweat clung to the man's expansive forehead, covering the Dominus rune marking it.

"What will it be?"

Kony slid a silver piece on the bar. "Two mugs of ale, good sir."

Without a word, the man swept the silver off the bar, replaced it with eight coppers, and turned away. Broland surveyed the room, his gaze settling on a woman dressed in leathers. She sat alone, staring at someone while a full mug sat on her table, untouched. Something about her screamed to him that she was a threat. He followed her eyes and tried to determine whom she was watching.

"What are you waiting for?" Kony asked.

When Broland turned, he found a foam-capped mug held toward him. He accepted it and tapped it to Kony's mug before taking a drink.

Broland had sampled ale a few times during his teen years, when his father's friends had visited the castle and decided to open a barrel. The results had been mixed. He had found the bubbly brew a little bitter, and he tended to prefer wine. Regardless, the Aspen Inn didn't seem like a place where one might order wine. Swallowing, the cool drink carried the bitter aftertaste he expected. The bubbles forced him to belch as they came back up. Kony turned and led Broland to an empty table.

With his mug held in a firm grip, Kony sat back and looked about the room before his gaze returned to Broland.

"Seeing so many people marked by vocation runes makes me wonder what it was like before…you know, before it all changed."

Broland took another sip, finding the ale tasting better with each drink. "I think about it from time to time. My parents tell me stories, most of them not good. Since they were both Unchosen, I suspect they endured the worst of it and that blackened their perspectives."

Kony's eyes flicked toward the table. "Is it true that they can both wield Chaos?"

"Yes. My brother and sister as well."

"What about you?"

With his eyes on the tankard before him, Broland replied, "No. Not me. My mother…she has divined me numerous times, hoping to discover that it might change. Unlike them, I don't possess the innate ability."

"So, you wouldn't have gone Unchosen."

Broland looked up, his eyes landing on the rune that marked Kony's forehead. "While I cannot touch Chaos, I do have an affinity with Order. I can even heal. If I had been born earlier, I'd have the same rune as you. Instead, they stopped performing the Choosing ceremony only months before I was born."

"Does it scare you…what your family can do with Chaos magic?"

"Not really. More than anything, it leaves me jealous of their abilities."

Kony's brow furrowed in thought. After a moment, his expression brightened. "You can heal, though. It seems like an extraordinary gift...something I wish I could do."

Broland shrugged. "I suppose. But it has limits. I can't even heal myself."

"Why not?"

"Nobody can. It's just...one of the rules."

"Why must everything have rules with you?"

Broland chuckled. "This is different. It isn't like I can choose it."

Kony took a deep drink from his mug, emptying it. He then held up his hand, waving to a pretty girl who wore a pale blue smock over a black dress. A moment later, she walked over and eyed Kony before turning toward Broland. With long strawberry-tinted hair, large green eyes, and freckled button nose, she had an attractiveness that Broland couldn't quite pinpoint. When his gaze fell lower, his eyes bulged and he turned away, blushing. After a moment, he looked back at her and hoped his cheeks didn't appear as red as he feared. The woman glanced down at her partially exposed chest, and she snickered.

"Shy one, eh?"

"He doesn't get out much," Kony replied.

The girl put a hand on the curve of her hip and tilted her head while her other hand teased her hair. *Is it hot in here or is it just me?* he wondered.

She arched a brow as she stared at Broland, half smiling. "I assume you waved me over for something other than leering at me?"

Broland felt his cheeks grow even warmer, and the girl chuckled again.

"Yes." Kony slid three coppers across the table, saving Broland. "Two ales, please. Keep the extra copper."

Scooping the coins off the table, the girl smiled and Broland found himself smiling in return, his heart racing as she winked at him and turned away. His eyes remained glued to her as she sauntered to the bar, swatting away groping hands during the journey.

"You like her?" Kony asked.

"There's something about her."

"I can see a few somethings of note."

Broland chuckled at the comment.

"Have you at least kissed a girl?"

Taken by surprise and the directness of the question, Broland stammered, "Well, I...one time when I was twelve summers, I kissed a wash girl."

"Twelve?"

"She was three years older than me."

"Pfft." Kony swatted the comment aside. "You barely know your head from your backside when you're twelve. Please tell me you have something more recent."

Broland grimaced. "You don't know what it's like to be in my position. I don't have the time to mess around nor do I know any girls my age."

"Listen." Kony leaned close, whispering. "You are the prince. One word from you and half the girls in Kantar would throw themselves at you. Why not take advantage of it?"

Looking away, Broland considered the idea but shook his head. "It wouldn't be right. That would be abusing my station. I...I can't do it."

Kony sighed. "Fine. I'll give it some time, but one of these nights, you need to take your shot. You don't know what you're missing."

"One of these nights?"

Kony grinned. "You didn't think this was to be our only outing? When I'm through with you, drinking, gambling, and girls will be second nature."

20

JUNGLE RUN

C huli squatted in wait while hiding behind the makeshift wall. The sky above was growing brighter, the stars now barely visible to the west. She held her bow ready, her mind calm – focused. Birds tweeted from the distant trees. A starfetch atop the stable roof chirped in response, joining in their morning serenade. All was peaceful outside, mirroring how Chuli was on the inside…until Thiron shouted.

"Attack!"

In a breath's time, Chuli readied an arrow and darted from behind the barrier. Her eyes scanned the field and she spotted a man's head poking above a hay bale. Slowing, she lifted her bow, focused on the man's head – a target that seemed to grow larger while she focused on it – and loosed the arrow. A moment later, she was behind the next barrier. In her mind's eye, she recalled what she had seen. A guard on the wall. One peeking from behind the shed. Another atop a horse near the stable.

She pulled three arrows from her quiver, nocking the middle one on her bowstring while she held the other two between her fingers. After taking an easy breath, she slid around the barrier, took aim at her target, and let go. The arrow struck the man on the wall as Thiron leaped out of hiding and threw an egg at Chuli. She dove out of the way, rolled, and came up on one knee to shoot at the man on horse-back. Her aim true, the arrow struck the mounted man in the chest, and she loosed the third arrow toward the man peeking around the shed. Another egg sailed toward her, and she rolled again, placing herself safely behind the barrier while the arrow struck the target and the egg cracked on the ground.

Thiron's voice rang out. "Good. You hit all four targets with your first four arrows." A squeaking sound emerged from the same direction as his voice. "Now, take out the moving targets."

Chuli pulled three more arrows and nocked her bow before swinging it around the edge of the barrier. She found her first target, focused on it – her arrow following it to gauge the speed – and fired. When the next emerged, moving at the same speed while hanging from the same moving rope, she fired again. She knew that hitting the third would be easy, a repeated motion from the first two. With a jerk, the target lurched forward, the squeaking louder as it moved at twice the speed of the others. She hastily drew an arrow and fired, missing when she led it too much. She pulled another, and missed with a shot that was a hair too late. Then, it was gone, lost behind the hay bales. The squeaking ceased when Thiron stopped cranking the winch.

"You grew complacent." The man's voice preceded him before he emerged from hiding. "Always assume that things can and will change at any moment. A gust of wind, another enemy, the speed at which they move, a distracting glint of sunlight…anything that might cause you to adjust your focus."

Upset with herself, Chuli pressed her lips together in frustration. "I can do better, Thiron."

The dark-skinned man stopped two strides away. "You *are* doing better, but better doesn't matter if you are dead. This is why I push you, Chuli.

"There is little doubt you have skill with the longbow," Thiron said. "You have also displayed an aptitude for tracking and stealth. The trip to Vallerton proved your readiness in the field, but I would be sad to see you killed because of a small slip, some lack of detail that you overlook.

"Now, get back into position. I'll pull arrows from the targets and create a new arrangement of enemies. Maintain focus throughout and it should go well."

A sword swept toward Chuli's head. She ducked and lifted her shield, the glancing blow sending the strike safely past while she lunged with her longsword. When Quinn twisted, Chuli's strike missed. Quinn's other sword trailed the first, sweeping toward Chuli's midriff and forcing her to leap backward.

The two girls eyed each other, focused. Gritting her teeth, Chuli leaped forward with her shield ready, her longsword colliding with Quinn's short sword. The wooden weapons met with an odd, dead *thud* rather than the loud *clack* she had grown used to at the combat school. The Elastic augmentation infused into the weapons made them bend slightly, bounce heartily, but never break.

Chuli spun, ducking below Quinn's other sword as she swung her shield and struck Quinn's leg. When Chuli rose to a ready stance, she recognized the look in Quinn's eyes – her usually blue irises now appearing steely gray and narrowing with anger. Having learned the hard way, Chuli watched Quinn warily. She knew that Quinn only grew more determined when challenged, the anger making her more dangerous than reckless. Neither girl moved save for their deep breaths – a moment of respite that lasted mere seconds.

Taking two quick steps, Quinn leaped up and twirled with one blade in the lead. Chuli jumped back and knocked the first blade aside, backing another step as she avoided the following blade. With a lunge, Chuli went for the kill, hoping to strike before Quinn could recover. Somehow, she missed when Quinn twisted and grabbed Chuli's wrist. An elbow to the face left Chuli stumbling backward, blinking through the tears. In a flash, Quinn's boot smacked the side of Chuli's helmet and the world spun.

The next thing Chuli knew, she was on her hands and knees. Red spots dotted the floor below her face, the blood sinking into the stone floor of the Atrium. She looked up and the room tilted, forcing her to fall on her side with a thump. There she lay with her eyes shut, the world still spinning.

"Are you all right?"

Quinn's voice sounded distant beyond the ringing in Chuli's ears.

"Is there a healer around?"

"I'm right here, Chuli."

"Ugh," Chuli groaned. *Why Jonah?*

His hand rested on her arm, the warmth of his palm giving something for her to focus on. A chill gripped her body and left her gasping for air. She opened her eyes and the world had stilled, the blur now gone. When she sat upright, she touched her nose and found it free of pain.

"Thank you, Jonah."

She found herself surprised that she meant it. A frown crossed her face and she scolded herself. *He means well. Don't let your annoyance from the trip cloud your opinion of him.*

"I'm sorry as well," Chuli muttered. "I...did not treat you well during our mission."

Jonah shook his head. "Don't worry about it. I know I tend to complain when I am uncomfortable. I suspect that may have worked your nerves. If so, you are not the first. If we ever again share a mission, I'll try to refrain from doing so or will at least reduce the sheer volume of my complaints." He held his hand toward her. "Let me help you up."

Chuli found herself grinning in response. "Fair enough." She gripped his hand and he pulled her to a standing position.

"Sorry about the elbow," Quinn said. "You have blood on your sparring vest."

Chuli glanced down and found blood spots on her chest. A frown crossed her face. "Another one, likely stained." She bent and scooped up her training sword.

A grunt coming from across the room flagged Chuli's attention. She found Brandt sparring with Bilchard, who stood a full head taller than the prince did. Brandt's quarterstaff was a blur, forcing Bilchard to defend himself with sword and shield as he was driven backward.

The taller boy burst forward, leading with his shield before swinging a heavy overhead strike at Brandt's unprotected head. Somehow, Brandt's staff redirected the strike and he slid inside to give Bilchard a hard kick to the groin. The big guy bent with the blow, and

Brandt elbowed his chin, sending him to the floor. Brandt backed away as Bilchard lay curled up, coughing.

"Excuse me," Jonah said. "It looks like I have another patient." The redhead ran over to the downed boy and knelt beside him.

Chuli noticed Quinn staring across the room, in the direction of the boys.

"What do you think of him?" Quinn asked.

"Who? Jonah?"

"No. Brandt."

Chuli turned toward him again and found the prince kneeling to one side of Bilchard while Jonah knelt on the other side. After a moment, the two helped Bilchard to his feet.

"I am unsure. He acts...entitled at times. At other times, he almost seems normal. In truth, I find him somewhat of an enigma. His sister is easier to read and a fair bit more level-headed."

A smirk appeared on Quinn's face. "Brandt runs a little hot, doesn't he?"

With a nod, Chuli said, "Not that I know anyone else who behaves that way."

Quinn's brow furrowed. "I'm working on it."

Chuli grinned. "No worries. You're my friend, faults and all. I'm not quite perfect either."

"Not quite?" Quinn's tone was incredulous.

"Close enough, I guess."

They both laughed. When the laughter settled, Quinn turned and looked up at the structure that loomed over them.

"Are you interested in a jungle run?"

Chuli considered it and nodded. "Yes. It would be a good way to end today's workout."

Quinn turned to look across the room, toward the three boys who were in quiet conversation. "I wonder if Brandt would like to give it a go."

"You could ask him."

She turned and held Chuli's attention for a moment before nodding. "You're right."

Without another word, Quinn headed across the Atrium floor, her stride confident, almost threatening. Chuli experienced a moment of pride for her friend. When Quinn reached the boys, there was a brief conversation with her pointing toward the jungle and Brandt staring up at it. Jonah said some words, clapped Brandt on the back, and turned to leave. Quinn spun on her heels and strode back across the floor with Brandt following close behind. When they neared Chuli, Quinn addressed her.

"Brandt says he will join us. Let's ditch the weapons and give it a go."

With a nod, Chuli pulled her sparring helmet off and shook her head to free the stray hairs plastered to her skull. She ran one hand down her braid and found it still intact. Quinn reached the side of the room before Chuli and tossed her swords and helmet to the floor. A moment later, Chuli's gear joined Quinn's. When Chuli spun around, Brandt approached them, glancing up at the twisted contraption.

"So, this Jungle, as you call it. Other than looking like a mess of beams and pipes and ropes, what exactly is the point?"

Quinn gave him a sidelong glance. "If you don't know, why did you agree to join us?"

He grinned. "It looks dangerous. When given the option, I'd rather be dangerous."

Chuli rolled her eyes. "Not another one." She then grunted when Quinn's elbow struck her ribs.

"You're not as cautious as you claim, Chuli," Quinn said. "Even despite Thiron's preaching."

Chuli chuckled. "True. And while my daring side drives him crazy, he would likely explode if one of you two were his pupil."

"No doubt," Quinn said before turning back to Brandt. "The Jungle is designed for training, just like everything else we do here. In addition to honing our scaling abilities, the Jungle is a great way to improve agility, strength, and balance. Don't lose your focus, though. Despite the Elastic augmentation on these floor tiles, a fall from this thing will hurt. Tumbling from the upper levels will break bones or even kill you."

He gazed up at the structure towering seven stories above him. "And the leaders aren't concerned?'"

Quinn shrugged. "I guess not. We have healers always ready if someone gets hurt. Should someone have a particularly bad fall and die...well, death is a risk every warden must face at some point." She paused in thought. "Save for the gadgeteers. They aren't supposed to be put at risk, save for some invention gone haywire."

Chuli recognized the look on Quinn's face and knew that her friend was concerned for Everson. Despite her brother's mechanical legs and the newfound mobility they afforded him, Quinn behaved like nothing had changed. Chuli wondered when Quinn would stop trying to protect him from the world.

"Do you guys want to race to the top?"

Brandt peered up again. "The top?"

"Sure. The ICON flag." Quinn pointed upward, toward the black flag, marked by a gold ring with a gold dagger running through it. "See. Right there."

He looked up and asked, "What are the rules?"

"What rules?" Quinn grinned. "Go!"

She scrambled toward the nearest pole and began to scale it.

Brandt barked. "Not fair!" as he ran to a rope and did likewise.

Rather than wear herself out on the lowest level, Chuli ran to the ramp beside the wall and scurried up it to the ladder above. After she had cleared the top rung, she turned and ran across a long beam to another platform. A glance revealed Quinn running up an angled beam thirty feet away as she rose above Chuli's current elevation.

When Chuli reached the platform, she scaled another ladder and emerged to the fourth level hub – a platform with beams extending in four directions and ropes dangling beyond the end of each beam. She ran down one of them and leaped, catching the rope to swing to a small landing fifteen feet away. Gripping a pole, she began to shimmy up. Another glance to the side showed Brandt even with her as he climbed a rope. Quinn was beyond him, scaling a ladder.

Reaching the top of the pipe, Chuli swung her feet over to a narrow beam, wobbling before catching her balance. She shuffled forward, careful to watch her foot placement and ignore the sixty-foot drop below. The beam ran to a narrow spiral stairwell that she scrambled up to emerge at the seventh level.

Quinn and Brandt were already on the level, heading toward the flag waiting at the center. The beams that connected the outer plat-forms to the core narrowed on this level, now barely four inches wide.

Chuli edged out on the beam, extending her arms to her sides for balance as she worked toward the center. A glance up showed Quinn moving much more quickly, throwing caution aside as she raced Brandt, who was coming from the opposite direction. The two reached the middle simultaneously and dove toward the flag as Chuli stepped onto the platform.

Spinning away from Brandt with the flag in hand, Quinn laughed and held it up.

"Give me that," Brandt said through his laughter.

"I got it first. I win."

When Brandt's eyes shifted toward Chuli in appeal, she gave him a shrug. "Get used to it. She doesn't like to lose...even to a prince."

21

A PIECE OF FURNITURE

Brandt focused on Master Alridge while she traced symbols on the black wall. Although her appearance still distracted him occasionally, he no longer found himself staring at the shapely woman. He couldn't decide if it was because he had grown used to her looks, valued her knowledge as an instructor, or if he cared what his fellow wardens thought of him…at least one of them.

He glanced to the side and found the others watching in rapt attention. Quinn sat between her roommate, Chuli, and her brother, Everson. All three were busy drawing their own version of each rune and marking it with the related augmentation. Brandt looked down and found his paper blank. Taking notes had never been his thing. He, instead, relied upon his memory. If he tried, if he focused, he knew he would recall every detail. Accordingly, he stared at the board and drank it all in.

He immediately recognized the two runes his parents had taught him – Illuminate and Reduce Gravity. His parents had considered the augmentations unlikely to cause trouble. Of course, Brandt and Cassie had proven them wrong.

The other runes they had covered over the past four weeks included Increase Gravity, Animate, Brittle, Elastic, Power, Truth, Enlarge, Courage, Fear, Heat, Cool, and Shockwave. Today, the woman added another new rune to the board, appearing like a series of intersecting diamonds. When she finished drawing it, she turned toward her students and tapped on the rune with the chunk of glowstone in her hand.

"This is the last rune known to us – one we must thank Master Firellus for sharing."

Brandt frowned at the oddness of the statement. *Sharing?* he sent to his sister.

Her reply rang loud and clear, *Be quiet.*

"All augmentations carry risk, some more than others." Alridge's glare carried a more serious weight than normal. "The Stamina rune can empower a person with a seemingly endless amount of energy. What it truly does is accelerate your ability to recover by sapping your natural reserves. If you push yourself too hard while charged with a Stamina augmentation, you will eventually hit a wall and collapse. We have seen people require as much as four days rest before they regain normal functions. As a result, I call this augmentation the last hope, only to be used when no other option will suffice."

She stood back and examined her work. Drawn with the pale blue of glowstone, runes and their names covered twenty feet of black slate walls. Each rune marked a potential use for Chaos, each symbol displaying the true form of the magical effect it represented.

"These augmentations are your tools, whether used in combat, to get out of a tight spot, or to enhance some mechanical invention. You must memorize these runes and maintain a firm understanding of what they can do…and of the potential side effects of each."

In the periphery, someone to Brandt's right shifted as a hand rose in the air.

"Yes, Everson?" Master Alridge asked.

"Where did we discover these runes, and why aren't there more of them?"

The woman stared directly toward Brandt and Cassie. "Over two hundred years ago, the Ministry made a bold move and attempted to erase Chaos…forever. They killed everyone who could wield the magic and then made it their mission to destroy any references of Chaos. From that act, the Choosing ceremony was born, enabling them to sort out anyone who possessed the latent ability to use Chaos and treat them as outcasts.

"Centuries of knowledge were lost during the Cleansing. Only two decades have passed since the return of Chaos, an event that was spurred by King Brock." Her voice grew quiet, her eyes distant. "Many of the runes before you were discovered by him just before the Battle at the Brink, a battle we surely would have lost if not for the use of Chaos." She turned and stared at the runes. "Regardless of what we have learned, a massive gap in the knowledge surrounding Chaos remains, and it leaves us believing that there is much yet to be discovered."

Brandt's eyes met his sister's, and he knew she pondered the same questions as he did. *How did our father discover these runes, and how can we unearth others?*

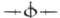

Brandt thought of his father, imagining the man leading the battle to save humanity. The man seldom spoke of the past and had never offered details as to what exactly had happened. Brandt's mother was no better, insisting that the story should come from Brock. As a result, Brandt and Cassie had decided that there was little to tell…that Brock and Ashland's role had been minor at best. The way Jestin and Alridge spoke of his parents told Brandt a different story. Their respect was obvious, the roles his parents played clearly more significant than he had ever considered.

He headed up the stairwell, not stopping until he reached the fifth floor. When he turned the corner, he found Quinn standing in the corridor, across from his room.

Brandt hesitated when she turned toward him. He ran his hand through his hair to tame it and then strolled toward her, attempting to appear nonchalant.

"Hello, Quinn."

"Brandt," Quinn said. "I…I…" Her eyes looked down, her lips pressing together. "I wanted to ask you for help."

When she looked up, her eyes met his, hardening. Before he could speak, she added. "If you make a big deal out of this, I'll hurt you."

Brandt held his hands up. "No big deal. I just never imagined you as someone who needed help."

She tilted her head and turned away. "It isn't...an easy thing for me to ask." When she turned back toward him, their eyes met again. "Before Delvin left, he gave me a new persona to practice."

Brandt asked, "Persona?"

She huffed a sigh. "Let's get out of the hallway and I'll explain."

He withdrew his key before unlocking the door. When he turned the knob, it opened to a quiet room. "Thank, Issal," he muttered.

"What?"

"It's Wyck. I'm sure he has some positive traits...I just have yet to figure them out." Brandt shook his head. "Why'd they stick me with such an arrogant jerk, anyway?"

Quinn closed the door behind her. "They have a reason. Trust me. Every move here comes with a reason – calculated and cunning."

"So, being stuck with Wyck is a punishment from my father."

She laughed. "No. My guess is that they sought out the only person more arrogant than you, hoping you might learn some self-awareness."

Brandt's jaw dropped. After a moment, he shook his head and laughed. "Fair enough."

"Besides, Wyck's personality is perfect for his role."

"And, what would that be?"

"He's a wildcat."

"A what?"

Quinn sat on the sofa. "A wildcat. You know, a fighter – a warrior, but one trained to battle with the advantage of a Power augmentation." She shook her head, her eyes reflecting wonder. "When imbued with that rune, you feel invincible and are able to do amazing things. It can make anyone superhuman. For a warrior like Wyck, who is scary under any circumstances, it can make him into a killing machine. He could probably defeat a squad of fifty soldiers if he were properly armed and charged with a Power rune."

"It sounds amazing. I'd like to try it."

"You will. Soon. We all practice it after eight weeks or so of training."

Brandt sat on the chair across from her. "I assume there are warden roles besides wildcat."

"Of course. My brother is a gadgeteer. His job is to invent things. My roommate, Chuli, is a ranger. Jonah is an arcanist. I'm training to be an espion – a spy."

"So, what am I?"

Her eyes narrowed in thought. "I suspect you'll be an espion or an arcanist. It is difficult to be sure since your training appears to cover both disciplines."

"What about an ecclesiast?"

"A healer?" She shook her head. "They only accept people who can wield both Order and Chaos. Healing comes with your other magic or you don't get the job."

He grimaced as he considered his inability to heal others. *What if I can't do it? Will they still want me?* Surprisingly, Brandt found that he cared. He actually wanted to be a warden.

Quinn said, "Now, about this new persona…"

"Wait," he interjected. "You still haven't explained this persona thing."

"We espions need to perfect a number of personas – fake identities that we can slip into at any moment. However, a persona is more than just a name and clothing. Each persona must have a history, a childhood, a family, wishes and desires…the things that make a person real. We must completely assume the identity so we do not stumble when faced by an odd question or compromising situation.

"I already have personas as a thief, a guard, and a trader," Quinn said. "Now, Delvin wants me to work on one as a castle servant."

"So you came to me?"

"You lived in a castle, right?"

"Yes. My entire life. Until I moved here, I really didn't know anything else."

"Well, if you think this place is reality, think again." She smiled. "I suspect your comfortable life in the Kantar Citadel was more real than the Ward."

His brow furrowed. "What makes you think my life in Kantar was so great?"

"What could be wrong with it? Don't your parents love you?"

He looked away. "Yes. They are very loving...and supportive. They go out of their way to ensure my sister, my brother, and I have everything we need. We are trained by private tutors, fed the best food, interact with the most important people..."

When he paused, Quinn interjected, "But..."

He turned toward her and stared into her steely blue eyes. "This is going to sound petty."

She sat back with a smirk. "Let's hear it."

"My brother, Broland, is the oldest. His role as heir prince is to take over should anything happen to my parents. His entire life, he has been prepared for it...and lavished in the attention that comes with the role. My sister and I were often the afterthought...just the other two kids who live at the citadel."

Quinn's smirk remained below a furrowed brow. "Did your parents favor him as well?"

Brandt shrugged. "Not directly."

"And they love you?"

"Yes, of course."

"So, you're jealous."

"No...well...in a way." He frowned as he tried to articulate his feelings. "Preparing to be the next king, regardless of when it actually happens, has given my brother a goal...and a challenge. Cass and I have no tangible goal and have rarely found ourselves challenged. As a result, we often designed clever schemes to get ourselves into trouble." He turned away again. "There were times when I thought my parents would just wish to be rid of us. When one recent prank went too far, they sent us here."

Quinn sat forward and took his hand. "You arrived at the Ward, what? Four weeks back?" He nodded and she continued. "Put your hurt feelings aside and tell me what you have found here. A sense of purpose? A challenge?"

He stared at her for a moment before nodding. "You're smarter than I thought."

She bent his fingers back, forcing his elbow down to the Ratio Bellicus table as he yipped. "Ouch!"

"You might want to be careful what you say next."

Brandt responded between gritted teeth. "I meant it as a compliment."

She let go and he sat back with a sigh, opening and closing his fist to work his fingers.

"By what you said, your parents care about you very much. They likely saw the gap in your life and decided that the role of warden would help fill it."

"You might be right. I will talk to Cassie about it." A smile crossed his face. "Thank you."

With a nod, she stood. "Good. Now that I helped you, you can help me with Glynnis."

"Who's Glynnis?"

With a tilt of her head, she thumbed toward herself while sharing a small smile. "Glynnis is me. Or, more accurately, my servant persona."

He laughed. "I like it."

Quinn turned and strode to the door, stopping with her hand on the knob. "I'm going out into the hallway. When you hear a knock, it will be Glynnis."

Without another word, she opened the door, stepped out, and pulled it closed. Brandt stared at the door, wondering what he was supposed to do. A thumping knock came from the door, drawing a frown on his face. He stood and crossed the room. When he opened the door, he found Quinn standing there with her hands clasped together at her waist.

"Hello, good sir. I'm Glynnis, here for the evening service – to clean the room and turn down your bed."

"Quinn…" he said before she smacked his shoulder, "Ouch!"

"I'm Glynnis, remember?"

"Yes. Fine." He backed up two steps "Don't hit me again. Just let me explain."

She stared daggers at him, her arms crossed, her toe tapping the floor while she listened.

"You made at least three major mistakes. I've been around servants my entire life. There are two kinds you'll find – the ones who run the place and the ones who do the work. The first are all full of themselves, obsessed with every propriety and having everything perfect. The second type, the type that you are to portray, are almost invisible…like a nondescript piece of furniture that is always in the room, but you never seem to notice it. You just walk past it every day and seldom give it a second thought.

"Your first mistake was the knock. Servant knocks are timid. If there is no response, they will try again, a little louder. After that, they will open the door to see if anyone is inside. If not, they will enter and do their business quickly in an effort to be gone before anyone returns.

"Secondly, you gave your name. I don't care what your name is, and if I did, I would ask for it. Telling the person *why* you are there is fine but until asked to do so, *never* give them your name. There are dozens of servants who have worked in my father's castle my entire life, and I don't know their names.

"Third, keep your eyes downcast. Giving them a hard glare is even worse than giving them your name. You must bottle up your real self and become timid, shy, and even awkward. The use of *please* and *sorry* are acceptable if for some reason you do something to capture their notice. Try not to. Remain as unnoticed as possible."

As Brandt spoke, Quinn's expression softened.

"Thank you." Quinn smiled. "I knew you could help with this one. Your being raised as a spoiled brat actually has some positive aspects."

"You're hilarious."

She stepped back into the corridor, facing him as she held the door open. "We'll try this again, but this time, I'll try to be nothing but a boring piece of furniture."

22

CHAOS TRAP

E verson tentatively touched the bronze and yanked his finger away. He tried again, his finger lingering longer this time. It was hot, but the metal didn't burn him. With the tip of a chisel, he gently pried it free from the casting. He held it up, squeezing the object between his finger and thumb. The pattern he had etched into the casting showed on the outer surface of the bronze piece like a work of art. Yet, he still needed it altered to compensate for the weight inside. When he saw Jonah approaching, he smiled.

"Perfect timing."

"What crazy contraption are you creating now?" his roommate asked.

Everson shook his head. "As usual, I'll not reveal it until I'm finished." He held the bronze piece toward Jonah. "Regardless, I think even you can guess this one."

"Even me?" Jonah's face took on a pained expression. "You cut me to the quick, Ev."

"Oh, stop." Everson chuckled.

Jonah examined the object in his hands, the ornate pattern in the domed-shape bronze piece glittering in the light. He flipped it over to the concave side and his brow arched. "You actually embossed this rune into a casting block?"

"Yes. I plan to make a number of these and that will save a step."

"I assume this rune is why I'm here?"

"Yes. I need it Infused."

Jonah arched his brow. "You want me to enchant this to make it lighter?"

"I need it lighter to compensate for the weight on the inside. When I'm finished, it should feel and appear innocuous as long as nobody attempts to open it."

"I assume something other than powder will be inside it."

"Good assumption," Everson tapped the disk in Jonah's hand. "Can you do this now? I need to finish this one today."

Jonah's gaze met Everson's. They both knew why it had to be finished today.

"I'll work on it now."

"Good. I'll finish assembling the body. By the time you're finished, I'll be ready for final assembly."

Jonah moved off to a quiet corner and sat facing the wall. Even from a distance, Everson saw the rune flash bright red, the glow quickly fading. While his friend applied the new technique, Everson recalled their final classroom session with Alridge.

As they had every day for the past five weeks, he and his fellow wardens in training met in the debriefing room. Seated at the tables arranged in a U, they listened as Master Alridge strode down the center of the tables and offered her instruction.

"We are nearing the end of our time together. You now know the extent of what we have discovered regarding Chaos augmentations and their application. Only one piece remains, the one that ICON holds most secret...because it is the most dangerous."

Alridge paused and stared at the floor, as if seeking the right words. After a moment, she looked up and spoke.

"What you might know of as Enchanting, is technically termed Infusion. This is because it involves the process of permanently infusing a Chaos augmentation into something. Why so secret? Because when the process is applied to a living thing, the consequences are dire.

"Very few people know the true nature of banshees. Chaos is infused into these monsters, giving them their massive size and powering their screams with debilitating fear. You see, at one point, each banshee was just a man. When augmentations of Enlarge and Fear were given to these men, they infused the augmentations for a reduced, but permanent affect. The intent was to create an army unlike any other. The truth was far worse.

"You see, to perform Infusion, one must use Order to trap and contain the Chaos used in the augmentation. Since living things are made of Order, it leaves the required boundary unstable. Eventually, the Chaos breaks free and corrupts the host, driving them insane. As a result, the men who were turned to banshees are wild, mindless creatures, so demented that they will eat humans, dead or alive.

"This is why we must maintain our secret. If the ability to Infuse got into the wrong hands, we might face another army like The Horde, or something even worse. This is why it is strictly forbidden to perform Infusion on a living thing. Anyone caught doing so will be executed by ICON, for it is among our core tenets." She paused and swept the room with a grim glare. "Executed."

The room fell silent, the mood somber. The woman's glare slowly swept around the room, her dark eyes meeting each student's before moving to the next. Finally, she nodded.

"Now that you have been warned, we can begin." She turned and strolled toward the black slate wall with a chunk of glowstone in hand. "Infusion begins with a Chaos augmentation, but requires the use of Order to seal it. How does this work? Imagine you hold a piece of metal that you wish to make lighter." She sketched a rune they all recognized. "When a Chaos augmentation is applied to a Reduce Gravity rune, the arcanist must immediately switch roles and become an ecclesiast. Once he or she finds their center, they will begin coaxing the Order that surrounds them to bind the Chaos into place. Only when the Chaos is fully captured by order can it be made permanent and not allowed to dissipate." Alridge sketched a circle around the rune, marking the circle with the word ORDER. She then turned back toward the room. "Since Order is connected to living beings, this is very challenging and requires far more time than if you were to attempt the same task on a human or an animal. While a skilled ecclesiast might trap the Chaos in twenty or thirty minutes, it often takes an hour or more to complete the process, leaving the person drained and exhausted.

"Also note that the effect of a permanent augmentation is typically around one fifth as effective as a temporary one. This is because the Order required to trap Chaos in place dulls the effect. We have also learned that…"

Suddenly, Alridge's voice faded and Ivy's voice replaced it.

"Everson!" She nudged him. "Are you listening to me?"

The memory of the classroom faded and he found himself in the Forge. He looked at Ivy and saw frustration on her face.

"What?" He blinked. "I'm sorry. I was thinking about Infusion and how we can utilize it."

Ivy rolled her eyes. "While I understand your fascination with Infusion, it can be frustrating when you don't listen to me. I don't enjoy repeating myself."

In spite of his attempt to resist, Everson grinned. "I like to see that fire within you."

Ivy's eyes narrowed. "What's that supposed to mean?"

"I know that there is more to you than your shy exterior might portray. This fire, this attitude…you should show it more often."

Ivy's frown shifted into a smile. "You really think so?"

"You're a smart girl, Ivy. Beyond that, you have more to offer than you think. You should be more confident in yourself and always be willing to express your ideas…and your feelings." He put his hand on her shoulder. "I believe in you."

Her eyes lowered toward the floor. "Thank you, Everson."

"Now, what was it you said before?"

"Oh. The trigger mechanism is ready. Now that the first one has been tooled and assembled, it should be fairly easy to create others."

He smiled. "That's wonderful. Can you bring it to my workbench? I can begin assembling it while Jonah finishes his enchantment."

Whirring from Everson's legs and the tapping of his boot heels echoed in the otherwise quiet corridor. Everson gripped his prize invention in one hand and gazed upon it. The bronze reflected the blue glow from the beams above him. A bellow from ahead claimed his attention. The door to Brandt and Wyck's room burst open and Brandt ran past Everson at a sprint.

Wyck stopped outside the door, his face twisted in fury. "Get back here, you twerp!"

Brandt laughed aloud as he reached the stairwell. The sound of footsteps followed, fading as he made his descent.

"What happened?" Everson asked as he neared Wyck.

With deep breaths that puffed his barrel chest and flared his nostrils, Wyck glared down the hallway in the direction Brandt had fled. After a moment, he pointed into the room.

"That brat did something to my chair. It was magic, I think."

Everson peered past Wyck and found bits of shattered wood covering the tiles near the table. A bowl lay upside down with spilled soup and a spoon beside it.

"Looks like he used a Brittle rune."

Wyck frowned. "What does it do?"

Everson swallowed his urge to chuckle when he saw the anger on Wyck's face. "It makes things brittle, causing them to shatter with little effort."

With a nod, Wyck looked back into the room. "That was it, then. This is the third prank he has played on me. Just wait until he comes back. He'll need his sister for healing when I'm through with him."

Without another word, Wyck walked into his room and slammed the door shut. Everson shook his head, *I wouldn't want to be Brandt right now.*

He continued down the hallway and stopped at the second to the last door. The rap of Everson's knuckles against the wood echoed in the corridor. The sound of footsteps came from within, drawing closer until the door opened to reveal a familiar face.

"Hello, Quinn."

She leaned through the doorway and peered down the corridor. "Did I hear yelling just now?"

"Yes. Wyck is upset at Brandt over a prank."

Quinn smirked. "Good. Wyck's head is the only thing more overgrown than his muscles. Perhaps Brandt can poke a few holes and deflate that ego."

"I'm not sure it will work. Wyck wants to punch a few holes in Brandt at the moment."

She chuckled. "I wonder if Brandt considered that. Perhaps he will just hide until tomorrow."

"Tomorrow?"

"Yes. Wyck is leaving on a mission."

"Where is he going?"

Quinn shrugged. "He didn't say, which doesn't surprise me. We *are* in the business of secrets."

"True." He gestured toward her room. "May I come in?"

"Sure." She moved aside, holding the door.

He walked past her and entered the room, his mechanical legs whirring and clanking. Rather than standing, he moved to the sitting area and sat in a chair. Quinn joined him, taking a seat on the sofa.

"I heard Delvin returned last night."

"Yes."

His eyes shifted toward the Ratio Bellicus board and found the pieces arranged in mid-match. "I also heard that…you are leaving."

When he looked up, his eyes met hers and found them to be more blue than gray. There were times when the gray dominated. Those times should be a warning to anyone who knew her as he did.

"Yes, I've been assigned a mission."

"When do you leave?"

"The day after tomorrow."

"What about Mother and Father?"

"Delvin promised me one night with them, and then we leave before dawn the following morning."

"Weren't you going to tell me?" he allowed his tone to reflect the pain he felt inside.

Her eyes softened further. "Oh, Ev. I wasn't going to leave without saying goodbye. Since Delvin told me last night, I've been busy preparing for the trip. I was going to come see you right after lunch."

Everson sighed. "I know you wouldn't leave without seeing me. I just…feel like I should have heard it from you, not from Jonah."

She reached out and gripped his hand. "You're right. I should have taken the time to come see you last night. Just remember, I'll always be your sister, and you'll always be my closest friend."

He choked back tears, nodding rather than responding with words that might draw those tears out. After a moment, he recalled his other reason to visit her.

"I have something for you."

She grinned. "Is it candy?"

He laughed. "Stolen candy?"

"Not lately."

"I still can't believe you weren't caught."

She took on a pained expression. "I do have skills, you know."

"Fine." He reached into his coat and withdrew something from his inside pocket. It made a faint metallic sound when he placed it on the table between them. The late-day sun coming through the open balcony doors shone off the embossed pattern in the bronze cover.

Quinn stared down at it. "You think I should wear powder? Is my complexion that bad?"

"I'll not comment on your complexion." Everson smiled. "However, that isn't makeup. I only intended for it to appear like a powder case."

Her brow furrowed and she picked it up, examining the metal case – an elliptical body four inches long, three inches wide, and an inch thick.

Everson pointed toward it. "The button on the front won't depress unless you also squeeze the release on the bottom. Try it and see what happens."

She put one thumb on the bottom release while the other went to the button on the front. When she squeezed, a narrow rod popped from the rear with an audible *click.*

Quinn blinked, eyeing it as she asked. "What does it do?"

Everson grinned, ready to share his secret. "This Chaos trap will enable you to perform an augmentation. Perhaps two if you limit how much you charge the first one."

"What do you mean? I can't do magic."

"Exactly. That's what makes this so useful." Everson reached out and took the Chaos trap from her. "Inside this unit, is a shard of rock, charged with Chaos. I have discovered that a Chaos rune can be charged from Chaos Conduction by touching a conductor to the rune itself." Everson pointed toward the thin rod sticking from the back of the unit. It only takes a moment to achieve a result The longer you hold the conductor to the rune, the stronger the augmentation. Note that this type of use will drain the Chaos crazy fast, and the capacity is limited by the size of the Chaos-charged rock involved. In this case, I can only use a thin shard, which cannot hold enough to equal a full augmentation."

Everson spun the object in his hand. "I chose this form factor for convenience, making it easy for a warden to carry with them. In addition, it will appear innocuous to anyone else. They will think it a common case for face powder."

"This is wonderful, Ev." Quinn smiled while she stared at it. "How do I get the thingy back inside?"

Everson stood and walked to the balcony door. "Find something that won't conduct Chaos. Glass is a good option." Holding the open door with one hand, he pressed the metal rod against a glass pane. The rod slid into the unit with a *click*. He then showed Quinn the rear of the disk, the rod once again hidden from view.

When he sat back down, he placed the disk before her. "I wanted to make something that might save you one day. Be sure to save it until the need is great, because it will only support a single use."

23

DEPARTURE

Quinn slung her pack over her shoulder, walked out of her bedroom, and found Chuli sitting at their small dining table. The Tantarri girl pushed her chair back and stood.

"You are all packed?" Chuli asked.

"Yes. I'm to meet Delvin in the Atrium."

"You still don't know where you're going?"

"No." Quinn shook her head. "He insists on maintaining secrecy to the very last. I don't know where I am headed, what I am to do when I get there, or when I will be back."

Chuli circled the table and looked Quinn in the eye. "You'll be fine. You are the strongest person I know."

Quinn smiled. "Thank you."

Without another word, Chuli hugged Quinn. They held each other for a long moment before stepping back.

Quinn walked to the apartment door and opened it, pausing to look back. "Take care, Chuli. Continue training hard. Your next mission could come at any time." She gave her friend a smile. "Until next time."

Chuli nodded. "Until next time."

When Quinn stepped into the corridor, she paused before heading toward the room next door. Her knock echoed in the empty hallway, and she heard footsteps from inside the room. The door opened to Jonah's grinning face.

"Did you miss me, Doll?"

Quinn winced. "Not you, too. You sound like Wyck."

Jonah chuckled. "I know. Pretty solid impression, wouldn't you say?"

"Too good." Quinn peered past him. "Is my brother here?"

Jonah shook his head. "He's already down in the Forge. He didn't want to see you."

"What?" Quinn frowned.

A familiar whirring sound preceded her brother emerging from his bedroom. "Careful, Jonah. Cross her, and she might hurt you." Everson grinned.

Jonah puffed his cheeks, blowing air out before replying. "Trust me. I remember."

"I did apologize for that," Quinn noted.

"I see you're packed." Everson said as he crossed the room. "I'll walk you downstairs."

She stepped back into the corridor as he followed, pulling the door behind him. The two siblings then walked down the hallway, shoulder-to-shoulder, in silence. Down the stairs, they went. Not a word was said until they reached the Atrium.

As Quinn expected, Delvin was already waiting, in discussion with Master Firellus and Master Hedgewick. What Quinn didn't expect was to find Brandt and Cassilyn there, the two sitting in a corner with their eyes closed in meditation. Quinn stared at the brother and sister while she and Everson crossed the floor to meet Delvin.

"Ah. My star student has arrived," Delvin said with a grin. "Are you ready to graduate?"

"Graduate?" Quinn asked.

"A mission – going undercover. This is the true test, Quinn." He glanced at Everson. "It will be dangerous."

Quinn smiled. "All things considered, I'd rather be dangerous than boring."

Delvin chuckled and patted Elias on the shoulder, causing the man to wince. "See Elias. Possessing skills will help her, but the attitude is not something I can teach."

"Yes, Delvin. Just be sure she understands her mission objectives. We don't need any international incidents."

Quinn noted Everson's grimace. *He's going to worry about me, now,* she thought. She then corrected herself. *He was always going to worry about me. Now, he feels he has just cause.*

"Are you ready, Quinn?" Delvin asked. "We have an appointment to keep, so we should get going."

"I'm ready. Let's go."

The man nodded toward Everson. "I'll give you a minute to say goodbye to your brother. Meet me in the stables."

Delvin spun on his heel and walked away.

Master Hedgewick patted Quinn on the shoulder. "You will do fine, Quinn. Just know that ICON is behind you, and we have resources at your disposal should the need arise."

Hedgewick and Firellus then moved away, the latter leaning on his cane as he hobbled toward the lift. When the lift began to rise, Everson turned toward her.

"We had best get it over with, since we only have a minute."

"Take care of yourself, Ev."

He shook his head. "No. Not this time, Quinn. You don't get to be concerned about me." The look in his eyes grew serious. "You heard what they said. This is real and will be dangerous. Remember your training and mission objectives, but please don't take unnecessary risks."

"I know, I know."

"Send word when you can. I'll be here when you get back."

His arms wrapped about her and squeezed, but not nearly as hard as she squeezed him. Everson groaned from the pressure, but didn't say a word. Quinn released her embrace, gave him a final nod, and turned away. The walk toward the stairwell at the far end of the room seemed to take an eternity. Beyond that stairwell was an unknown future, one for which she had prepared but knew nothing of what to expect.

Her path brought her close to Brandt and Cassie. The siblings' eyes were both now open, and they watched her approach. Brandt rose to his feet and stared at Quinn, their eyes locking – his green and intense and intriguing. A mixture of feelings stirred inside Quinn. She slowed to say something, but the words would not come. When Brandt's mouth opened, her stomach wrenched in a mixture of anxiety and anticipation. Before he could say anything, his sister interjected.

"Take care, Quinn," Cassie said. "We'll see you soon."

Quinn replied, but her gaze never left Brandt. "Thank you, Cassie."

Brandt stared in return, but the words – whatever they might be - remained unsaid. Unable to say goodbye to him, Quinn turned toward the stairwell and pushed thoughts of Brandt aside. Down the stairs, she went to meet her destiny.

24

WAYPORT

The setting sun painted the walls of Wayport orange. Thick with traffic, the road outside the city was lined with farmers selling produce from wagon beds. Delvin slowed his horse from a trot to an easy walk and Quinn did likewise. Of Tantarri stock, the steeds seemed to have many miles left in them, despite two consecutive long days of travel. Unlike most Tantarri horses, these mounts had been taught to accept a bridle, ensuring that the riders would not attract undue attention. Attention was the last thing Quinn and Delvin needed.

As they approached the gate, Delvin gave the guards on duty a nod. Dressed in the black, red, and gold of Kantaria, the guards ignored Delvin and continued to monitor the incoming traffic. Quinn noted the ready stance of the guards, who appeared to take their job seriously. *Well trained*, she thought. *Either that, or on alert because of a warning of trouble.*

When they entered the city, the gravel roadway ended and cobblestone streets began, fanning out from a square just inside the gate. A breeze came from the direction of the bay, carrying salt air with it. Quinn tugged on the front of her tunic in hope of allowing the breeze to cool her. The tunic was damp with sweat – a reminder of the thick humidity, if she needed a reminder. While autumn had begun to take hold in Fallbrandt valley, summer still held Wayport firmly in its grip.

Delvin pulled his reins, stopping his horse as Quinn did likewise. Dismounting, they each took their reins and began leading their horses down one of the narrow streets.

People on foot traveled in both directions. A cart came toward them, pulled by an ox that lumbered slowly and left Quinn wondering if the beast suffered from the humidity as she did. The cart passed them, filled with barrels that she suspected came from the harbor. A woman exited a shop door with an armful of cloth and walked past them. Quinn looked up and found a sign that read *Wayport Looms* above the shop's door. Her focus shifted to the building beside it and found a sign that read *Gulley's Inn*. Delvin angled toward an alley just past the inn and led his horse around back with Quinn and her horse a step behind. A gravel yard and stables waited behind the building, the area covered in shadows. Quinn spotted a workhorse drinking from a trough and an empty wagon beside the stables. A man kneeling beside one of the wagon wheels turned toward them, stood, and wiped his hands on his trousers. The man's skin was dark, his black hair shorn close to the scalp. The arms of his tunic were pushed up to his elbows, the laces loose to expose his chest, which was visibly covered in sweat. He gave them a grin as he approached.

"You're back with company, I see."

"Yes, Furley," Delvin replied. "We'll only stay for the night, but the horses will remain for week, perhaps longer."

The man nodded. "I'll get them fed and check their shoes. You go on in and settle with Libby."

Delvin handed the reins over and led Quinn inside. They ducked through a door that led them down a corridor with stairs to the upper levels beside it. The hallway opened to a taproom with half the tables occupied, as were half the stools along the bar at the far end of the room. Without pause, Delvin led Quinn to the bar and took an open stool. Quinn rested her pack on the floor and sat beside him, placing her elbows on the bar to emulate the man.

A thin woman with long black hair stood behind the bar, pouring a tankard of ale. She slid it onto the counter before a man with a thick black beard and then turned toward Delvin. A grimace crossed her face, and she strolled over to him.

"I see you're back," she said.

"You are most observant, Libby."

Her eyes flicked toward Quinn. "I hope you're not teaching this innocent girl anything unsavory."

He held his hands up in surrender. "What do you think of me?"

Libby snorted. "I'll let you guess at the response." She leaned closer. "No gambling. Keep your dice in your pocket."

Delvin's face took on a pained expression. "You can be most hurtful, Libby. I did learn my lesson last time."

"I wish I could believe that." Her mouth twisted, and her brow furrowed. "How long are you here?"

"Just tonight. The girl and I have an appointment in the morning."

"One room or two?"

Delvin thumbed toward Quinn. "Two. The girl can take care of herself."

Libby's large, dark eyes shifted toward Quinn. "Good to know."

"Now that we have the chit-chat out of the way, I'd love an ale and some food."

The innkeeper turned toward Quinn with a questioning look. "And you?"

Quinn replied, "The same."

The woman spun about, walked the length of the bar, and opened the door to the kitchen. After poking her head inside and saying a few words, she turned to a cabinet on the wall. Two keys tied to cords dangled from her fist when she closed the cabinet door. She then grabbed two mugs from a shelf and opened the spigot on the barrel beside her.

Having never tried ale had Quinn a little concerned, but she was determined to drink it. Blending in was about adapting and that meant making as little fuss as possible. This might be the first time of many where drinking ale was the best way to remain unremarkable. When the woman returned with two foam-capped mugs, she placed the tankards and the keys on the bar before moving along to help another customer. Delvin picked his mug up, took a sip, and smacked his foam-covered lips before wiping them dry.

"Ahh. Nothing like a cool mug of ale after a long, hot day on the road." He swiped the keys from the bar and turned toward Quinn. "Give me your pack. I'll put it in your room and open the window.

'Trust me. You'll want the room to air out for a while before you head up there. The sun will soon set. Given a couple hours, the room might cool down enough to be almost tolerable."

Bending down, Quinn scooped up her pack and handed it to him. Delvin slid past her and disappeared into the hallway as she turned back to the bar and her waiting mug of ale. Quinn grabbed the handle, surprised by the weight of it. She lifted it to her lips and slurped. The flavor of the cool, bubbly drink reminded her of bread. When she swallowed, a bitterness lingered and triggered a desire to pucker her lips, which she resisted with a conscious effort. She took a deeper drink. Bubbles and foam slid down her throat. The cool drink tasted better, as if the first attempt had beaten down her defenses and convinced her taste buds that the hoppy flavor was acceptable. She put the mug down with a nod as she decided it was not bad. Turning, she began to examine the other patrons in the room.

In one corner, she spotted a man slumped over to the side, his wide-brimmed hat partially covering his face. Near him, four men sat together, laughing over something said. A waitress approached their table, and one of the men tried to grab her. The woman swatted his hand and twisted away with laughter while exchanging insults. Further down, two men leaned over their table in quiet discussion. When the server approached, they shook their heads and she turned away to return to the bar. Quinn's gaze followed her, and she counted four others sitting at the bar.

The two men beside Delvin's stool were comparing stories of their travels. Beyond them were a man and a woman, both appearing to be hunters. From the grimace on the woman's face, she didn't appear to be in a good mood. The man sipped his ale while his eyes flicked about the room nervously.

Quinn turned and found a big man seated by the front door with his arms crossed, his head tilted as he dozed. The man had a cudgel in one hand, bruised knuckles on the other. Not far from that man, four men and two women sat around a table playing dice. Two of the men had shorn hair and stubble on their faces. The other two wore hats and sported trimmed beards while the women had their hair in braids – one blond, the other brunette. One of the women threw the dice and groaned while the others cheered. She handed the dice to the man beside her and took a drink of ale.

Motion from the periphery tugged at Quinn's attention. She spun about to find Libby emerging from the kitchen with two steaming plates. The woman slid them on the bar and turned away as Delvin reappeared and took his stool.

"What is it?" Quinn asked with a frown.

"Corn," Delvin said with a grin.

A sigh slipped out. "No. This" She pointed at the fish on her plate.

"Fish."

She rolled her eyes. "I know *that*. But, why the odd things on its face?"

Delvin cut through the fish's crusty baked skin to reveal tender white meat beneath. "That is a Bootslick Fish. Bottom feeder. From the river." He pointed toward her plate. "Try it. They're good."

With a shrug, Quinn cut into her fish and took a bite.

Over an hour later, Quinn and Delvin sat at a table in the same taproom. Their conversation had waned as they ran out of innocuous things to discuss. The entire time, Quinn had surveyed the room, noticing things that struck her as odd. When the dice players staggered out the door, it left her and Delvin alone in their corner. The moment of privacy prompted her to ask him a quiet question.

"What is this place?"

He gave her a smirk and turned toward the bar. "It's an inn, like any other."

Quinn shook her head. "Not like any other. "

Delvin took a drink of his ale while giving her a sidelong glance. He put the ale down and wiped his lips dry. "Tell me."

Quinn stared at him for a moment as she assembled her thoughts. "When we arrived, the stable hand and the bartender knew you."

He shrugged. "Not uncommon. Travelers typically frequent the same inn repeatedly."

"True. Yet, neither of them said your name. Places like this will go out of their way to use the names of repeat customers. It helps to establish a personal connection and to encourage a return visit. They want you to feel like they care. Besides, you did not use my name when you spoke with Libby." Quinn's eyes narrowed. "You are trying to blend in without identifying yourself."

He sat back and took another drink before setting his mug down. "Fair assessment, but not quite surprising, given our circumstances."

"Oh, there is more." Quinn leaned forward. "What about coin? The woman gave us drinks, food, and rooms without one mention of coin. I have yet to see a business owner hand out things without establishing the price or payment in advance." Quinn gestured across the room. "The man in the corner with the hat half covering his face. He has been watching…listening. I caught his eyes open twice. His breathing is too shallow, too rapid for him to be asleep." She turned toward the bar. "The two men exchanging stories at the bar have been there since before we arrived, yet their mugs have yet to be refilled. And then, there is the bartender."

Delvin's brow rose.

"She apparently owns…or at least runs this inn. Yet, she had no rune on her head despite being well north of thirty summers. That makes her an Unchosen. I know things have changed since the Empire and the Ministry were disbanded, but I suspect she has come into such a position in an uncommon manner." She locked eyes with Delvin, the man staring at her for a long moment before he nodded.

"Good. You didn't catch everything, but enough to prove yourself." He downed the last of his ale and plopped the mug on the table. "You're correct. This place – without naming names – was purchased about ten years back by the father of a certain pair of twins you know. He then put Libby in charge of the inn because she is someone he trusts." He ran his fingers across the table. "We use it as the center of our business in Wayport, and we have similar facilities in cities throughout Issalia."

Quinn considered his words and realized that the network she was now part of was more extensive than she had imagined. "Those who are in the Ward – they are just the trainees."

"Yes and no. The gadgeteers likely will remain there. As will many of the arcanists, for they are required to enchant objects. A few, such as

Thiron and Wyck, come and go. The others will likely move on when they are ready and a suitable assignment arises."

"What about my assignment?" Quinn asked. "Will you finally tell me?"

He grinned. "Not yet."

"When?"

"Soon."

She rolled her eyes and sat back, frowning.

Delvin stood. "Now, we can go to our rooms."

"What? Why now?"

"Because I was waiting until you proved that you are observing as you were trained."

Quinn rose from her chair. "That's why we've been sitting down here?"

"That and the fact that our rooms are likely to feel like someone locked them tight and then left a kettle boiling on an open flame."

25

MISSION OBJECTIVE

Twilight from the purple sky above offered faint illumination to the quiet streets. Waning glowlamps at the intersections added little light to aid Quinn and Delvin's passage toward the harbor. Every couple intersections, Delvin would turn from a wide thoroughfare to a narrow alley, dark and foreboding. Quinn found her hand searching for the pommel of her sword more than once, but her hip was bare. Once again, she wished she hadn't been forced to leave her swords behind at the Ward. *They are too noticeable*, Delvin had said. *They also do not fit the persona you will portray.* She understood his point, but she didn't have to like it.

As they neared the south wall, she began to spot others moving about. Unlike the sleepy city behind her, when they passed through the harbor gate and the view opened to the docks, Quinn found them awake and teeming with life.

Warehouses and holding yards occupied the area between the city and the wharf. A boardwalk of wooden planks encircled the harbor while long wooden piers stretched out into the bay. Without pause, Delvin lead Quinn down one such pier, toward the three ships moored beside it.

Quinn examined the first ship as they walked past where dockworkers were busy loading barrels into the hold, forcing her and Delvin to circle around them. The vessel had two masts and a wide, low body. Sailors lounged on the deck, chatting as they waited to set sail.

The next ship was also being loaded. Dockworkers emptied a wagon filled with crates into the hold while another wagon waited behind it. It was a freighter, like the first – its hull built to carry cargo.

When they approached the third ship, Quinn observed differences in its construction. Taller, but with an aggressively shaped hull, it had the look of something built for speed. A long black beam – narrowed at the end – jutted out from the prow. Matching the beam, the rails that surrounded the ship were coated with a shiny black lacquer. With three masts and a high quarterdeck at the rear, Quinn stared in awe, thinking it a thing of beauty.

Delvin stopped and shouted. "Yo! Star Razer!"

A moment later, a man stood at the railing. He rested his bare arms on it, his skin exposed from the shoulder of his sleeveless cream tunic. The man pushed his long dark bangs from his forehead, exposing the Order rune that marked it. With dark eyes, tanned skin, and an affable smile, Quinn decided she might find him attractive if she were fifteen years older.

"You made it," the man said.

"Did you miss me, Parker?"

"I'll admit that I miss watching you and Tenzi exchange barbs," Parker chuckled.

"It's wonderful to find someone who appreciates my talents."

"I'll not comment on that." Parker moved toward the middle of the ship. "I'll have the plank extended."

He turned from the rail and faded from view. Moments later, two men removed a section of the railing while two others fed a long plank over the edge until it tipped, the far end landing on the dock with a thud. Without pause, Delvin walked up the plank, using the boards nailed to it to keep from sliding down. Quinn trailed behind him as memories of her adventures on the Jungle surfaced. In comparison, walking up a foot-wide plank was nothing of note.

When she reached the top, Quinn climbed off to find Parker and

Delvin clasping forearms and patting each other's opposite shoulder, Parker then turned toward Quinn.

"So, this is the girl?"

Delvin nodded.

Parker's gaze lingered for a moment. "She isn't much to look at."

Quinn's face clouded over, her knuckles turning white, her eyes narrowing as she glared at the man.

"Careful, Parker. Don't poke this one. Her bite is far worse than her bark." Delvin smirked.

"I know another female with those traits," Parker said. "If you are ready, we'll set sail."

"We are ready. You know our destination?"

The man spoke over his shoulder as he walked across the deck. "I do, but more importantly, the captain knows."

He stopped before the door below the quarterdeck and knocked. "Captain! Our guests are here and are ready to set sail!"

A moment later, the door opened and a woman emerged. "If they are ready, call the order. I'll take the helm."

Quinn was surprised when Parker nodded toward the woman and responded, "Yes, Captain."

The captain shook her blond hair and pulled it behind her head before slipping a black hat on. With a wide brim and white plume, Quinn thought the hat looked quite dashing. The woman then strode toward Delvin, her mouth turned up in a sardonic smirk.

"So, the miscreant returns for another voyage."

Parker's voice called out, relaying orders as he strolled the length of the ship.

Delvin flashed a wide grin. "Admit that you missed me, Tenzi."

She snorted. "Yes. Much like I miss the feeling I get the morning after I over-indulge. I recall how little I enjoy it, yet I continually return for more."

His expression was one of pain. "You cut me to the quick, Captain. Am I not a most gracious guest when aboard your ship?"

"Yes. You continuously gift me with your childish humor and snide remarks. And then you steal my men's coin before making off like a bandit."

"Wait. I did not steal a thing. They lost fairly."

"Whose dice were you using?"

Delvin shrugged. "Mine were handy."

She snorted again. "I'd just as soon dice with a demon."

"There is no such thing as a demon."

Her brow arched. "Are you so sure? Have you not seen a few things you thought could not exist?"

"Good point."

The woman's blue eyes settled on Quinn. Despite standing over a half-head taller than Tenzi, Quinn experienced a rare moment of self-doubt when staring into those eyes – as if Quinn's own steel gaze was directed back toward her.

"This is the girl?"

Delvin nodded. "Yes."

The woman extended a hand toward Quinn. "I'm Captain Tenzi. Welcome aboard."

Quinn shook the woman's hand and found a firm grip. "Thank you. I'm..."

"Names aren't necessary," Tenzi interrupted and then turned toward Delvin, gesturing toward the bow. "Your usual cabin is ready. The one across the hall is for the girl."

Delvin waved for Quinn to follow while sailors scurried about the deck, preparing the ship. She looked up as the first rays of morning light struck the top of the main mast. *My first time sailing on a ship,* Quinn thought, *and I have no idea where I'm going or what I am to do when I get there.*

Quinn pulled the door open to the sound of the surf. She climbed the stairs and emerged on the deck to find the rising sun split by a dark slice of distant land. A long stripe of reflecting sunlight rippled in waves between the ship and land, forcing her to squint. With her hand above her brow, she scanned the horizon and found nothing in all directions save for the slice of land to the east.

"Good morning."

She turned to find Delvin approaching with a biscuit in one hand, a metal cup in the other.

"The galley is open if you wish to grab some food." He popped a chunk of biscuit into his mouth. "Mmm." He chewed and swallowed. "Warm biscuits with honey – a good way to start the day."

As Delvin took a drink from the cup, Quinn looked toward the bow, the rising sun, and the land mass ahead. Shouting arose as Tenzi issued orders from the quarterdeck.

"We are coming into enemy waters! Raise the flag! Take down the false name!"

The captain now wore a bright red vest, easy to spot from a distance. Quinn wondered at Tenzi's odd commands, so she turned to ask Delvin.

"What does she mean by 'false name'?"

Delvin smiled. "Follow me."

He turned as a man walked past, armed with a sword at his hip and dressed in a sleeveless leather jerkin. The man held a long black cloth in his hand as he headed toward the main mast. Quinn stared at the man while she walked to the starboard rail, watching as he tucked the cloth into his jerkin and began to scale the mast. When she reached the rail, she found Delvin leaning over it. She slid in beside him and turned toward the bow where he pointed.

A woman had slid beneath the lowest cross-rail and was detaching something from the side of the ship. A small board came loose, and a longer one joined it, revealing what lay beneath. Quinn stared intensely as she tried to read the word from the odd angle.

"Razor?"

"Yes," Delvin said. "The other name, Star Razer, is just a persona – not dissimilar from the ones you have developed."

She turned toward him, thinking. "Why keep a ship undercover?"

"Because this persona, as Razor, is a pirate ship...or at least pretends to be one."

"Pretends?"

"We are moving into enemy waters. Transporting you is not this ship's only mission. Tenzi, also known as Red Viper, has been terrorizing trade ships in the east for some time now, acting as a thorn in the side of this upstart Empire."

"Why the subterfuge?"

He looked toward the quarterdeck, staring at the woman at the helm. "As pirates with no apparent political affiliation, Tenzi and Parker can upset the workings of the Empire without giving them cause for war. At least, that is the plan."

Nodding, Quinn considered the idea. "So, they are causing the enemy pain while not risking anyone but themselves."

"Precisely."

The sailor who had altered the vessel's name walked past them – a rough-looking woman with short hair and a Custos rune on her forehead. Quinn frowned in thought. She had expected a Nauticus rune like she had seen on other sailors in the past...like the one on Tenzi's forehead. Pieces began to come together, forming a picture that created another question.

"Who is she?"

"Tenzi?"

"Yes. Not only her...Parker and the rest of the crew as well. They appear to be fighters as much as sailors. The guise of the ship and their willingness to cause the Empire harm for the greater good..."

"Yes. You see it, now." Delvin stared at a seabird, circling overhead before diving toward the water. Moments later, the bird emerged with a fish in its beak, shook its head once, and swallowed it whole. "Tenzi is a tough woman. She and Parker have been together for a long time. Tenzi was in charge of the Kalimar Navy before the kingdom was conquered. Some might know her as Admiral Thanes, although Thanes is Parker's last name and not her own."

"Are they married?"

"Not that I know of. They have a...complicated relationship. I would term them as companions and even partners, but I don't think they ever took the vows."

"And now, they are pirates?"

"Sort of. They act as pirates, but operate under the direction and support of ICON. Although he would never publicly admit it, using this vessel and its crew was King Brock's idea. For all I know, there may be others. This was the one ship I was offered to use for missions and it is all I know."

"Speaking of missions, can you finally tell me where we're headed?

We've been sailing for two days, and I've seen nothing but water until now."

Delvin tilted his head and arched his brow, as if considering her request. Finally, he nodded. "Yes. Knowing now will do you no harm. In fact, you'll need the next few days to prepare yourself."

She glanced toward the bow again and found the land taking shape as the sun slid above it. "Days? That land can't be more than a half day away."

"True. What you see ahead is the west coast of Kalimar. We must sail around the peninsula to the Sol Mai Ocean, for our port is in Vinacci."

"Vinacci?"

"Come."

He led her toward the bow and sat on the circular bench at the base of the foremast. Quinn sat beside him with her elbows on her knees. Delvin took a drink from his cup, emptying it before turning toward her.

"I don't keep secrets to torture you."

"I know."

"I do it for your protection…and for the sake of the mission."

"I know that as well."

"Good." He patted her shoulder. "Before I explain your mission, I must explain what we are up against.

"It is not commonly known, but a secret sect called The Hand ran the Ministry before the Empire's collapse. These people are fanatics. They despise Chaos and see the use of such magic as an abomination. They are the force that kept Unchosen as outcasts while claiming that Issal determined those poor peoples' fate. In truth, labeling those who had the ability to wield Chaos as Unchosen was a means to prevent the return of the magic. That is why the Ministry created the vocation runes they used to dictate the lives of empire citizens. Those who lacked a rune lacked the education and access to information that might help them discover their abilities. I believe that The Hand hoped that those capable of magic would just die out and fade from existence."

Quinn turned the information over in her head and thought of her friends who would have suffered under such laws. Anger at such treatment began to boil inside her until Delvin reclaimed her attention.

"As you know, Vinacci's king died a few years back and a council took over to rule in his stead," Delvin said. "We have determined that The Hand was behind the king's death and their people were who replaced him to rule Vinacci.

"As you might suspect, their ambition did not stop there. A few years later, they attacked eastern Hurnsdom, splitting the kingdom in half as they brought the eastern coast under their rule. Emboldened by their success, and backed by a secret weapon, they turned their sights on Kalimar. Their territory now extends from the southern tip of the Kalimar peninsular, to Yarth, the entirety of Vinacci, and eastern Hurnsdom. These people have taken away lands by force, have outlawed the use of Chaos in those lands, and have turned to persecuting anyone capable of the magic. This is our enemy...one who we understand far less than they understand us. We need information. We need to know what they plan and how we can stop them. Are you with me thus far?"

"Yes."

While she had known some of what the man said, his story painted the picture more clearly, filling in the gaps and fleshing out the scene.

Delvin pointed east. "Our destination is Vinata. There, you will stay a night at an inn, much like the one in Wayport. From that point on, you will be on your own.

"Glynnis, the most recent persona you developed, was for a reason. You will assume the identity of a lady's maid, journeying to Sol Polis with Vinata just a stop along the way."

Quinn's brow furrowed. "If I'm heading to Sol Polis, why not just sail there now? We could be there in a few hours."

"Perception and detail are critical to success in these things. Your story as Glynnis, requires her arriving from the road that leads to Port Hurns, where she worked for Baron Rimini before he was deposed last summer. After a year of working for a local merchant, your uncle, Weldon Mor, sent you to work at the citadel in Sol Polis.

"You see, a serving position on the citadel staff has recently opened, and you are traveling to the city to fill this role. While working there, you will watch and listen as our eyes and ears. Get close to the Archon, discover what the Empire is planning, and unearth any secrets we might use against them should it come to war."

The thump of Quinn's heartbeat pounded in her ears and combined with the rush of the surf. An unexpected anxiety filled her as she realized that her training was at an end. She would be on a mission in a foreign land, surrounded by enemies, and alone. Very much alone.

26

STOLEN KISSES

A gust of wind ruffled Everson's hair as he climbed off the ladder and onto the tower roof. He looked to the north and found dark clouds beyond the grey mountain peaks. The temperature had dropped dramatically since morning. Buttoning the last few buttons on his coat to keep the wind at bay, he walked toward the north edge of the roof. As he moved past the pyramid of glass at the center, he found another person standing along the four-foot wall that encircled the rooftop. He didn't need her to turn to know it was Rena. Everson would recognize those auburn curls anywhere.

He walked toward her, and she turned toward him.

"I didn't expect to find anyone else up here," he said.

She gave him a sad smile. "Hello, Everson. I came up here…to think."

The tone of her voice matched the lack of joy in her smile. Sensing her sadness, the question on his mind remained unsaid.

Everson settled beside her with his elbows on the wall. He was happy just to be near Rena, to share a moment with her as he drank in the scenery. As always, the view of the valley was breathtaking, more so now that the leaves had begun to change color and left the hillsides covered in yellows, oranges, and reds to go with the deep green of the pines.

Below them was the Ward Training Yard, boxed in by a wall a mile deep. Two people were pushing a flying machine from the corner storage shed to the gravel path that ran adjacent to the wall. It was the first machine that received Everson's modifications, but they had lacked a pilot to test it until today. The wait to see the result had been gnawing at him for weeks.

"Petra agreed to test the flyer that Ivy, Henrick, and I modified."

Rena gave him a sad smile, "That's nice."

The two people pushing the flyer stopped and moved away. Petra, the smaller figure who had been walking behind the flyer, moved beside it and climbed in. Everson gripped the wall as anticipation took ahold of him.

"I hope she remembers what I told her," he said to himself.

The blades mounted to the wings began to spin, the buzz reaching the rooftop. With a lurch, the flyer began to speed down the road until it caught air, cleared the top of the wall, and turned to circle over the training yard. Up and up it went as Petra guided it toward the tower where Everson waited. When the flyer approached the tower, she dipped and turned, waving to Everson as she sped past. Petra whooped in joy as she banked again, circled around the west side of the tower, and flew toward the south end of the valley. In moments, she was miles away.

"It worked," Everson said. "Chaos conduction not only eliminates the need to pedal, but it makes the flyer faster – far faster with the added augmentations to the flyer components."

He turned toward Rena and found her grinning. "That's wonderful, Ev."

Unable to resist, he smiled in return. "Thank you, Rena."

Her eyes lowered to her feet. "I'm sorry. I shouldn't let my problems get in the way of our friendship."

"Is there anything I can do?"

"No. Not really. Torney and I had a fight. It isn't a big deal."

"A fight?"

"Yes. He volunteered to go on a mission with Jonah, Chuli, and Thiron."

"Jonah's leaving?"

Rena looked up, her eyes meeting his. "I'm sorry. I...should have let him tell you. Please don't say anything."

"Don't worry. I won't," he replied. "I assume you don't approve of his leaving?"

"When we agreed to join ICON, he and I also agreed that we would remain at the Ward. There is plenty for us to do here with a long list of Infusion augmentations for smart people like you. In addition, there is healing to be done and the possible need to help defend the complex should we ever fall under attack."

Everson nodded. "True. Did he say why he volunteered to leave?"

She turned away and leaned against the wall, the north wind blowing her hair backward like auburn tendrils of the finest cloth. Her beauty again struck Everson.

"He claims he is bored and he wants to help at the front."

"The front?"

She shook her head. "I shouldn't say anything."

"Rena. It's me." He gripped her hand. "You know you can trust me."

A smiled crossed her face, this one laced with honest joy. "I know. If there is anyone I can always count on, it's you."

She squeezed his hand back, hers feeling warm compared to the cool wind. The heat from years of longing stirred inside Everson, and his pulse began to thump in his ears. He stared into her sparkling green eyes and felt them drawing him in, her pink lips pulling him toward her. After a lifetime struggling with his insecurities, he thought of Quinn's brave nature and allowed his sister's strength to push him toward boldness. Everson darted forward, his lips meeting Rena's as he poured his emotion into the kiss. It lasted for a moment before she jerked backward with a gasp. He immediately realized he had crossed a line uninvited.

"I'm sorry." He blurted.

She shook her head. "No. Don't be sorry, Ev. I...I value your friend-ship and I love you, but like a brother...not in the other way."

In her eyes, Everson saw something he had never seen in them before. Pity. It crushed him. He swallowed and blinked repeatedly at the tears that blurred his vision. He turned away and began walking back toward the ladder. After a few steps, he stopped and spoke over his shoulder, unwilling to look at her.

"Please forget this happened." He wiped his cheeks dry with the back of his sleeve. "I'll see you tomorrow."

Everson resumed his walk toward the ladder as thunder boomed in the distance, as if Issal himself were laughing at him.

— ◇ —

With a grunt, Everson pulled on the wrench. It broke loose from the bolt, and his fingers struck the metal frame. He cried out in pain and sat up with his fingers in his mouth.

"Are you all right?" Ivy asked, her face reflecting concern.

He grimaced. "I'll survive."

Rising to his feet, Everson walked away from the steam carriage. The project was coming along well, but he found no joy in it. Thoughts of Rena kept seeping in, his damaged heart poisoning the passion he normally experienced when working on an invention.

He rested his hands on a workbench and stared at his torn knuckles, the pale skin peeled up. The exposed flesh made him think of how he had exposed his heart to Rena two days prior. He couldn't face her now, not with the stolen kiss as a wedge between them. The thought of not being able to talk to her hurt him more than restraining his desire all those years.

"Everson?"

He turned and found Ivy standing behind him. "You've hardly spoken all day. We've been working together for hours, and each time I try to talk to you, you grunt or offer a single word answer before falling silent." Her eyes were pleading. "Please, tell me what's wrong. Is it something I did?"

"No." He shook his head. "It has nothing to do with you."

"So, there *is* something."

A frown crossed his face as he realized what he said. There was no avoiding it now. "I'll get over it. I just need…some time."

She brushed her dark hair back and tucked it behind her ear. "I can give you time. Just know that you can talk to me about anything. I'm always here for you."

Despite his mood, a smile crossed his face. "I know. You are the best. I don't know what I would do without you."

"Do you mean that?"

"Yes. Of course."

"What if I made you angry?"

He shook his head. "You have a good heart. You are compassionate and caring. There is almost nothing that could make me think badly of you, or change things between us."

"Good."

An odd look came across her face as she took a deep breath, her brown eyes locked with Everson's. Ivy lifted her hands to his cheeks, her palms gripping them as she pulled his head toward hers, and she kissed him.

When their lips met, Everson stiffened, caught off guard and unsure of how to react. The moment made him think of Rena and her reaction to his kiss. Rather than fight it, he chose to wrap his arms about Ivy and enjoy the kiss. Moments passed while their lips remained intertwined. A warmth ran through Everson, beginning at the tips of his tingling fingers and running down his body. By the time Ivy pulled away, Everson found himself breathing hard, his heart thumping like a drum. There was a fear in her eyes – a fear he recognized. He knew well the fear of rejection. While he was unsure of how he felt about Ivy, he would not reject her – not without giving her a chance.

"Thank you," Everson said.

Her face darkened. "Thank you?"

"Yes. I...I feel better now."

She hit him on the shoulder.

"Ouch."

"You idiot. This was not to make you feel better. I'm not some tavern wench who kisses men on a lark."

"I..." Everson struggled for the right words. "I'm sorry. I didn't mean it that way."

"How did you mean it?" The look on her face was a challenge.

Everson fought through his emotions and considered his response, fearing that the wrong word would send her away.

"I was hurting inside, and I felt sorry for myself." He reached out and took her hand. "You are a wonderful person, Ivy. I hope that...kiss meant something to you, because it meant something to me. I have always enjoyed spending time with you, but perhaps I need to now try and spend it in another way."

Her expression softened as he spoke. "Such as..."

He chuckled. "Why are girls always challenging what boys say? I feel like I am Jerrell Landish, seeking to avoid a trap that might burn me alive with one misstep."

"That is our prerogative. Now, please continue."

"It's almost dinner time. Perhaps you would like to stop by the kitchen, grab some food, and find a quiet place to eat together? Just you and me."

When she smiled, he knew he had somehow navigated the pitfalls and had come out unscathed.

"I would love to, Everson."

27

IN A FLASH

Quinn stood atop the quarterdeck, the fast moving wind blowing her hair back and forcing her to squint. An Empire ship sailed before them, now barely a quarter mile ahead.

"We're closing on them," Tenzi said. "When we draw close, fire the warning shot and we'll see how they respond."

Parker drew an arrow from his quiver and wrapped the note around the shaft before tying it in place with twine. He then slid his bow from his shoulder and descended toward the main deck.

A glance toward the west revealed land perhaps ten miles away and no city in sight. At the current rate, they would close on the other vessel within minutes. The Empire freighter had no hope of outrunning the Razor and her crew.

Quinn stared at the sailors on the other ship and tried to imagine the panic that might run through the crew when they saw the black flag approaching.

"Do you plan to kill them?" she asked.

Tenzi shook her head. "It rarely comes to that any longer. When we first began attacking Empire ships, we encountered resistance. After making a few examples, and firmly establishing the legend of the Red Viper," she tapped on her red leather vest, "ship captains began to surrender rather quickly. Over the past four months, we have captured more than a dozen ships with little loss of life." Tenzi looked at Delvin. "If we have to board her, what do you plan to do? Help or remain here?"

"I would hate to miss the fun," he said with a smirk.

Tenzi nodded toward Quinn. "What about the girl?"

"Her mission is more important. We shouldn't risk it."

Quinn grunted. "I'm no flower. I'll not wilt under a little heat."

"Oh, of that, I am aware." He patted her shoulder. "Still, I'd rather have you remain here. No need to take an unnecessary risk when there is little to gain."

"What about you, then?"

"While I should do the same, I seldom get to have fun anymore, and I'd hate to miss the opportunity."

"Don't worry, girlie," Tenzi said. "You can hold the wheel if I need to engage."

Despite the scowl on her face, Quinn let the subject drop and turned to look forward. They were drawing close, now two ships' length behind their quarry and about the same distance to the side of it. Parker stood with his hips against the prow railing and lifted his bow. Drawing it back, he held it steady for a long moment before loosing the arrow. It arced over the open water, bent with the wind, and landed on the deck of the opposing ship. A moment later, Quinn saw a man scramble to it and pull it free before heading to the quarterdeck.

"Joely! Shashi! To the foremast and mizzen mast!" Tenzi commanded. "Take down the topgallant sails!"

A thin man with dark hair scrambled up to the quarterdeck and began scaling the mizzenmast while the rough-looking woman with short hair ran toward the foremast. In moments, each was up their respective mast and had the topgallant sails furled, causing the ship to slow slightly. By that time, Razor had drawn even with the other craft, a freighter with the word *Galvanizer* painted on the side.

Three sailors emerged from the door beside galley. The two men in front carried a ballista, already loaded with a grappling hook. The third man held a long coil of rope, tied to the hook. Another trio of sailors ran into the room and reappeared seconds later with another loaded ballista.

While the Razor's crew placed both ballistae along the port rail, aimed at the other ship, Tenzi focused on the other ship. She then looked up and shouted, "Joely! Drop one more sail. We're still too fast! If we don't slow, we will slide past her."

The man in the rigging did as commanded, causing the ship to slow further. On Razor's deck, armed sailors waited at the port rail as they stared at their quarry. Quinn counted the crew – eighteen strong. Some thickly muscled. Others lean and wiry. All appeared rough and battle-tested.

Quinn shifted her focus toward the empire freighter as two men descended from the quarterdeck and ran toward the main mast, where something hid beneath a white sheet. The men fumbled with a rope for a moment, while two other men ran over to join them. The sheet rippled in the breeze as it loosened. It tore away, whipped across the deck, and flattened against the wall of the quarterdeck. The sailors then began pushing two large, black objects across the deck to the starboard railing. The objects were shaped like tubes, the open end facing the Razor.

"Launch Ballistae!" Tenzi called out before turning toward Delvin. "What are they doing? Do you recognize those things?"

Delvin shook his head. A sailor crossed the freighter's deck, pushing a handcart. When he stopped, the man lifted a black ball from the cart and slid it into an open hole of one of the black tubes. Something was familiar about the object. Quinn suddenly recognized why.

"Those look like the projectiles the academy uses for catapults," Quinn said.

Tenzi glanced at Quinn, her eyes widening. "Cut the ropes! Now!"

While the sailors drew swords and began hacking at the two ropes, a man with a torch appeared on the other ship. After he extended the torch toward the rear of the black tube, the men on the Galvanizer scrambled from the black object with their hands over their ears. An explosion of green flame blasted from the open end of the black tube, accompanied by a boom. A black ball hurled out, struck a sailor in the chest, and launched the man across the deck. He and the ball blasted through the Razor's starboard rail and disappeared. Splintered wood from the rail twirled and fell into the ocean, leaving a six-foot gap in the rail.

"Burn me!" Tenzi swore. "Hold on tight!"

Joely, still up on the mizzenmast, began wrapping rigging around one wrist and twisting it around an ankle. Shashi did the same on the foremast. Once the sailors were secured, Tenzi spun the wheel, her hands moving incredibly fast as she cranked it and sent the Razor turning from the Empire ship.

Still near the prow, Parker raised his bow and began firing at the Galvanizer's crew. The sailor holding the torch dropped first, with an arrow through his throat. The torch hit the deck and another man grabbed it before scurrying behind one of the black, iron weapons. Another man jerked and spun before falling to his knees with an arrow in his shoulder. The next shot struck his back and he collapsed face-first to the deck.

"Stein!" Tenzi shouted.

A middle-aged man ran up to the quarterdeck. Unlike the other sailors, he did not look much like a pirate. With brown hair and short-cropped beard, he wore a simple tunic and breeches.

"Yes, Captain?"

"Can your magic do anything to help us?"

He glanced toward the other ship as a deep boom and a burst of green flame came from the other weapon, sending another projectile toward the Razor as it was turning away. The ball clipped the port side railing and careened toward the ocean as splintered railing parts rained across the deck.

Tenzi then spun the wheel again and the Razor returned to its original course.

"I can't think of any rune that'll work for this, 'cept maybe making the ship a bit lighter."

Tenzi nodded. "Do it, then." As the man scrambled toward the bow, Tenzi looked up and shouted. "Unfurl those sails, Joely! We need to reach full speed before they get those things reloaded."

Stunned by the entire ordeal, Quinn stared at the Galvanizer while men scurried about, pouring sparkling powder into each tube. Parker ran toward the stern and shot another arrow. An enemy sailor, who was loading a projectile into a tube, suddenly stiffened. With an arrow in the eye, the sailor flipped over the railing and vanished into the sea, a splash briefly marking the man's grave.

Parker ran up the steps to the quarterdeck, took aim, and fired again. The Razor was picking up speed, now three lengths ahead of Galvanizer. His arrow missed the mark, striking the enemy ship's rail.

"They are too far behind us, now," Parker said.

With the sails unfurled and the lines tied off, Joely dropped to the Quarterdeck while Shashi climbed down the foremast.

"They're pushing the weapons to the fore of the ship," Delvin said while watching the enemy. "They intend to fire at us again."

"You do know that is obvious, right?" Tenzi said in irritation. Her head spun about, glancing from the enemy behind her to the sea before her. "I don't know the range of those things, so I'm not sure how much lead we need."

A deep boom answered her statement when one of the weapons fired. The ball arced through the air, toward them.

"Oh, no," Quinn backed two steps and gripped the rail.

While Quinn feared that it would land right on her, the projectile struck just shy of the quarterdeck. A burst of wood shards filled the air where it hit, and then the door to Tenzi's cabin blasted off its hinges and tumbled across the deck as the ball rolled toward the bow. Unaware, Stein had his back to it as he was tracing a rune on the deck. Just before the ball struck him, the Razor heeled hard to port, and the rolling ball curved, just missing him before it shot through a gap in the rail and disappeared.

"My ship!" Tenzi growled with her fist squeezed, knuckles white.

At the bow, Stein stood over a rune twenty feet in diameter, the symbol glowing a bright red. The captain cranked hard on the wheel, turning the ship starboard when another boom arose from behind. Again, the ball arced through the air toward them. When it fell, it narrowly missed the port side before splashing into the sea. The glow faded from the rune and the ship suddenly rose up ten feet, picking up speed. Tenzi turned the wheel again and set the ship back on course, the Razor now moving faster than ever.

"The Empire will pay for this," Tenzi said with a snarl. She then turned to Parker. "Take the wheel. The Razor will be well beyond their reach by the time they reload."

Parker moved to the wheel, his eyes locking with Tenzi's "Where are you going?"

Her scowl deepened. "I'm going to inspect my cabin...or what is left of it."

As the woman stormed down the ladder to the main deck, Quinn turned to Delvin.

"What kind of weapons were those?"

"The worst kind," Delvin said. "This confirms something we feared. They have discovered new ways to use flash powder." He looked Quinn in the eye. "Your mission just became far more critical. Thousands of lives may depend on the information you seek."

Quinn emerged from her cabin and smoothed the front of her dress. Her hair was tied in a bun behind her head. While wearing a dress seemed odd to Quinn, it was a critical aspect of her persona. As a handmaid, Glynnis always wore dresses.

She shifted aside and turned to watch Hex and Garrard climb the stairs, grunting under the weight of the chest they carried. The polished brass panels on the wooden chest glinted in the afternoon sunlight and offered a stark contrast to the dark stained wood from which it was constructed. The two men had shed their leather jerkins in favor of simple cream-colored tunics, now appearing more like sailors than soldiers. They passed by Quinn and headed toward the planks that had been extended to the dock. Her attention was drawn away from them as Delvin approached.

"The rune looks good," He grinned. "Perhaps I should become an artist."

Quinn's hand went to her forehead. She needed to remember the fake rune and wash it as little as possible. At least she no longer had to endure the smell of the dye he had used to create it.

"I will go ashore with you. We'll spend the night here, and you'll leave on a carriage in the morning." Delvin held a folded sheet of paper toward her. "When you arrive in Sol Polis, head to the citadel with this and ask for Abner Sheen. He manages the citadel staff and will be expecting you."

Quinn accepted the note and stared at it for a moment. "There will be an opening for me in the staff?"

"Yes. One of the handmaids will be taking a leave of absence, if she hasn't already."

"How did you arrange that?"

Delvin smirked. "She quite pregnant by now and it will be difficult to hide it. Abner will be forced to remove her from her service, which he surely has by now."

Quinn shook her head. "I don't want to know how you orchestrated this."

"It happened in the usual way, I can assure you." His grin widened. "Numerous times."

"How could you do that to the poor woman?"

Delvin's grin dropped away. "I *do* have a conscience, and I considered the repercussions. She has been compensated with a significant dowry, and she should have little trouble finding a suitable husband who will care for her and her babe. It is the best I can do under the circumstances."

"And what of the child?"

"I'm sorry, Quinn, but we are at war. While not ideal, I'm willing to make concessions so I might save the lives of thousands of other children. Let it go."

Quinn grit her teeth and pushed past him, toward the plank. Walking in slippered feet seemed as odd as wearing the dress. She had grown used to her boots and would miss them dearly. Reaching the dock, she joined the men with the chest and waited for Delvin to say goodbye to Tenzi and Parker. Moments later, the man was on the pier and leading her toward the city.

Vinata was located at the mouth of a river, the docks downstream from the city itself. A river delta of sand and scrub occupied the heart of the bay. White gulls dotted the island and circled high above it.

The city itself was a half-mile from the docks, closer to the river. Quinn wondered if the two men would be forced to carry the chest all that way. Her concerns were erased when they approached a wagon parked between two warehouses built along the shore. Delvin spoke with the driver before climbing on the seat and gesturing for Quinn to join him. The two sailors slid the chest onto the wagon bed, closed the rear gate, and pinned it in place before turning back toward the docks.

"Take us to Pintalli's Inn, please," Delvin said.

The driver snapped the reins. "Get!"

As the wagon climbed up the gravel road toward the city, Quinn gazed out over the countryside, covered with grapevines that climbed man-made trellises. For miles and miles, green vineyards stretched across the hills, occasionally interrupted by driveways that led to small clusters of buildings.

"Much of the wine we drink comes from this region," Delvin said, apparently reading her thoughts. "It would be a shame if tensions between the Empire and the kingdoms continue. Wine has already become difficult to purchase in the kingdoms, the cost rising each week. At the same time, these vineyard owners suffer because they are producing more wine than the Empire consumes, which has driven the local prices down." Delvin gave the driver a sidelong look. "I wonder if the situation has led to smuggling goods."

The driver's eyes flicked toward Delvin for a breath before returning to the road.

As they approached the city, Quinn observed portions of the wall two shades lighter than the rest. Similar to Cinti Mor, Vinata had been destroyed and the people slaughtered during The Horde invasion. Now, nearly two decades later, the city had been rebuilt, but scars remained. The entire east coast lived with those very same scars.

The wagon rolled through the city gate, the driver tipping his hat to the guards posted there. The soldiers were dressed in mail armor, their tabards white with blue accents and the rune of Issal, also known as the Order rune. The same rune marked their shields. With narrowed eyes and scowling faces, the soldiers watched the wagon roll past.

At the second intersection, the wagon turned up a winding, uphill street. When the horses reached the top of the hill, the wagon turned again and proceeded down a narrow alley that led to a cobblestone courtyard. At the back of the yard was a roof held up by a dozen wooden posts. Two horses stood beneath the roof, busily eating hay. The driver drove the wagon in a tight circle and stopped with the horses again facing the alley.

"Pintalli's Inn, as requested, good sir." The driver tipped his hat.

"Thank you." Delvin placed coins in the man's palm and climbed from the wagon. He then extended an arm toward Quinn. "If you please, Miss Glynnis."

She gripped his hand, lifted her skirts with the other, and climbed down. Two boys, both a few years younger than Quinn, emerged from the open stable and waved to greet them. Both were stout of stature and had dark hair, one with curls and large eyes while the other boy's hair was long and straight.

"Hello, Miss," the curly-haired boy said as he drew near. "We're here to take your chest."

Quinn nodded. "Very good. I will be staying the night."

"Go on in and ask for Pintalli. He will set you up. We will be right along with the chest." The two boys each stood to one end of the wagon bed gate and began pulling the pins.

Without a word, Delvin headed toward the green door at the rear of the red brick building. Quinn followed him inside and realized that this was the last night before her mission truly began. Tomorrow, he would leave her, and she would be on her own, entering the den of the enemy. The fate of thousands might rest upon her success. One misstep might lead to her death. Her stomach squirmed at the thought.

The carriage ride from Vinata to Sol Polis was quiet. Lost in thought, Quinn stared blankly out the window. The coastline and the ocean beyond it faded from view in intervals when obscured by foliage growing along the road. Hours passed before the carriage turned inland and the view changed to rolling hills of yellowed grass as the road headed west, toward her destination.

After months of longing to go on a mission, chomping at the bit for a chance to prove herself, Quinn found her eagerness buried beneath a mountain of anxiety and self-doubt. In the past, her determination and relentless drive had overcome most obstacles. In contrast, the nature of her new task required finesse, patience, and a subtlety that were outside her comfort zone. Her thoughts drifted to Chuli and the jealously she had experienced when her friend had been offered a mission before Quinn. *Why couldn't they just send me off to kill a monster?* When the wagon crested a rise, the white walls of Sol Polis came into view. Quinn sat forward and peered out the window in curiosity.

Outside the city walls, dilapidated buildings lay in ruin. As with every other city east of Yarth, Sol Polis had fallen to The Horde and the city had yet to return to its full glory. Within minutes, the wagon neared the buildings, broken, overgrown with weeds and moss – an abandoned graveyard of what once was. Quinn wondered if the city would ever again spread beyond the walls as it had during its prominence.

The carriage approached the gate and slowed. Quinn stuck her head out the window as a pair of armored guards dressed in white tabards stepped forward. The rune of Issal stood bold on their chests, sewn in blue to contrast the white. The taller soldier, a thin man with broad shoulders, addressed the driver.

"State your name and purpose to enter the city," he said in a deep voice.

"My name is Lester. Lester Mastin. I was hired to bring the woman in the carriage to the citadel."

The guard narrowed her eyes at Quinn. "What is your business at the citadel?"

"My name is Glynnis Mor. I journey from Port Hurns for work." She held the note out the window and the man moved closer to take it. After a moment, he handed it back to her and waved them forward. The carriage lurched into motion and entered the city. As the arched opening slid past, Quinn spotted the pale spires of the citadel towers stretching toward the sky. A moment later, buildings lining the road obscured the towers. Quinn's focus shifted to her immediate surroundings, seeking something that would help her better understand life under Empire rule. Instead, she found everything to be quite...normal.

They passed a bakery, a cobbler, a butcher, a tailor, a jeweler, and a smithy. The people on the streets were dressed in short sleeves, light dresses, and loose tunics – suitable for the summer-like heat that lingered far longer than she was used to, having grown up in Cinti Mor. Otherwise, she saw nothing that might distinguish them from citizens anywhere else. Here and there, she spotted Empire soldiers dressed in white and blue, strolling the streets in pairs, and she saw how their hands rested on their weapons. Was there an air of tension? Or was it just her own anxiety that clouded her vision?

The street ended at an open square with a hill in the center. Walls atop the hill encased the citadel inside them, and stairs led to a gate at the top where guards stood to inspect those who would enter the grounds. The carriage turned and headed north, up a shallow incline, and then turned west at the next intersection. Here, at the rear of the complex, the citadel hill and the street behind it became level. At the middle of the north wall was a guarded iron gate. When they reached the gate and the driver stopped the team, a ruddy-faced woman approached the carriage. The gold stripes on her white and blue tabard marked her as an officer.

Rather than wait, Quinn leaned out the window and waved the note. "Good afternoon. My name is Glynnis Mor. I have been hired to work for the citadel staff. Here is a letter from Abner Sheen, inviting me."

With a grimace, the female guard walked over to take the note. As she read it, Quinn examined the woman. Tall for a female, her black hair was tied back in a tail. She had severe eyebrows that Quinn decided would make her look angry regardless of her mood. The woman's dark eyes and stern disposition made it that much worse. When she finished, the woman handed the paper to Quinn.

"Open the door and step outside."

"Yes, of course." Quinn did as requested. Contrary to her nature, she did her best to appear timid, looking toward the ground and shuffling her slippers as she shifted away from the carriage.

The woman leaned into the carriage and poked around for a moment. She then stepped back and circled to the rear. "What's in the chest?"

"My things. Mostly dresses, shoes…smallclothes."

"Open it."

Quinn pushed her frustration aside, swallowed her pride, and moved to the back of the wagon. After fumbling with the straps that held the chest in place, she loosened them and flipped the latch.

The woman pointed toward the chest. "Lift the lid."

With a sigh, Quinn opened it and shifted aside. The woman began to rummage through it, pushing clothing, shoes, and other items aside.

After a moment, she pulled out an oval-shaped metal disk, the bronze glittering in the afternoon sunlight. Quinn's heart began to pound when she recognized the item.

"What's this?"

Stifling anxiety, Quinn forced anger into her response. "What do you think? That's my makeup, you ninny." She then took up a haughty expression. "Or, perhaps you remain unaware of what makeup is. Judging by your complexion, you could use a bit, you know."

The woman's grimace twisted to a sneer, and she tossed the item into the chest before slamming the lid shut.

"Get back in the carriage before I throw you inside."

Without a word, Quinn scrambled into the carriage.

The guard thumped the carriage door closed and climbed up beside the driver. "I'm riding in with you to make sure everything is as it seems."

Quinn sat back in relief, knowing she had just dodged a trap. How many more would she face?

Abner Sheen was a small man. Balding and possessing a pinched face, he barked orders to the people standing before him. The servants, consisting of women in navy blue dresses and men wearing white coats with navy trousers, exited the room and headed toward their posted positions. When the last person exited, Abner turned toward Quinn with a frown.

"Now, what is this about?"

She glanced toward her escort and took a breath. The female guard's stern glare remained fixed on Quinn, her face a grimace. Quinn took a breath and extended the note toward the man.

"My uncle Welden sent me from Port Hurns with this note. I understand that there is an open position as a handmaid."

Abner's eyes narrowed. He took the letter, opened it, and read it before nodding. "Thank, Issal. I was hoping that Weldon might have someone suitable." He looked at Quinn. "You have some experience with the position?"

"Yes. I was working as a handmaid for Baroness Rimini before the

Empire stormed the city." Quinn looked down, her voice quieting. "She was a fine woman, yet demanding. I am saddened that she died…" She shook her head and moved past the emotion. "Once things settled, I found work with a local merchant, but I was under-used there…and underpaid. Working for nothing but a roof and food leaves much to be desired. Working for a merchant also lacks a greater purpose, which is something I had come to relish. So, when uncle Weldon told me you were seeking help, I begged him to hire a driver to bring me to Sol Polis, promising to repay him with my earnings here."

The man frowned. "That is somewhat presumptuous. You have not yet been hired."

"If you give me a chance to prove myself, I am confident you will be satisfied."

A yellow-haired woman burst into the room, pushed Quinn aside, and stood before Sheen with her hands on her hips. Pretty, with pouting lips and plenty of curves, the woman carried a haughty air despite wearing a dark blue dress like the other servants.

"Archon Varius requested that her dinner be served in her chamber," the woman said. "Be sure it arrives on time and that it is still hot. If it is cold like the last time you served her in her chamber, you will feel the depth of her wrath."

Sheen scowled at the woman. "Don't tell me how to do my job, Jeshica. I will deal with it."

"Good." Jeshica turned toward Quinn. "Who are you?"

"My name is Glynnis. I've come for a position as a handmaid."

A sardonic grin twisted the woman's lips. "Huh. You'll be working for Larrimor, then. Good luck with that woman." She pushed past Quinn again but stopped to look back before exiting the room. "Be sure to keep your skirts lowered. You don't want to find yourself with child and end up like the last girl in your position. Larrimor almost killed her when she found out. A repeat of the situation might put the old hag over the edge."

Quinn glared at Jeshica's back as she disappeared into the corridor. When she turned back toward Master Sheen, she found him doing the same.

"That girl is insufferable," he muttered.

"So I've heard," the female guard said.

Sheen turned his focus on Quinn, staring at her for a long moment.

"I'll give you a week." Sheen pointed toward the door. "Head down the corridor, take the stairwell up three levels, and knock at the first door on the right. Tell Magistrate Larrimor that I sent you. She will inform you of your duties for now. Attend to her needs well. I will meet with her in seven days for a report…if you last that long."

28

MONDOMI

C huli closed her eyes, embracing the thrill of riding – focusing on the connection she felt with Rhychue beneath her. The horse's muscles flexed with each stride, and Chuli flowed with the rhythm of the gallop, the two as one. She opened her eyes and gazed toward the cloud-covered sky overhead. Autumn was upon the plains, and storms came with the drastic temperature swings that accompanied the season. Riding in the rain was less than ideal, and she would rather reach Mondomi before it began.

The tall grass surrounding her flowed past while the horse sped across the rolling fields, vast and sprawling. Wind-driven ripples flowed across the plains, the sea of grass appearing as if it were an ocean. A backward glance revealed her companions trailing behind.

Thiron rode a white and brown piebald, the man's horse one length to Chuli's right and three lengths behind her. To her left, and further back, Torney rode with a grimace and a fraction of the grace Thiron displayed. At the tail end of the group, Jonah stood in his saddle, doing his best to keep up without getting tossed. Chuli shook her head at his poor form, his lack of ability to flow with the chestnut mare he rode. After three days in the saddle, his discomfort was well known to the others. Jonah was not known for keeping his opinions to himself.

When she turned to look forward, the red-tinted hills at the southwest edge of the plains had drawn close. A dozen narrow canyons split those hills, each possessing steep inclines that made one appear much the same as any other. Chuli spotted a pale gray boulder atop a bluff and headed toward it, slowing as she approached the ravine below the rock.

The others stopped beside her, their horses shifting nervously.

"We are near Mondomi. Please follow, but be aware that you are entering protected grounds. The wrong move might result in a few arrows sticking from your ribs...or worse."

"Or worse?" Jonah frowned. "First, you beat us into submission by racing your blasted horse across the plains and now you threaten to have us shot with arrows."

Chuli tilted her head, her tone serious. "When you agreed to stop by my home during our journey, did you think it would be without a price?"

Torney and Jonah looked at each other. Thiron, held his hand over his mouth to cover his smile. The dark-skinned man behaved much like a Tantarri and left Chuli to wonder at his background. Other than his birth in Sunbleth and his teen years spent in the forests surrounding the Skyspike Mountains, she knew little of her mentor.

"Come," Chuli waved them forward as she kicked Rhychue into a trot. The horse hardly needed direction as it returned to its former home. A half mile into the canyon, the horse slowed to a walk and angled up a rocky slope that appeared to lead nowhere. When Chuli crested the rock, she rode Rhychue up a narrow ledge that ran along the canyon wall. They turned a corner, and the ledge grew wide enough that two horses could ride in tandem. Without waiting, Chuli led the party upward with the canyon floor falling farther and farther below them.

Cresting the top of the trail – yet still three-hundred feet below the upper reaches of the surrounding hills – the horses entered a wide tunnel and slowed to an easy walk. Two Tantarri emerged from the shadows as Chuli coaxed Rhychue to a stop. Both Tantarri had the shaved heads of warriors, each with a black topknot hanging in the rear. The shorter of the two stepped forward to greet Chuli.

"Welcome home, Chuli Ultermane," the woman said with the tilt of her head.

"It is good to see you, Bruxi Hornblower."

"You bring Outlanders to Mondomi?" The tall man crossed his muscled arms over his chest, his face bent in a grimace.

"Yes, Gothan." Chuli slid off her horse.

"And you have permission to do so?"

"No. However, these men are wardens, like me. They are allies of the highest calling, and they can be trusted"

The man grunted. "We will see what the head clanswoman says."

"Good," Chuli replied as Thiron stood beside her. "I must speak with my aunt regardless."

"Come, then," Bruxi waved for them to follow.

Chuli glanced back and found Torney helping Jonah dismount. Jonah's foot became stuck on the saddle horn, and he fell on his back-side, taking Torney with him. Torney landed on his back with Jonah atop him. A sigh slipped from Chuli's lips. She chanced a glance back at Bruxi and found the woman smiling. Chuli squeezed her eyes shut in a moment of embarrassment. When she opened them, she found the two boys climbing to their feet.

Chuli said, "When we enter, allow me to do the talking until I tell you otherwise."

Thiron gave a slow nod of agreement, as did Torney, while dusting off his trousers.

Jonah said, "I would really prefer to complain. My backside is likely permanently damaged, and it will kill me if I can't complain about it for a while. In fact, I may need hours to do it justice."

"It *would* be odd if he did not complain," Thiron added.

Chuli found herself unable to restrain a chuckle. "I understand that you find riding uncomfortable – something you have made perfectly clear. Regardless, I beg you to save your whining for later. I'll be sure to give you a proper platform, and you can then complain as much as you wish. But for now, please be silent."

Chuli followed Bruxi while the others trailed behind with Gothan at the rear. They entered a curved side tunnel, wide enough for three people to walk together. Ancient drawings marked the torchlit walls, depicting battle scenes from an era long past. Having seen them count-less times, Chuli ignored the artwork and considered what she must tell Puri. The tunnel opened to the receiving chamber, a natural cavern with one tunnel to the right and another entrance at the far end. As usual, orange coals from a brazier at the center offered light for those passing through. Chuli turned and found her companions staring upward as they eyed the uneven dome above them.

Without pause, Bruxi led them down the far tunnel, which curved until it came to a stairwell cut in stone. Chuli knew that the stairwell down led to the city. Bruxi instead led them up another staircase, curved and illuminated by a torch at each end. When they emerged from the stairwell, daylight greeted them. Chuli stopped beside Bruxi and surveyed the scene.

Head Clanswoman Puri and her husband Cameron were seated at a table on the high terrace, in the midst of a quiet conversation with the new elder, Kiananni. Chuli experienced a moment of sadness at the loss of Yuranni. She missed the kind, old elder, despite his idiosyncrasies. However, oddness was to be expected from someone who walked dreams and interacted with the spirit world. To young Chuli, the former elder had seemed as old as the stone walls of Mondomi. When he had finally died four years prior, there was much conjecture as to his real age, but nothing was ever confirmed. Rumors among the Tantarri placed the man somewhere north of one hundred summers. Some clan members believed the man had lived many more years than that. Unlike Yuranni, Kiananni was young and virile and would likely hold the position for many decades to come.

Chuli looked up at the half-dome of rock, fifty-feet above her. The limestone ceiling extended for hundreds of feet until it met daylight. The sheer vertical face of the opposing canyon wall was visible from where she stood. On sunny days, hues of red, orange, and amber shone from that canyon wall, oftentimes the minerals within it sparkling in the direct light. Today, however, was a dreary overcast day that muted the colors that she so admired.

Puri glanced toward Chuli as the others emerged from the stairwell. The woman said something to Kiananni, and the man rose to his feet.

The elder was of a height with Chuli, his long dark hair tied into a tail. At perhaps thirty-five summers, he might be old for a warrior, but he was quite young compared to the elders who had come before him.

His body also lacked the scars and body art that warriors bore, his skin pale for a Tantarri since the sun had seldom touched it.

"It is good to see you returned to us, Chuli Ultermane."

"Thank you, Elder Kiananni. It is good to be back, if only for one night."

He shook his head. "I am saddened that you must depart so quickly." He stepped beside her and placed a palm on her shoulder. "Be well and may the Spirits guide you."

With those words, he walked off and faded into the stairwell that led up to his quarters.

As Chuli approached the table, Puri and Cameron stood. Chuli had grown used to being among the tallest females in Fallbrandt, both at the combat academy and at the Ward. Even so, Puri's presence was imposing, her height exceeded Chuli's by an inch or two. The woman wore her long dark hair down, held back from her face with a jewel-encrusted headdress.

"Welcome home, Niece." Puri held her arms out, and Chuli moved close for a hug.

"It is good to be back, Aunt Puri."

Cameron's thick arms wrapped about both Puri and Chuli. "We missed you, Chuli."

He stepped back with a smile on his face. Standing at six-and-a-half feet tall, Cam towered over most crowds. His blond hair made him an oddity among the Tantarri. Of course, his parents were Torinlanders – a fair complexion and light-colored hair and eyes quite common there.

"Who are your friends?" Cam asked. "I recall seeing the dark one the last time I visited the Ward."

Not waiting for an introduction, Thiron gave a shallow bow. "My name is Thiron Hawking. I am a ranger, like your niece."

Puri arched a brow at Chuli. "A warden?"

"Yes. Since last spring. Thiron is my mentor, teaching me to hone my ranger skills."

A grin crossed Puri's face and she gave Chuli a nod. "You honor the Tantarri with your commitment, Chuli. Cameron and I know well the importance of wardens with the threat in the east."

Pride filled Chuli's heart. She could not help but bask in the glow of her aunt's approval. After a moment, she shed her smile and refocused, waving her other companions over.

"These two are Jonah Selbin and Torney Jacobs. Both are arcanists."

"Selbin? From Nor Torin?" Cam asked. When Jonah nodded, Cam added, "You are among my father's recruits."

"Yes, Sir. I trained at the citadel for a year before heading to Fallbrandt."

Chuli addressed Puri. "We need to talk. I must tell you of what we have learned and what we are planning. ICON prepares for the worst. The Tantarri must prepare as well. And…there is more. I must speak to you about Curan."

A grimace crossed Puri's face as she glanced toward Cam. "Curan?"

"Yes. The leaders have requested that he join us. They believe that his skills can be better utilized with training."

"They wish him to become a warden?" Cam asked.

"Yes."

Cam stared at Puri for a long moment. "Benny would only send a request for Curan if it were important."

With narrowed eyes, Puri took a deep breath, exhaling slowly. "We will discuss Curan later…in private." She turned to Chuli. "I must send a message for the clan leaders to join us. They must also hear the news from Fallbrandt. I believe all are currently in Mondomi, so we can meet this afternoon. Afterward, I invite you and your friends to join us for dinner. Please extend an invitation to your mother as well."

"Yes, Puri."

Puri headed toward the stairwell with Cam trailing close behind. While she watched her aunt and uncle depart, Chuli considered the information she needed to share with the clan leaders…and of the request she must extend to them.

"Look at this!"

Chuli turned to find Jonah standing at the low wall surrounding the terrace and she, along with Torney and Thiron, crossed the open space to stand beside him. The sight of her home brought a smile to her face.

"It's a city," Torney said, his tone filled with wonder. "A city made of stone, carved from the mountain itself."

Mondomi stretched out below the terrace, with narrow streets and open plazas that divided square stone buildings. Running fountains occupied the two primary plazas, drawing citizens to the running water. Children played in one square, while carts of produce filled the other. Above everything, stood a series of rooftop plazas, the plaza directly below Chuli being the largest.

'Welcome to Mondomi," Chuli said. "Only a handful of Outlanders have ever seen it and lived."

Jonah turned toward her. "Lived? You killed people who came here?"

Chuli shrugged. "So I am told. It was years ago, before I was born...when the Empire still ruled Issalia. While our war with them was not one of our choosing, the secrecy of our home is also its best defense."

Jonah's eyes narrowed at the thought before nodding. "Fair enough."

The clopping of hooves drowned out the sound of the surf below. Shrubs lined the road, filling in the narrow space between the gravel and the cliff's edge – the drop exceeding two-hundred feet. The white-capped sea below appeared rough, the sky overhead dark and cloudy. Chuli expected rain to fall soon, and she was thankful that they neared their destination. Rounding a bend, the city of Hipoint came into view.

Tucked back in a bay that acted as a natural harbor, Hipoint was constructed in tiers that lined a steep hillside. A single two-masted ship and three smaller boats were moored in the harbor. Sailors and workers on the docks looked like ants from the distance, milling around as they went about their business. A wide row of steps led from the pier at the bottom to the road atop the hill. Beside the road, stood the garrison – their destination.

The road turned, and Chuli lost view of the city. She glanced toward her companions and found them staring toward the sea. Moving at a trot, her fellow riders bounced along with their steeds.

Riding to Chuli's side, Thiron appeared at ease, although the man's hawk-like eyes never ceased scanning his surroundings. Torney appeared worn, exhausted from their journey. As usual while riding horseback, Jonah's face was a grimace of discomfort. Chuli chuckled to herself. *You would think that six days of riding would have forced him to adapt.*

Chuli turned to look forward as they rounded another bend. The garrison came back into view – this time far closer than the previous glimpse.

Wooden palisades encircled the structure, fifteen-feet tall with each log sharpened to a point. Hundreds of feet beyond it, rows of thinner logs had been wedged into the ground at an angle that faced southeast, each also sharpened to a point. *Like honed arrows, all pointing toward the Empire*, Chuli thought.

The group slowed their horses as they neared the fort and the stairs down to the city. Two porters finished loading a wagon atop the steps. The driver climbed into his seat and gave his team a shout while snapping the reins. The wagon lurched into motion, the man tipping his hat to Chuli as she rode past him.

As Chuli's horse approached the gate, a tug on the mane brought Rhychue to a stop. Thiron's horse settled beside her while Chuli dismounted. He dropped to the ground, and the two approached the garrison. Two soldiers dressed in the black, red, and gold of Kantaria stood beside the gate – a squat, husky man with shorn brown hair and a taller, thinner fellow with black hair that touched his shoulders. The taller one had dark eyes and a few days growth of a dark beard on his young face. The other had a scar from his forehead down to his cheek. Also unshaven, he seemed to be the more seasoned of the two guards.

"State your business," the shorter man said.

"My name is Thiron Hawking and these are my companions. We have been sent here by Captain Goren." Thiron removed a piece of paper from his jerkin and handed it to the man.

After reading it, the guard folded it and handed the paper to Thiron. "Wait here."

The man rapped on the gate. "It's Olusk. Let me in."

When the gate eased open, the man slid inside. Three minutes later, he returned with a woman beside him. Her red hair was tied back, her green eyes measuring, her lips pressed together. Matching Chuli in height, she was tall for a woman, but was easily ten years Chuli's senior. Gold stripes on the woman's shoulders marked her as an officer.

"Greetings. I am Captain Marcella. The Hipoint garrison is under my command."

Thiron gave the woman a nod. "Thank you for meeting us, Captain. We have been sent here to lend assistance. May we come inside so we can discuss things in a more private setting?"

Marcella frowned. "How do I know I can trust you? Your letter might be forged."

Thiron leaned close the woman. She twisted her head and listened as he whispered in her ear. Marcella's eyes widened, and she stepped aside.

"Come inside. Bring your horses. We have stables, food, and water for them."

Chuli led Rhychue through the gate and found the interior bustling with activity. In moments, she counted hundreds of soldiers, along with other men wearing clothes stained with red dirt. They had arrived in Hipoint and now had work to do. Thoughts of war lingered in thoughts and left her wondering what dark days the future might hold.

29

THE COLOR PURPLE

"And when you are through scouring the floor, you had best run down to the laundry room and bring up the fresh bedding I requested yesterday. I'll not wait for those useless porters to do the job or another week will pass before it arrives."

"Yes, Magistrate." Quinn maintained an even tone that hid her frustration.

Quinn scrubbed Magistrate Larrimor's hair, wishing she could dig her nails in to the hateful woman's scalp until she drew blood. With each day that passed, she despised the woman more than the day before it. She turned, dipped her hands into a bucket of water to rinse the foam away, and grabbed the pitcher beside it.

"Ready to rinse," Quinn announced.

The woman sat forward in the copper tub and faced the ceiling. Quinn poured the pitcher of hot water over her head, rinsing away the soap. She then put the pitcher down and squeezed water from the woman's gray hair. The woman stood and water ran down her wrinkled body into the tub as she waited for Quinn to dry her.

"Hurry with the towel. I don't have all day."

Quinn did as instructed while wishing she could wrap the towel around the Larrimor's neck and strangle the old hag. *Restraint.*

Patience, Quinn told herself. *Killing the woman would also terminate the mission.*

With the woman dried, Quinn scrambled to snag the woman's blue velvet robe from a hook and draped it over her shoulders. Magistrate Larrimor climbed out of the tub and onto the rug, waiting while Quinn knelt to towel off her lower legs and feet.

"I changed my mind," The woman said. "I'll dress myself today. Remove the quilt and sheets from my bed and take them down now. Don't come back until you have fresh bedding. Once you do, make the bed and then scrub the floor. When I return to my chamber after court, I expect to see the room's appearance pristine, the bedding made and turned down."

Quinn stood and turned toward the woman's bed, thankful she didn't have to help her dress again. She pulled the summer quilt off, a thin version of what was used in the coming winter months. The sheets came next. When the mattress was bare, she added the wet towel to the pile and gathered it all into her arms before heading toward the door. Fumbling with the knob, she opened it and stepped into the hallway before pulling the door closed.

Down the stairs she went, careful to watch over the bundle in her arms. Quinn's descent continued until she reached the basement, the same floor where she and the other servants lived. Following a long corridor lit by glowlamp sconces mounted to the wall, she continued past her room and approached a pair of closed doors that led to her destination. She grabbed the knob and twisted it, stepping into a room busy with activity.

A long counter divided the front from the storage and work areas. Behind the counter, rows of tall shelving occupied the far end of the room. Towels, bedding, soaps, and other supplies filled the shelves, while carts of clean clothing stood in a line beside them, ready to return to their owners. Launderers moved about as they gathered items into baskets. Once a basket was full, they would bring it to a cart, where it would sit until a porter picked it up.

Quinn glanced toward the open doorway at the side of the room. Through the door, she saw four women sitting on stools, busily rubbing clothing up and down ribbed boards. Foam covered their hands, their dresses wet on the front. A man walked past the women, handing each another piece of laundry while taking the articles they had just cleaned. He then faded from view as he headed toward the rinsing station.

"May I help you?"

Quinn turned and found a short, heavy-set woman staring from behind the counter. Her graying hair was tied back in a tail, the white smock on her blue dress marked with stains. With her fists on her hips, the woman glared as if Quinn were interrupting something important.

"Yes," Quinn approached the counter with a smile, her voice full of honey. "I'm sorry to bother you, Mavis. Larrimor forced me to come down to retrieve new bedding. To save the porters a trip, I brought her dirty bedding and towel with me."

The woman's grimace softened as she snorted. "That woman can be quite trying. I don't envy you, Glynnis."

"I do what I can to…" A woman's voice from behind interrupted Quinn.

"Excuse me." Jeshica shouldered Quinn as she walked past and put her hands on the counter. "The Archon sent me to get fresh towels, soap, and a new bottle of dye."

Mavis scowled as she stared at the woman. "I was speaking with Glynnis, Jeshica."

The woman gave Quinn a sidelong look, her blue eyes assessing her as she pursed her lips. "I hardly think that this girl's needs are more important than the Archon's."

"Are you here, Archon Varius?" In an exaggerated manner, Mavis surveyed the room and then glowered at Jeshica. "I don't see the Archon. It appears that only her handmaid is present, a handmaid who does not know how to act civil and wait her turn."

Jeshica leaned across the counter, eyeing Mavis. "If you don't bring me the requested items immediately, I'll report you to the Archon. I'd like to see how you respond when she comes down because you refused her request."

Fire burned in Mavis' glare. After two heavy breaths, Mavis sneered. "Fine. Wait here."

The woman turned, grabbed a basket, and disappeared down one of the aisles. Jeshica looked back at Quinn with a smirk on her face. Quinn's eyes narrowed, and her lips pressed together. She longed to punch the pretentious woman, maybe even break a bone or two. While there were many other servants at the citadel, Jeshica was the only handmaid besides Quinn, with the Archon the only female on the Council and Larrimor the only female magistrate. The manservants assigned to the male officials all treated Quinn with the respect of a peer. Jeshica was another story. Quinn suspected that Jeshica's looks, if one were attracted to a simpering blond with a curvaceous figure, contributed to her entitled behavior. The woman's position as the Archon's handmaid seemed to have further inflated her self-opinion.

Mavis reappeared with a basket filled with fresh towels, a clean robe, a bar of soap, and a corked bottle. "Here are the items the Archon requested, save for the dye. We had one bottle of black left, but it broke yesterday when it fell off the shelf, staining the tile forever. The next delivery won't arrive until sometime next week."

"What?" Jeshica sounded outraged. "This is unacceptable. What is the Archon to do? You know her hair will gray without it."

The grimace returned to Mavis' face. "That is not my problem. When a new delivery comes in, I will gladly send the bottle up to the Archon. Until then, I can do nothing."

Jeshica's eyes narrowed, her face pinching as if she smelled something rotten. "I suppose I will have to go buy some myself."

"That is not my concern."

"Fine." Jeshica said with a huff before taking the basket and storming out the door.

As the woman's stomping feet faded down the corridor, an idea began to form in Quinn's mind. She recalled a story Brandt had shared regarding one of his many childhood pranks. An opportunity had presented itself, one that required boldness. She decided it was time for action. Although risky, if successful, her gambit might solve two problems at once.

"Sorry about that, Glynnis," Mavis said.

"I understand, Mavis. The Archon is an important person."

"True, but I would like to strangle Jeshica."

"Perhaps she will be gone soon."

"Oh, if that were true, I'd drop to my knees and kiss the ground while thanking Issal."

"In that case," Quinn grinned, "Where does one purchase dye in this city?"

The stairwell was quiet save for the soft footsteps of Quinn's slippered feet. Rather than sneak, she walked as if she belonged, while internally praying she remained unnoticed. She turned the corner at the landing and continued upward until she emerged at the fifth level. A guard on patrol had his back facing her as he walked toward the opposite end of the corridor. She eased forward, walking such that her footsteps matched the beat of the armored man. When she reached the third door on the right, she turned the knob and found it locked.

She lifted her skirt to withdraw her picks and dagger from the sheath strapped to her leg. A glance down the corridor showed the guard's back still facing her, the man now beyond the midpoint of the hallway. She inserted the first needle, shifting it until she sensed resistance...as Delvin had taught her. When the tumbler clicked, she slid another needle into the lock. Her pulse thumped in her ears, her armpits damp with sweat. Resistance, a twist, and a click. Praying that the lock had only two tumblers, she slid the dagger tip into the slot. When the lock turned, she glanced down the corridor and found the guard approaching the far end. She pulled the needles from the lock, opened the door, and eased it shut. A ragged breath blew from her lungs as her eyes closed in relief. She opened them, sheathed her dagger and picks, and turned to survey the room.

The suite was massive, long enough to use as an archery range. Quinn stood in what she assumed was the office portion of the chamber, which contained a wall of shelved books, a pair of padded chairs, and a desk covered with papers. Her mind raced as she considered sifting through the notes for information. *No. Focus, Quinn,* she told herself. Instead, she crossed the room, passing the sitting area before she reached a section of the suite furnished with a copper tub, a mirror, and a vanity. Upon the vanity was a vial filled with dark liquid. She picked it up while removing a similar vial from the pocket of her white smock. When she held them together and compared the color, she found the difference slight, too slight to notice at first glance. After placing the new bottle atop the vanity, Quinn hurried to the door. With her ear against it, she listened.

The sound of footsteps echoed through the wood, fading as the distance increased. She opened the door and peeked out to find the guard's back facing her again. Moving quietly, she pulled the door shut and eased toward the stairs. Thoughts of her plan ran through her head as she considered what remained. Disposing of the black dye would be simple enough. The receipt she had given to Mavis was far more critical. Once the woman placed it among Jeshica's clean laundry, a porter would bring it to her room, and the trap would be set.

Quinn stood in line, waiting for her turn. Norden and Wol, two of the porters, were collecting cleaned laundry and other items for council members. Mavis dealt with each methodically as she sorted through the lists provided. As usual, when Jeshica entered the room, she ignored the line, strode past those who were waiting, and leaned against the counter to address Mavis.

"You'll pay for this," Jeshica growled.

Mavis narrowed her eyes. "What are you going on about, Jeshica?"

"The Archon's hair. The dye. You know what I mean."

"I told you. We will get another shipment next week."

Jeshica slammed her hand on the counter. "You know what I mean! I know you did it!"

Mavis put her hands on her hips and grimaced. "I have no time for this, woman. Explain yourself or get out."

"You changed the dye! The Archon...her hair...it's purple!"

Mavis blinked, her eyes flicking toward Quinn before returning to Jeshica. "I assume she did not intend to have purple hair?"

"Of course she didn't!" Jeshica shrieked. "She is angry. Heads will roll for this mistake!"

Quinn stepped forward. "Didn't you procure the dye, Jeshica? I was in here two days ago when you stated you were off to purchase dye yourself because the storeroom had run out."

"Stay out of this, Glynnis. This is none of your business."

Mavis said, "She has a point, Jeshica. If you bought the dye, then it would be your mistake."

"I made no mistake, and I'll not go down for this!"

"Where is your receipt?"

"What?"

"Did the apothecary provide a receipt when you purchased the dye?"

"Yes, but I don't have it. I threw it away."

A voice emerged from behind Quinn. "Odd that you might say that."

Quinn turned to find a middle-aged woman, a bit shorter than herself. Archon Varius was dressed in white with a gold cloak over her shoulders, her arms crossed over the rune of Issal on her chest – a rune that matched the one on her forehead. The purple in the woman's hair almost caused Quinn to laugh, but she restrained herself. Even if she wasn't the Archon, the hard look in Varius' brown eyes, along with the armed guards standing behind her, gave Quinn cause to remain serious.

The purple-haired Archon held a slip of paper out. "Look what was discovered in your wardrobe. An apothecary receipt for purple dye."

Jeshica stammered, "But...but....that isn't mine."

Varius arched a brow, black in contrast to her purple hair. "Did you not say that you personally visited the apothecary to purchase the dye for me? As I recall, you made it sound as if you had committed a significant sacrifice to ensure I did not have to wait."

"Yes, but I..."

"I have suffered your impertinence for too long, Jeshica. You treat others with disrespect, as if you are their superior." Varius crumpled the receipt in her fist, her knuckles turning white. "I have sent an envoy to the apothecary. If the man confirms that a young woman with blond hair and blue eyes purchased purple dye, you will wish you had never met me." The Archon's mouth curled up in a smile, an expression that did not touch her eyes. "In the meantime, you will enjoy your new accommodations. The cell won't be as spacious or well-lit as you might wish, but you'll have plenty of time to think."

—+ φ +—

Quinn picked up her navy maid dress and smelled it, thankful to have one freshly laundered. Larrimor worked her hard, yet she scolded Quinn the moment she began to smell of sweat. Thankfully, Quinn's training had her muscles toned and her body in excellent condition, so it usually was not until late in a long, grueling day that she reached that point.

She stepped into the dress, pulling it up over her shift and sliding her arms in before tying the sash behind her back. Using a length of navy ribbon, she gathered her hair together and tied it in a tail before securing the button behind her neck. As she reached for her white smock, there was a knock at the door. A glance toward the window revealed a milky fog lit by twilight, the mist not yet touched by the rising sun. *It's early. Who would be here at this hour?*

A glance in the mirror revealed a golden-haired serving woman, properly timid in nature. Pure Glynnis. Satisfied, she opened the door and found a small balding man standing in the corridor.

"Master Sheen," Quinn said with surprise in her voice. "I was just about to head upstairs to wake Magistrate Larrimor."

He shook his head. "No need. You are to pack up your things. I need you out inside the hour. A new porter is expected this morning, and he is to take your room."

Anxiety struck Quinn. "But, Sir. I have done everything that woman has asked of me. Please, give me another chance."

"You misunderstand. You have proven yourself capable and surprisingly patient. Anyone who can satisfy Larrimor should do well in your new position." Sheen held out a cord with two keys dangling from it. "You are relocating to the fifth floor. Go up the south stairwell and use this to open the fourth door on the right."

Quinn accepted the key as she turned the news over in her head. Excitement brewed inside her, brought on by hope that seeds carefully planted had now blossomed.

With her face free of expression, Quinn said, "Sir, if I may ask, what is my new role?"

"You will take over Jeshica's position as handmaid for Archon Varius. I'm sure you are aware of the responsibility that comes with the position, for the Archon is the most important person in the Empire.

Do not fail or you will feel her wrath. Worse yet, you may join Jeshica in the dungeon."

—+ ⏀ +—

The rap of Quinn's knuckles striking the door echoed in the corridor. She looked to the side and smiled at the guard. He gave her a nod in response as if to give her encouragement.

A woman's voice called from within the room. "Come in."

Quinn turned the knob and slipped inside. When she closed the door, she found the Archon sitting at her desk, her hair now as black as ink. The woman stared at Quinn, who quickly lowered her eyes and clasped her hands together in a demure pose.

"You may come closer. I don't bite…unless provoked."

As commanded, Quinn shifted forward to stop two strides from the desk. Varius stood and rounded the desk before circling behind Quinn. When the woman reappeared on her other side, Quinn turned toward her.

"I was told your name is Glynnis."

"Yes, Archon. Glynnis Mor."

"Hurn?"

Quinn nodded. "From Port Hurns."

"Follow me."

Varius turned, walked past the sofa, and sat the cushioned chair across from it. The woman pointed toward the sofa and Quinn sat, glancing toward the game board on the table between them.

"Do you play?" Varius asked.

Quinn hesitated as she considered her response. Deciding that her ability to play the game might give them common ground, she took a chance and nodded.

"Interesting. You don't find many handmaids who play Ratio Bellicus."

"I…have had an interesting life."

"I was told that you worked for Baroness Rimini."

The words sunk in as Quinn realized that Varius had known of Quinn's background before their conversation. "Yes."

"I'm sorry that your mistress had to die." The Archon pressed her lips together. "However, we needed control of the entire east coast if the Empire were to be self-sufficient. In addition, certain tactical advantages were gained by capturing Port Hurns and Cinti Mor."

Quinn remained still, unsure of how to respond. She considered the tactical advantages of having those cities under Empire control. *Of course, they wanted to control the coast. Taking those two cities removed any near port other than Hipoint, a location that is impossible to defend.*

"How old are you?"

As instructed by Delvin, she lied, adding years to the truth. "I know I appear young, but this is my twenty-first summer."

"You are quite fit," Varius noted. "Your arms don't look like the arms of a handmaid."

"Yes. My father was a blacksmith. I spent many hours with him in the smithy." Quinn paused and realized she needed further explanation. "My last employer, the merchant I worked for after Rimini died, he tasked me with a great deal of physical labor as well, which erased any softness I had earned while working for Rimini."

For a long moment, one that felt excruciating, the woman stared at Quinn, measuring her. Quinn fought her inclination to stare back defiantly and allowed herself to look down, look to the side...look anywhere but at the woman's eyes. Until Varius spoke.

"You arrived here three weeks ago?"

Again, Quinn nodded.

"And you served Magistrate Larrimor during that time?"

Hearing the woman's name evoked a grimace on Quinn's face before she even realized it.

Varius laughed. "Yes. I suspected that working for that woman might be distasteful. Larrimor is good at her job, but she is unreasonable at best, a bitter old hag at worst."

While Quinn ached to agree, she knew that Glynnis could not, at least not out loud. "One might say that working for Larrimor is...challenging."

The woman laughed again. "Well said." She then put her forefinger and thumb on her chin while staring at Quinn. "I think we will get along fine. You will find me less demanding than Larrimor, but that does not mean I don't have high expectations. Your tasks will be plentiful and varied in nature. Perform them as expected, in a timely manner, and all will be well."

She pointed toward the far wall, where a door and a vanity stood beside a four-poster bed.

"That door leads to your room, which provides you direct access to my quarters. This will allow you to be at my call when needed and will enable you to perform your duties with as little resistance as possible. Take heed that you must always remain clear of my desk. I will clean and organize whatever is there, while you are responsible for the rest of the chamber. Break this rule, and you will discover what it means to cross me. Understood?"

"Yes, Archon."

"When we are alone, please call me Meryl."

"As you wish," Quinn smiled and added, "Meryl."

30

SECRET WEAPON

A puffy white cloud blocked the sun, darkening the city before it drifted eastward. The sun reappeared, shining upon Quinn as she weaved her way through the busy streets of Sol Polis. She glanced up and saw a familiar shop, the sign on the front with the words *Denali's Apothecary* carved into it. A moment of regret struck when she thought of Jeshica being held in the citadel dungeon, but it quickly passed. The mission required Quinn to get close to Varius, and no position could equal the access to information that came with being the woman's handmaid. *You had no choice, Quinn,* she told herself. *Worse, you could have killed her instead, but that might have created other complications.* The mere thought left a sour taste in Quinn's mouth.

At the next intersection, she turned the corner and dodged to the side, narrowly avoiding a horse pulling a small wagon. The wheels squeaked under the weight of its load as it rolled past, the wagon bed filled with bricks. Quinn chose to stop and watch the wagon, an act that allowed her to see if anyone had followed her. After a full minute, she continued on, relieved when nobody had rounded the corner from whence she came.

Another turn at the next intersection led her down a less-trodden street. When she spotted a narrow alley beside an inn, she slid into it and removed the note she carried.

The archon's seal, an Order symbol encapsulated by flame, was stamped into melted wax. She frowned, considering how to open it without breaking the seal. Her gaze fell on an open window. Inside, the inn's cook turned a whole jackaroo over an open flame. The man wiped sweat from his forehead, turned, and walked out of her view. *Heat melts wax*, Quinn thought.

She continued down the alley and opened the back door to the inn. Within, Quinn walked past an open storeroom door and heard the cook inside, rummaging for something. Acting quickly, she pushed the kitchen door open, lifted her skirt, and drew the dagger strapped to her thigh. After holding the blade over the flames for a few seconds, she eased the knife-edge between the wax and the paper, the heated blade slicing through the wax until the seal popped free.

A furtive glance toward the door revealed that she remained alone. She opened the letter and read the contents.

Master Jarlish,

I have reports that the flash cannons have proven a success. One of the armed ships was able to repel that god-forsaken pirate, Red Viper. While she was able to escape, with such a weapon, we may yet see the end of that scourge. Yet, most of our ships remain unprotected.

I am officially placing an order for one hundred more cannons and two thousand projectiles. Increase production as quickly as possible. In addition, continue developing other weapons. We must have something that tips the scales in our favor, for our enemies have Chaos on their side. Focus on weapons of a smaller scale, something a soldier might carry alone. The threat of war looms and our days of peace might be limited.

The Avatar of Issal,
-Archon Varius

Quinn folded the paper with a grimace. *The weapon that fired at Razor must have been a flash cannon. A hundred more could sink an entire fleet of ships.*

She held the knife in the fire again and then pressed the heated blade against the seal. Although the stamp in the wax was now less visible, the letter was once again sealed. The kitchen door opened and she turned toward it.

Startled eyes from the overweight cook stared at her. He held a pot in his arms, pressed against his ample stomach.

"Who are you and why are you in my kitchen?"

"Oh. Sorry. I took the wrong door." She slid past the man before turning back to him. "The food smells delicious. I'll be looking forward to dinner."

The man stared at her with an open mouth while the door swung shut behind her. She then scurried out the back and hurried along her way to deliver the message to the rider she was to meet at the east gate.

When Quinn returned to the citadel, she chose to head toward the rear entrance rather than travel through the main hall. The route took her through a quiet garden at the west side of the building. The path ran past flowering shrubs, dotted in yellow and purple. Beyond the shrubs were trees, tall compared to the rest, but not even two decades old. Quinn knew that Sol Polis had been devastated when The Horde attacked. The scorch marks remaining on one of the citadel towers were a constant reminder. The tower remained sealed, unsafe for use. Beneath one tree, she found a lonely bench. There, she stopped and thought about the note she had read.

From where she sat, a gap in the trees provided a clear view of the square before the castle and the wall that bound the citadel proper. She spotted a stark white section of wall, a few shades lighter than the rest. Memories of the attack on Cinti Mor returned as Quinn realized what had happened and what it meant.

When the Empire took Sol Polis, they had used some sort of explosive, just as they had when capturing Cinti Mor. That explosive is what created the green flame when the flash cannon launched its projectile at the Razor. If the Empire intends to create more weapons, I must find a way to stop them. The idea of a war with Chaos on one side and explosives on the other frightened Quinn. Her imagination conjured images of destroyed buildings and piles of dead, burned bodies.

As she considered the situation, a streak of bright orange and blue sailed past her. Her eyes followed it as a starfetch landed on a branch and began to tweet. The lilting song carried with it a sense of peace and happiness – an aria that lifted Quinn's mood. After a few minutes, the bird flew off and disappeared beyond the citadel walls. Quinn took a breath to gather herself, stood, and resumed her journey. The path emerged into an open area patrolled by an armored man dressed in a white and blue tabard. She fell into character, looking down as she walked past the man.

A firm grip wrapped about her wrist, stopping her abruptly. She turned, ready to scold the guard for stopping her, but the words slipped from her tongue and her mouth dropped open.

"Hi, Doll." the man said.

"Wyck?"

"What are you doing here?"

She looked around and found them alone before responding in a hushed tone. "I'm on a mission. Why are you here?"

He released her wrist. "Same as you, I guess."

Quinn moved closer to him, her whisper heated with anger. "You're not an espion. You should not be here."

"Well, I am."

"Does Delvin know?"

Wyck's brow furrowed. "I suppose not."

"Explain why you are here, then."

"Well, Firellus sent me off to Cinti Mor when an opening came up to work for Prelate Dorlan. It was nothing significant, just a typical guard position at the citadel. For a few weeks, I found it more boring than you can imagine. The only thing I discovered is that listening to judges and court sessions is a form of cruel torture.

"Then a day came where I was guarding the side door in Prelate Dorlan's courtroom, and I spotted a flash of metal. I burst into a run, dove, and a dagger struck my shield just a stride in front of Dorlan. Lucky, too, because the blade was poisoned. The woman who threw it was arrested and found herself in a dungeon cell. The act won me praise, and the next thing I knew, my captain told me I was getting promoted to Sol Polis. So, here I am."

Quinn listened to the tale and wondered how Wyck could possibly be useful in this situation. The man might be an outstanding warrior, but he had the subtlety of a bear in a sweetshop. When Quinn looked past him, she noticed a curtain move in a fifth story window. She gasped when she realized it was Varius…watching.

"Kiss me," Quinn said with urgency.

Wyck grinned. "So, you *did* miss me."

"Kiss me. Now!"

The man put his hand behind her head and pressed his lips against hers. She allowed it for a moment and then pushed away, slapping him.

His face held the look of shock as his hand went to his cheek. "Ouch! What was that for?"

"Just walk away. We're being watched," Quinn said quietly between clenched teeth. She then screeched, "Stay away from me!"

His face turned red and he snarled, "You crazy wench!"

Wyck reached for her but Quinn was faster, reacting on instinct. Her hand flashed out and grabbed his thick fingers, bending them back as she leapt to his side. With a knee up against his rear, she twisted his arm behind his back and lifted the elbow with as much pressure as she could apply. Even then, it was a struggle to hold it. Quinn grunted and strained while he did the same. However, she was in a position of advantage – one that countered his superior strength.

"Argh." He grunted. "Let go of me."

"I'll let go, and you just walk away," she said aloud before lowering her voice. "The Archon is watching," she hissed.

Quinn released him and stepped backward. Wyck turned toward her while holding his arm, his face red as he breathed heavily through his nose. "I'll remember this."

"Good. Now, move along."

Without another word, the big man stomped down the path and faded from view. Quinn then turned the opposite direction and made her way back to the castle, hopeful that Varius would see the interaction between Quinn and Wyck as nothing more than a man's unwanted pursuit of a woman. But she knew that Varius was intelligent. Quinn hadn't meant the situation to go as far as it had. Trained to defend herself, Quinn's instincts had taken over and revealed far more than she might wish.

31

DISCOVERY

"Good, Cassie. Concentrate. Hold it."

Jestin's voice carried through the mist of Cassie's mind. Her eyes remained closed as she maintained her focus. She felt him place his hand to her forehead. His palm was warm compared to the cool peace she found inside herself. Like a ghost slipping into a room, she sensed Jestin extend his awareness, probing her mind.

Order was her most prevalent inherent trait, and she allowed him to divine it. When his presence dove deeper, she held the false image she had created – a representation of a Dominus rune, masking the true symbol that resided there. Satisfied, he dove deeper and read the Cognitio rune, Artifex Altus rune, and the Medicus rune that lay deep within herself, all inherent traits, each weaker than the one prior.

When Jestin lifted his hand from her forehead, Cassie opened her eyes. The man gave her a nod. "Very good, indeed. I couldn't sense anything false, nor could I see the Chaos rune in you."

Cassie turned toward her brother, who sat cross-legged on the floor a few strides away. "It actually worked, Brandt. Somehow, your idea worked."

"Thank, Issal." Brandt's jaw set as he turned toward Jestin. "Try me. If I can't make it work, Delvin won't send me out, regardless of how I progress with the other skills."

Brandt shut his eyes and slipped into meditation while Jestin shifted to squat beside him. The master ecclesiast placed his hand on Brandt's head. Cassie bit her lip as she watched. She knew how badly Brandt wanted this. Despite her misgivings, she understood his desire to make a difference…as well as his thirst for excitement. Besides, only one of them would go into the field, and she knew it should be him.

When Jestin opened his eyes, he shook his head with the look of awe on his face. "It worked. I see Famulus as your primary trait and no hint of the Chaos rune you are hiding. How did you think of this anyway?"

When Brandt opened his eyes, a grin spread across his face. "It was something Delvin said before he and Quinn left. He was explaining personas to me, and I began to understand the depth he wanted us to achieve when we adopt them. Knowing that others divining my inherent ability to channel Chaos was a risk, I wondered if we could somehow use Order to mask Chaos with a different vocation rune – as if it were a persona of another trait."

"When Brandt came to me with the idea," Cassie said, "he and I began testing it right away, one divining the other while attempting the mask. It took a few days to master before the mask appeared like a proper symbol, but once we had the method perfected, slipping the mask rune over the true one became as easy as slipping on a glove."

Jestin stood and began to pace. Cassie watched him from their dark corner of the Atrium. The sun was low; the upper portion of the building still bright while shadows filled the lower reaches. It was quiet since the others had left to clean up before dinner.

"The pair of you continue to press the boundaries of what we know about Order. Considering the strength of magic your parents possess, you two may be just scratching the surface of your full potential."

Cassie heard Brandt in her head. *If we are so strong with Order, why can't I heal yet?*

We've been over this. It will come in time. Even Jestin believes so.

The man continued his speech. "Despite the academy class sessions that now occupy my days, I would like to continue to work with you. Perhaps I can help you discover other things Order can achieve."

He stopped pacing and faced them. "In the meantime, continue with your meditation when your other duties allow it. I will make time to visit a few times each week, and we shall see what else you might achieve." The man gave them a final nod. "Enjoy your dinner."

"Thank you, Master Wykatt," Cassie said.

Bootlicker, Brandt said.

Troublemaker, she replied.

"Come on." Brandt stood and stretched. "Let's get some food."

As Brandt led her toward the dining hall, Cassie considered the man's words.

A lack of purpose had been hanging over her since she had yet to find her place within ICON. It had become clear to her that Brandt was training to be an espion like Nalah...like Quinn. While Cassie had helped Everson with a number of augmentations, she found the process of infusion dull and repetitive. Despite the worthiness of the cause, she desired something more – desired to make a greater impact. Walking beside her brother, she glanced toward him and found herself envious. The life of an espion might be fraught with danger, but danger meant excitement – something that they both had craved since they were young.

Jestin had a point. If she could develop new abilities using Order, perhaps she might find herself a new purpose.

The thuds of Elastic-augmented weapons colliding filled the Atrium, along with the grunts from those who wielded the weapons. Cassie opened her eyes, yet maintained her connection with Order, something she had been practicing. The calmness, the peace of it, surrounded her as she watched Brandt and Bilchard training.

Bilchard stood practically a foot taller than Brandt and seemed almost as strong as Wyck. His wooden longsword repeatedly connected with Brandt's staff, with both fighters exchanging vicious attacks. While Bilchard possessed an obvious edge in strength, Brandt's advantage was his speed.

The quarterstaff whirled in his hands, expertly blocking one strike after another. Occasionally, he would alter the course of the staff and connect with Bilchard's leg, his shoulder, his hip – each drawing a grunt from the overgrown teen. Rather than attempt to block what he could not reach, Bilchard kept his shield held before his torso to ensure that Brandt never struck his most vulnerable areas.

When Brandt smacked his opponent's thigh a third time, it drew a roar of anger from Bilchard, who charged with his shield in the lead. Brandt twisted and dove aside, lightning quick. A red symbol materialized before Cassie's eyes, holding in the air near her brother. The image startled Cassie, and she lost her connection with Order, the vision of the rune fading with it.

The two opponents faced each other with intense glares. Bilchard shifted forward but Brandt retreated a step, waiting, measuring.

Cassie closed her eyes and took a long, calm breath as she sank back into meditation. The cool blue aura of Order enveloped her inner self, and she embraced the connection. Still holding it securely, she opened her eyes to see Brandt lunge forward with a flurry of strikes, fast and furious, exhibiting his exceptional quickness. The symbol materialized as it did before. Cassie gasped in awe. She suddenly knew what the rune meant, yet she was sure to maintain her connection. With concentration, she stared at the glowing emblem and memorized the lines, curving and crossing to create a rune she had never before seen.

A low sweep of Brandt's staff connected with Bilchard's ankle, and the larger boy fell to the ground, clutching at his leg.

"Hold," Bilchard said between clenched teeth. "I think you broke it."

"Huh. It's about time." Brandt pulled his helmet off and wiped the sweat from his brow. "I was growing tired of hitting you."

Realizing she was needed, Cassie stood and approached the two fighters.

Brandt turned toward her. "It's a good thing you decided to stick around while we dueled."

Cassie knelt beside Bilchard. "Yes," she mumbled as the memory of the odd rune remained in her head. "Hold still, Bilchard."

Still embracing her own source of Order, she shut her eyes and extended her inner self toward Bilchard. A storm of red symbols swirled about his lower leg. She seized his source of Order and used it to smother the crimson invaders. They began to unravel and dissipate, shedding tiny red threads before fading away. Bilchard's body shook beneath her palm, and he gasped for air. She opened her eyes and stood.

"I know you are hungry from the healing. Although I don't have any food, lunch should be ready by now," she said.

Bilchard gave her a nod as he stood. "Thank you, Cassie." He turned toward Brandt. "If we were allowed to fight with a Power augmentation, I know I could win."

"You are already crazy strong. Adding a Power augmentation..." Brandt snorted. "Let's just call that a scary thought. Thankfully, we don't duel under those conditions because one of us might kill the other."

A sigh slipped from Bilchard. "True. Yet, training to fight while charged with a Power rune is the point of being a wildcat. How can I truly test my enhanced fighting skill before I face a real battle?"

Brandt gave Bilchard a friendly thump in the shoulder. "I'm sure you'll get a chance to test it in the field soon. Your strikes already feel like they are coming from an Ox in heat. I shudder to think of how hard you'll hit when charged with an augmentation."

"Thanks," Bilchard said. "You know, waiting for my first mission was already difficult before the others left. But now..."

"I know. Trust me. I've been pushing Delvin to let me go out ever since he came back."

A loud rumble caused Bilchard to put his hand on his stomach. "Huh. Hear that? I feel like I could eat a herd of cattle. I'll see you two later. I'm off for some food."

He turned and walked away. Cassie waited until he was beyond earshot and then she turned to her brother. "I saw something while you were fighting."

His brow furrowed. "What do you mean?"

"I saw...a rune. It came from you, first when you dodged, the second time when you attacked. I...think it has something to do with your nature."

"What are you talking about?"

Cassie sighed. "I was holding a tight connection with Order while I was watching you two fight."

"You can do that? With your eyes open?"

"I've been practicing." She shrugged. "Anyway, while doing so, I was thinking of how much faster you are than Bilchard. You then dodged him, and the rune first materialized."

"Can you draw this rune?"

"Sure."

Cassie reached into the satchel at her hip and withdrew a chunk of glowstone. Kneeling, she sketched the rune on the stone tile floor. When finished, she looked at Brandt.

"I haven't seen that one before," he said.

"That's what I thought."

"What does it mean?"

"I...I can't explain how I know this, but I think it has to do with speed or quickness"

He stared at her for a long moment before a grin crossed his face. "We need to test it."

The sun was kissing the tall peaks west of the Ward. Cassie pulled her coat tight about herself to keep the cool breeze from sneaking inside. Now full autumn, and the nights were as cold as the most bitter winter weather in Kantar. While Cassie was eager to experience snow for the first time, she feared how cold it might become in the valley when winter had it firmly within its grasp.

She walked beside Brandt, down the road that ran along the inner perimeter of the training yard wall. Over the hours since she had revealed the strange rune to her brother, he had been acting like a young boy on Libra Te, unable to wait for the food, music, and games that marked the event. His desire to test the new augmentation almost caused him to ignore her caution. Thankfully, she was able to talk him out of trying it on himself. She shuddered at the thought of Brandt exploding or being fried to death by uncontained Chaos should the rune not prove capable of harnessing it.

Brandt angled away from the road and led her toward a waist-high boulder surrounded by long, yellowed grass.

"We'll use this for our test." He sounded confident.

"What if it doesn't work?"

"That is why you and I will keep a distance from it."

"Are you sure we need to perform both augmentations?"

He sighed. "You heard Everson. He said that we needed to apply a Speed augmentation to something animated. Machines require the conversion of energy to propel them. A Power rune works in that instance. A Speed augmentation would not."

"We don't even know that this *is* a Speed rune."

He stared at her for a moment with concern in his eyes. "What has gotten into you? Why are you so pessimistic about this?"

Her mouth twisted in a grimace. "It...just seems too good to be true."

"What?"

"The idea that I could discover a new rune this way. It can't be that simple."

"Listen. Just because nobody else can do it, and that a new rune hasn't been discovered in Issal-knows-how-many years, doesn't mean it can't happen." He gripped her shoulder. "I believe in you, Cass. You say you saw it, twice. I believe it."

"All right."

"Good." He smiled and handed her a chunk of glowstone. "I'll draw the Animate rune. You draw the other one."

They each took position and began to trace a rune atop the boulder. When Brandt finished, he backed away. Cassie did the same, both of them backing up until they were a dozen strides from the rock.

"I'll charge the Animate rune. Once it comes to life, you do yours."

He closed his eyes for a long moment. When they opened, red sparks sizzled in his irises. The rune on the rock glowed, pulsed, and faded. The boulder trembled, as if the earth were shaking. In a sudden blast, shards of rock sprayed from the boulder. Legs formed, lifting the boulder from the ground, pushing a mound of dirt aside, and revealing that the rock was bigger than Cassie had believed since a fair portion of it had been buried from view. With a grinding sound emitted from each movement, the boulder began to walk toward Brandt.

"My pet has come to life." Brandt smiled. "Your turn."

Cassie clenched her eyes shut, embraced her anxiety, and reached for Chaos. The surrounding energy poured into her until she was ready to burst. She opened her eyes and focused on the other rune traced atop the boulder. The stored energy poured into the rune, setting it ablaze with a crimson hue. A wave of exhaustion washed over her, leaving her empty and feeling lethargic. Even so, she and Brandt backed away from the thing they had created.

The movements of the headless rock-monster grew faster and faster as it blazed toward them. Brandt dove to one side, Cassie to the other as the thing sped past in a flash. A swirl of dust arose when it blazed across the gravel road before colliding with the wall. The rumble of the impact was immense. Rock sprayed through the air with bits pelting Cassie as she covered her head with her arms. When the noise settled, she lowered her arms and looked at Brandt, who stared back at her with wide eyes.

His voice rang in her head. *I'm afraid to look.*

Cassie swallowed hard and turned toward the wall.

Swirling debris filled the air, lit by the last rays of the sinking sun. As the dust settled, the extent of the damage they caused became clear.

A section of the wall, eight strides across, had crumbled to the ground. Broken square blocks lay piled atop pieces of the living boulder. Those pieces twitched violently, still charged with the speed rune, yet trapped by the weight of the wall.

"What have we done?" Cassie said aloud at the extent of the damage.

Brandt smiled and put his arm around her. "We found a new rune! You can do it, Cass. You discovered how to identify new Chaos runes!"

32

THREAT OF WAR

W ith a sealed message held in one hand, Quinn opened the door and stepped onto the terrace. A balding man in a white-trimmed blue coat leaned against the railing. He was tall and had an athletic build that spoke of his excellent physical condition, despite his advancing years. Quinn glanced toward the desk at the center of the loft and spotted a map, black notations and arrows marking an area near Yarth. On the wall behind the desk, weapons dangled from hooks – a massive great sword, a halberd, a shield with the rune of Issal on it, and a pair of short swords that crossed one another. The noise of wooden weapons clacking together, along with the grunts of those involved in the duel, came from below. A cry of pain arose, followed by cheers.

Quinn walked toward the man, but rather than turning toward her, he continued to watch the action in the sparring yard below.

"He is a beast...a one-man army." The man said aloud.

When she reached the rail, Quinn saw Wyck in the training yard below, facing two fellow male soldiers. A female guard lay in the dirt behind Wyck, holding her leg as a healer ran in to help her.

One of the men facing Wyck circled to the wildcat's side, trying to get behind him. The other man attacked, drawing Wyck's attention. Wyck blocked the first man's strike with his shield and thrust with a low kick that struck the man's knee, sending him to the ground. The guard behind him attacked, but Wyck's backswing forced the man backward and gave Wyck time to recover. The man snarled and tried again, leading with a lunge that Wyck sidestepped. Wyck then swung a vicious swing, striking the man's shield so hard that the sword shattered, splinters raining down as the man staggered backward. The loss of his weapon didn't appear to affect Wyck's bravado. Instead, he charged the man, his shield smashing into him with an upward thrust. The impact was thunderous and launched the man into the air. He landed in a heap eight feet away and didn't move. As the healer ran in, the man beside Quinn turned to her.

"Did you see that? He destroyed the other three soldiers like they were children using pretend weapons."

"Yes. Quite impressive." Quinn was unsure of what else to say.

The man looked down at the sealed message in Quinn's hand. "I assume that is for me."

"That depends on who you are, sir."

He smiled, his thin mustache curling up with his lips. "I am Captain Sculdin. And you are…"

"Glynnis Mor, sir. I am Archon Varius' handmaid."

"What happened to the other girl? The pretty one with the lips and curves?"

"She…she upset the Archon."

Sculdin snorted. "I am not surprised. That girl seemed to think much of herself. With looks like that, I can understand why. She likely could get away with it if she were working for a man, but not even the Archon herself acts as if others are that far beneath her."

Quinn held the missive toward him. "I am to give you this. You are to send a trustworthy man with it, first thing tomorrow."

A frown crossed Sculdin's face as he broke the seal and opened the note. As Quinn waited for him to finish, she found herself wishing she knew the information it contained. She looked down toward the sparring yard and saw the healer helping the last man to his feet. Despite having been healed, he staggered when he stood, and the woman helped him toward the exit. Wyck ignored it. He stood amid a cluster of guards, laughing at something Quinn was unable to hear. When she turned back to the captain, he folded the piece of paper and gave her a nod.

"Tell the Archon that I will have the messenger on the first ship tomorrow morning."

With a nod, Quinn spun about and headed toward the door. She crossed a long corridor lit by angled beams of sunlight coming through narrow windows overhead. With concerns of an impending war between the kingdoms and the Empire preoccupied her mind, the return journey to her room passed far more quickly than the outbound trip. Those thoughts slid away as she exited the stairwell near the door to her room.

Quinn removed the cord from beneath her dress and slid it over her head. Her fingers found a key, a glance revealing it as the wrong one. She released it, grabbed the other key tied to the cord, and slid it into the lock. With a twist, she opened it and entered her room.

A thin sliver of sunlight streamed through the curtain on the far wall. Quinn circled her bed and opened the curtain, the angle of the sun forcing her to squint.

Still well above the horizon, the bright orb hovered over the Sea of Fates, painting the blue waters with aqua tones. The harbor stood a mile away, but at five stories above the castle grounds, Quinn had a fair view of the busy docks, teeming with activity. With red tiled rooftops between the citadel and the docks, the view was among the things she enjoyed most about her stay in Sol Polis. Releasing a sigh, she turned from the window and walked to the door that connected to the Archon's chamber.

Knocking soundly, Quinn paused and listened. When Varius didn't respond, she used the other key on her cord and unlocked the door. She then slid the cord over her head and peeked inside.

Sunlight streamed through open curtains and provided sufficient light for Quinn to confirm that the Archon's suite was empty. Since Varius spent much of her time there, it was difficult for Quinn to maintain the room and remain out of the woman's hair. *I had best get some cleaning done.*

She stepped back into her room, grabbed her basket of cleaning supplies and the bucket of water she had prepared earlier in the day, and entered the Archon's quarters. After walking to the bathing area,

Quinn set the bucket and supplies down before standing and stretching her back. Cleaning the copper tub was among the duties Quinn most detested – yet it was better than half the things Larrimor had forced on her. The Archon had Quinn doing things that actually seemed to hold value, such as taking notes during a meeting or carrying missives to council members and local officers.

Quinn's gaze landed on the Archon's desk, covered in papers. A longing stirred inside as she stared at the paperwork from a distance. Varius had specifically forbidden her from going near the desk, yet secrets might reside there, waiting for Quinn's discovery.

With a deep breath to firm her resolve, Quinn walked toward the office. When she neared the desk, muffled voices came through the door at the end of the room – the door that led to General Kardan's office. Instead of searching the desk, Quinn walked to that door and put her ear against it.

"…isn't the point, Leo." Varius said. "I'll not go into a war blindly and without regard."

Quinn heard Kardan reply. "We've been over this before, Meryl. Half of the Council is with me and they agree."

"And, yet, half of them are not. Nor am I."

"If we attack now, we could capture them by surprise," he insisted. "Hipoint and Wayport are ready for the taking, which would extend our reach. From there, we could push up toward Fallbrandt before winter hits."

Varius sighed. "I know how much you would like to take control of the schools, but what about the garrison at Hipoint? Reports are that King Brock has reinstituted it." The woman's tone made it seem like saying *King Brock* was rancid to her tongue. "We cannot claim Hipoint without addressing the garrison. How many soldiers are stationed there?"

"Last report tells me three hundred, perhaps three-fifty."

"What about arcanists?"

"Yes," Kardan admitted, "They likely have those as well."

"With their access to Chaos, you know well the destruction they can render. Imagine a war with flash powder on one side and Chaos on the other. How many would die without even getting near an enemy?"

"Why have we taken Kalimar if we had no intention of further expanding our borders?" he demanded.

"We took Kalimar because Sol Polis is rightly ours, as it was centuries ago. This is the seat of the Empire and the holy center of the Ministry, as it was always meant to be."

A long moment of silence left Quinn wondering if she should rush back to cleaning the tub. The thought was squashed when the Archon resumed speaking.

"The Empire controls the eastern seaboard, Leo. We have a home and laws that protect the people from Chaos, just as we did twenty years ago. Yes, our lands are not what they once were, but neither is our army." Varius paused briefly. "The call has gone out, and we are already gathering new followers who journey from the west to join us, to live a life free of Chaos. Given time, our forces will grow and our enemy will grow weaker in the process. Gambo is out feeding that frenzy while he gathers more soldiers to support us.

"Perhaps Jarlish will discover another means to utilize flash powder, something that will give us an edge and limit the casualties should it come to war. Until then, we must wait. More importantly, I need you to back my position. Arguing amongst the Council members is one thing – for that will happen on most subjects – but you and I must lead together with a unified message and a clear agenda.

"Give my plan more time, Leo. The order has been issued, and my son will do what is required. If Kantaria crumbles from within, we can swoop in and capture it with little resistance. The Empire can then advance and occupy the south. With winter coming, the weather will slow the northern kingdoms and offer us time to solidify our position. By spring, it will be too late. Kantaria will be ours and then we can focus on Fallbrandt."

After a long pause, Kardan finally replied. "Fair enough, Meryl. I'll back your stance and will push the issue no further. However, should your plan fail, we must rethink our position. A war with Chaos and flash powder might be frightening, but I'll not give up what we have earned nor will I return to that god-forsaken prison. Thirteen years there was more than enough for me, and I suspect you feel the same way."

"Thank you, Leo," she said with gratitude in her voice. "You are correct about one thing: Returning to that prison will never happen. I will end my own life before accepting such a fate. Still, I pray this situation does not come down to a direct clash of our armies – of our weapons against their magic. If it does, the blood of thousands will be on our hands. I don't know if that is something I can willingly accept."

Soft footsteps tapped across the tile and carried through the door. Quinn gasped, spun, and sprinted away. She launched herself over the sofa, landed, and slid on her knees across the marble floor to slam against the side of the copper tub. When she heard the door open behind her, Quinn turned and lifted the sponge from the bucket as she gave Varius a nod. Quinn then wiped her forearm across her brow, turned back to the tub, and began scrubbing to the beat of the heavy thumping in her chest.

33

ASSASSIN

The pale aura of glowlamps lit the citadel receiving hall, the light too weak to reach the recesses of the vaulted ceiling. A pair of guards with white and blue tabards stood beside the doors to the council chamber. Occasionally, one of the guards would fidget, the rings of their mail jingling as they stretched out a kink from standing so long. Inevitably, Quinn would turn toward them and then stare at the doors, wondering what might cause the meeting to run so late. She glanced down at the basket beside her on the bench. The food was assuredly cold by now as it was hours past dinner. Still, she waited. The Archon had to eat at some point.

A thud startled her when the doors burst open. Eight men poured out into the hall, each wearing a blue-trimmed white cloak. Four of the men appeared weary, but satisfied. The other four grimaced as they walked past her. Moments later, the door opened with Kardan holding it for Varius as she exited the chamber. Quinn scooped up the basket and stood, ready to greet her master.

When Varius saw Quinn holding the basket, she stopped and turned toward Kardan.

"It appears I won't miss dinner after all. Would you like to join me, Leo?"

Kardan shook his head. "No. I need to get these new orders to

Sergeant Mollis. He's stationed at the western gate, so I'll take two soldiers and head there now to tell him myself."

Varius nodded. "Very well. I will see you in the morning."

Without another word, Kardan strode across the hall, toward the doors that led outside. Varius turned toward Quinn, her eyes landing on the basket.

"I don't suppose there's a hot meal in there."

Quinn shook her head. "Sorry, Archon. I waited until the kitchen staff had cleaned everything else and then assembled the basket. There is a jackaroo leg, two hard rolls, and steamed carrots. None are warm, but all can be eaten while cold."

Varius pulled a note from her cloak. "Give me the basket. I'll go to my room and eat. I need you to bring this message to Master Sheen. He must receive it tonight so he can prepare first thing tomorrow morning."

Holding out the basket, Quinn handed it to the woman in exchange for the sealed message. "I'll run down and see him right away."

"Good. When you are finished, you may go to bed. I will see you in the morning."

With a nod, Quinn trailed Varius to the stairwell. The Archon began her ascent while Quinn descended to the lower level. Glowlamps mounted on the wall lit the basement corridor, guiding the way to the servants' chambers. At the first door, Quinn stopped and knocked. A moment later, a man called from within.

"Yes?"

"It's Glynnis Mor, Master Sheen. I have a message from Archon Varius."

The door opened to reveal the short man dressed in a blue robe. His eyes squinted and blinked at the pale light in the hallway.

"I'm sorry to wake you, sir. Archon Varius said that you needed to read this now so you could properly prepare first thing tomorrow."

He stared at the note with a furrowed brow. "What's it say?"

"I don't know, sir. The message is sealed." Quinn held it out to him.

The man grimaced and snatched the note from Quinn before closing the door. She snorted as she stared at the door. *I wonder if that man has ever been happy.* Turning about, she followed the corridor to the stairwell and began her ascent. Her mind began to drift as she recalled the conversation she had overheard between Varius and Kardan a week earlier. Varius was against any further invasion of kingdom lands, and she had convinced Kardan to back her. The long council meeting may have centered on that topic. Half the council had emerged upset, while Varius and Kardan appeared at ease. Kardan delivered orders to Mollis himself, so they must be important. *I wish I knew what those orders involved.*

When Quinn emerged from the stairwell, she walked down the empty hallway to her door before removing her key and opening it. She removed the cloth from the glowlamp beside the door and shook the lamp, bringing the blue glow back to life and lighting the room. Her bed called to her, begging her to lie down and rest. After a long day of errands, cleaning, and waiting hours past dinner for the meeting to end, Quinn felt compelled to accept her bed's request. She sat at the edge of it and kicked off her slippers. After removing her smock and untying her sash, she unbuttoned the neck, stood, and dropped the dress to the floor. Now in her cream-colored shift, she bent to pick up the dress before draping it over a chair.

A crack and a thud came from the room beside hers. Quinn frowned at the door. She moved closer and put her ear to the door. The thump of heavy footsteps vibrated the wood – too heavy to come from Varius. Alarmed, Quinn grabbed her keys and the bronze disk beside them before unlocking the door to the Archon's quarters. Her heart was racing as she opened the door, and it then skipped a beat at the sight beyond.

Wyck stood over Varius, who lay upon the floor just beyond her bed. Blood ran down the side of her head and a broken bedpost lay beside her. The woman's eyes were closed, her body still.

Quinn cried, "Wyck. You mustn't!"

The big man looked at her and shook his head. "I can end it here, Quinn. I kill the evil wench. If I chop the head off the snake, I'll end this war."

She ran into the room. "No. It doesn't work like that. Besides, she is *against* going to war. She might be the only thing stopping the council from attacking the west."

He stared at her for a long moment before drawing his sword, the ring of the blade echoing in the quiet chamber. "I can't pass on the opportunity. I eliminate her, and I strike a blow against them."

Quinn scrambled between Varius and Wyck and held her palm toward him. "I can't allow you to kill her."

"How are you going to stop me?"

Quinn drew the dagger strapped to her thigh and held it ready. Wyck snarled and swung his blade in an arc intended to slice Quinn in half. She used her knife to block the blade, but the force of his strike was tremendous, and the dagger flew from one hand while the makeup case fell from the other. He leveled another swing toward her and she leaped onto the bed, rolled across and off it, and grabbed the glowlamp on the nightstand. He turned toward her, and she flung the glowlamp at him. He raised his arm and it struck his bracer, breaking and showering him in glass and glowing blue dust. Other than a glowlamp at the far end of the suite and the light coming through the open door to Quinn's room, the only light came from the glowing powder on Wyck and on the floor around him.

Jumping atop the bed, Quinn pushed off the footboard and leaped high, twisting around Wyck's wild swing. As she flew over his head, she wrapped her arm under his chin and pulled him with her. He stumbled backward, tripped over the copper tub, and fell into it as Quinn landed in a crouch. The man's sword clanked to the tiles and slid across the floor while a wave of water splashed from the tub. Without hesitating, Quinn tore Wyck's helmet off and hit him with it. A loud clang rang in the room and vibrated her hands with the impact. The man sat up and held his arm to protect his head as she swung the helmet again, this time striking his bracer. She stepped forward to take another swing, but her bare foot slipped on the wet marble floor and she fell, the helmet tumbling from her hand and rolling away.

Wyck climbed from the tub, water pouring from him, blood running down his face from a gash above his brow. Quinn scrambled to her feet and moved toward the sitting area rug for better footing. The man was bigger and stronger than Quinn, and he had the protection of his mail chain armor. Speed was her advantage, but if she ran, Varius was dead.

When Wyck drew close, she decided to attack. With a leap, she pushed off the back of the sofa and kicked toward his head. Wyck was ready and was faster than anticipated. He grabbed her leg, spun, and launched her across the room. Quinn hurled past the tub and landed hard on the marble floor before colliding with the bed. Her head struck something hard, the thud rattling her teeth as everything went black.

Pain. Quinn tried to breathe and knives of pain pierced her ribs and ran down her shoulder. The throbbing in her head was in time with her pulse. She opened her eyes, lifted her head, and blinked at the blue glowstone powder on the floor, streaked with blood. Through bleary eyes, she saw Wyck walking toward Varius, his bloody face grim. On the floor beside her, Quinn spotted a bronze disk – the false makeup case. Hope sparked inside her, weak but present.

She moved, gritting her teeth at the pain as she wiped a finger across the glowstone powder. On the back of her other hand, she traced a Chaos rune. Wyck stopped and bent to pick up his sword, the metal tip scraping across the tile with a streak of sparks. Quinn grabbed the makeup case, squeezed the release on the bottom, and pressed the trigger. The short metal rod popped out and hope's trickle became a stream. With ragged breath accompanied by searing pain in her ribs and blackness encircling her vision, she pressed the rod against the rune drawn on her hand. A burning sensation made her cry out and drop the case as the rune began to glow. It pulsed and faded.

Raw energy arose inside her, and white spots invaded the black tunnel that had been compressing her vision. Quinn slowly began to rise. The pain slipped away, replaced by the familiar vigor of a Power augmentation, but much less powerful than what she had experienced in the past. She turned toward Wyck. The man's back was facing her as he lifted his blade over his head. Quinn lunged and kicked him in the back. The man launched forward and smashed against the wall with a grunt. He turned toward her, staggering, angry, and bloody. Bending, Quinn picked up the broken bedpost and prepared to face him.

Wyck advanced past the prone form of Varius, who was beginning to stir. He swung his sword and Quinn dodged it. She jabbed with the bedpost and struck his midriff. The man bent over with an *oof*, stumbling backward. Snarling, he came toward her again, swinging his sword left and right like a scythe, forcing Quinn backward. She then leaped on the bed, ran across it, and off the far side. Wyck turned toward her as Quinn stood beyond Varius with the bedpost extended toward him. When he advanced, Quinn lifted the post like a spear, and she launched it at him, forcing him to duck beneath it. Before he could recover, Quinn burst toward him, leaped, and drove both her bare feet into his chest before falling to the floor. The big man launched backward, flew six feet before he struck the corner of the bed, and stopped with a sudden lurch. His eyes bulged, his mouth hanging open as he coughed blood. The splintered end of the broken bedpost stuck through his chest, pushing his mail and tabard up like a tent. Crimson drops stained the white cloth. Blood began to drip from his ribcage, down the footboard, and onto the floor. A gurgle came from Wyck as his hand fumbled for the post sticking through him, his other arm dangling limply to the side. More blood oozed from his mouth. His hand fell away, his head dropped to the side, and he stilled.

Quinn rose to her feet, turned toward Varius, and found the woman awake, blinking as she attempted to sit up.

"Glynnis? You stopped him?"

Quinn ignored the question, "You're hurt, Meryl. Where can I find the nearest healer?"

34

SENSE OF DREAD

F rom the comfort of his own chamber, Broland laughed heartily at Kony's animated retelling of the previous night's events.

"The look Stigg gave you when you tossed that last throw…" Kony shook his head as he moved a game piece on the Ratio Bellicus board. "Needing three winning tosses in a row, you nailed all three and the crowd went wild. Stigg, however, looked like he wanted to stick a knife in you. A gold piece is a lot to lose for someone like him."

"That's why I snuck him two silvers and bought him a drink afterward," Broland sat back in his chair. "I don't need anyone hating me, especially if they figure out who I am."

"Good idea, as it was for you to purchase a round. But when you grabbed the barmaid and kissed her, you surprised even me. The way she shoved you back into your chair and glared at you…I figured she would surely deck you. Then, she climbed atop you and gave it back to you tenfold." Kony laughed and slapped his leg.

Broland laughed with him. "After weeks of dreaming about it, I took a chance. I felt lucky after winning that throw. Somehow…it seemed right." Broland grinned at the memory. "I'll admit I don't have much experience with girls, but that was one I won't soon forget."

Leaning forward, Broland moved an archer into position and shook three dice.

"What happened when she pulled you into the back room?" Kony's shake was a losing one and he was forced to remove an infantry piece.

"Let's just say that she was *very* appreciative of the extra silver I had given her when I bought that round of drinks earlier." The grin on Broland's face was so wide, his cheeks hurt.

"You dog..."

A knock at the door interrupted Kony. Broland turned toward it and called out.

"Come in."

The door opened and Nels stepped inside. "Sorry to interrupt, Prince Broland. There is a courier here for Master Kearns."

Broland glanced toward the window and found it dark outside. "At this hour?"

"It is odd, but he says it's urgent," Nels replied. "This young man calls himself a purser, whatever that is. He has a message bearing the Duke of Wayport's seal, along with a package for Kony. He is waiting downstairs."

With a furrowed brow, Kony stood and approached the door. "I'll be right back."

The guard shut the door, leaving Broland alone. He gazed down at the game board and counted the pieces, finding him up by one piece. After months of playing the game together, Kony had improved his skill and now won almost as often as he lost. As a counterpoint, Broland had similarly improved in the sparring chamber. Before Kony first arrived, Broland had considered himself good. However, facing a highly skilled opponent every day had raised the bar and Broland's skill with it. Having a competent sparring partner was certainly a benefit of Kony staying at the castle, but Broland now found it among the least important benefits.

As the weeks passed, Broland had come to value Kony's company, and he had discovered what it was like to have a true friend. They were together every day, spending hours inside the castle in addition to evening adventures in the city. Over the course of their shared experiences, an unexpected bond had formed. A cavity had been filled with Kony's friendship – one that Broland hadn't realized existed until life occupied the dead space. Now that he had this connection, he found it to be like a drug – an addiction that fed portions of his soul that had gone hungry for far too long.

The door opened, drawing Broland's attention. Kony stepped into the room, but his eyes were downcast, refusing to meet Broland's gaze.

"What's wrong?" Broland asked, sensing the change in his friend.

"I...received news...bad news. My adopted father, Baron Rhone, has fallen ill. I must go see him."

Broland stood, concerned for his friend, but also fearing how this might affect their friendship. "When will you leave? How long will you be gone?"

Kony closed his eyes, in obvious pain. "I must leave tomorrow. I... don't know when I might return."

"I could come with you," Broland offered.

Kony looked up and Broland saw something in his eyes. Shock? Pain? Sadness?

"I could not ask you to come with me, Broland. You are the heir prince and you must remain here."

"If you are concerned for my safety, I can request a retinue of guards to accompany us. My father does so whenever he travels to Fallbrandt."

Kony's face clouded over. "No, Broland." He shook his head. "Leave it be. I must go alone."

Startled by the response, Broland blinked and softened his tone. "All right. You do what you must." He gestured toward the game board. "Come. Let's finish our game."

The cloud drifted from Kony's face as he stared at the game board, the anger lifting to reveal a sadness. "I...cannot. I am no longer in the mood, and I must prepare for my trip." He stepped back with his hand on the doorknob. "Goodnight."

With a gasp, Broland opened his eyes and sat upright. He found himself panting as if he had run for miles rather than just waking. His room was dark, the starlight coming through his window providing just enough light to see the furniture within. A sense of dread lingered from his dream and bumps dotted his arms while another chill ran down his spine. Something felt off – a wrongness in the very air. He fumbled for the cup on his nightstand, found it, and took a long drink of water. After setting the cup down, he stood and padded to the door.

Unlocking it, he eased the door open and pale blue light bled into the room. He peeked out, glancing to his left, and then to his right. Other than the glowlamps mounted to the walls in both directions, he saw nothing. His brow furrowed. *Where are the guards?*

He stepped out and walked down the hallway, careful to remain quiet although he couldn't explain why. The other doors were closed – Brandt's room, Cassie's room, Kony's room – save for the door to General Budakis' room, which stood slightly ajar.

Broland knocked softly and held his ear to the door. Hearing no response, he eased it open and was met by darkness.

"Gunther?" he said in a hushed voice.

When there was no response, he fumbled for the glowlamp beside the door and removed the cloth. The sight before him caused him to gasp, his chills returning in full force.

Burke lay on the floor, his throat sliced from ear to ear with blood pooled around his head. The guard's sword lay beside him, glinting in the light of the lamp. Beyond Burke, Gunther lay in his bed with a pillow over his face. When General Budakis was younger, he was strong, viral – a man to be feared. Since his poisoning years earlier – an assassination attempt that had almost taken his life – Gunther's ability to function had greatly diminished, taking his strength with it. Whoever killed him knew this.

Gathering his wits, Broland picked up Burke's sword and turned toward the door. He peeked out again and found the corridor quiet. Crossing the hallway, he tested the knob to Kony's room. It was unlocked. With his lips pressed firmly together, Broland swung the door open and jumped back. The room was dark...quiet. The glowlamp on the wall behind him offered just enough light for Broland to see that Kony's bed was empty. The fear simmering inside him instantly boiled over to panic.

Broland turned toward the stairwell and sprinted up to the next level. At the top, he found Lorna on the floor, her head bent in an unnatural manner, her eyes staring into nothingness. He knelt with his hand on her head, his eyes closed while he found Order at his center.

He extended his awareness toward her, but her body was an empty shell, her life force expended. Broland stood, stepped over her, and tested the door to his parent's room. The knob turned in his hand, unlocked. This time, he opened it quickly and dove inside, rolling to a crouch beside the desk. He tore the cloth off the glowlamp his father kept there, and the darkness fled to the corners of the room, revealing an intruder at the room's midpoint, standing beside an open balcony door.

Kony turned toward him with a dagger in hand. When Broland saw a horrible sadness in his friend's eyes, he felt his heart wrench, and he staggered with his hand to his chest.

Shocked, Broland blurted, "Kony...how could you do this? *Why* would you do this?"

Kony looked toward the floor, and he shook his head. "You don't understand, Broland."

"What are you doing in here?" Brock voice came from the far end of the suite as he climbed out of bed, his hair a mess.

Like Broland, his father was dressed in nothing but his small-clothes. The king's athletic physique remained in impressive condition, despite his being twenty years older than Broland. The man shifted toward the corner near the bed, and he grabbed his metal-reinforced quarterstaff.

Grimacing, Kony glanced from Broland to Brock and lifted his dagger up, the tip still dripping blood.

"I'm putting my blade down," Kony said. He slowly knelt and put the knife on the floor before sliding the pack off his shoulder. "I'm going to open this pack. I have something to show you. It will... explain everything."

Broland eased closer while his mother wrapped a robe about herself. When Kony's hand emerged from the pack, he held a jar with a bronze dial on the top. Stepping even closer, Broland kept his sword ready while Kony placed the jar on the floor. Brock and Ashland shifted forward with Brock standing in front of her, his staff ready, his eyes narrowed as he watched the intruder.

Kony turned the dial and stood as it began to tick. He looked Broland in the eyes and said, "I am truly sorry. Goodbye."

He turned, darted across the balcony, and grabbed a rope tied to the railing. When he climbed over and began to lower himself, Broland moved to follow.

"No!" Brock bellowed. "Get out! Now!"

Brock grabbed Ashland's hand and sped past Broland, toward the door. Confused, but alarmed, Broland ran after them. His parents darted out the doorway with Broland three strides behind. A flash of bright green blazed around Broland as a thunderous boom deafened his ears. Heat seared his body when a massive thump from behind launched him through the door and drove him into the corridor wall. Empty blackness followed, swallowing him entirely.

35

REDEMPTION

G ritting her teeth at the pain, Quinn lifted her hand and knocked. A moment later, a familiar voice called out.

"You may come in."

She opened the door and found Varius sitting at her desk. The woman appeared quite well and showed no ill effects from the assassination attempt the night prior. Without looking up, Varius finished writing a note and then placed her pen back in the ink well. The archon sat back and stared at Quinn for a long moment.

"Come closer, please."

Quinn did as she was asked, wincing at the pain from her bruised knee.

"Didn't Numi heal you?"

"No," Quinn replied. "I refused it. Sometimes there is value in living with pain. It can be a reminder of sorts."

"A reminder that you saved the Archon? That you are some grand hero?"

Quinn shook her head.

"What then?"

"A reminder that I was forced to take someone's life."

Varius narrowed her eyes, her glare measuring Quinn.

"You lied to me," the woman said.

The statement carried weight, tension accompanying the accusation. Quinn could not deny it, so she responded with the truth.

"Yes."

"Come here."

As commanded, Quinn circled the desk as the woman stood. She placed a hand on Quinn's forehead and closed her eyes. *Is she going to heal me?* Quinn wondered. When the woman opened her eyes and Quinn's pain remained, she found herself confused.

"How did you learn to fight? I saw you in the garden the other day...and what you did last night."

Quinn had considered the question, expecting she needed a plausible tale to explain herself. The truth, or a version of it, seemed the best route. "I was a cadet at the military academy in Fallbrandt."

"I see. Why are you now a handmaid?"

"I...I was removed from the school after two fellow students died and two more went missing."

"Did you kill them?"

Quinn shook her head. "No."

"Yet, you took the blame?"

She gave a non-committal shrug. "When I returned to Hurnsdom, I needed work. My uncle secured a handmaid position for me, and that has been my job ever since."

Varius moved away, walking slowly with her hands clasped behind her back. "Do you know what I did when I placed my hand on your forehead?"

"No, Archon."

"It is called Divining. It is an ecclesiast ability that enables me to determine your natural abilities." She turned and looked at Quinn. "Although you have a rune that marks you as a server, your primary trait is that of a warrior – Custos."

Quinn did not react. She had never considered the woman discovering something about her in this manner.

"I assume you were marked with a Famulus rune for a reason, although it is your third strongest trait." Varius walked toward Quinn, staring her in the eye. "How good are you, Cadet?"

Quinn considered her response and steered toward the truth. "I was among the best in my squad. Some would say I was the best, although my skills are not exactly traditional."

"Good, because I have a new job for you."

"A *new* job?"

"I have less need for a handmaid than I do for a bodyguard." Varius turned toward the window and stared at the sea. "Trusting someone armed to be around me at all hours, often when alone, offers challenges, particularly since I am a woman. As you can see with the guard last night, this man named Warrick from Cinti Mor, even a man in an Empire uniform can betray me."

The woman spun to look at Quinn. "When you could have let me die, you risked your life to save me. You have listened to my orders with patience and have performed every task I have placed before you with efficiency." Varius shifted close and took Quinn's hand, holding it in her own. "I can trust you, Glynnis. You have training, training that we can further enhance, and I can trust you. Be my personal guard."

Quinn stared at the woman – the leader of the Empire, the enemy power who would seek the end of Chaos with the intent to control the entire continent – and found herself unable to dislike her. Without understanding why, she found herself grateful for the opportunity offered.

"I would be honored to protect you, Meryl."

Dressed in her new padded leather armor, sleeveless with metal bracers on her forearms, Quinn stood against the wall and watched the people seated at the table. Varius sat at one end, Kardan at the other. Prelates from across the Empire sat between them – six men and two women. Voices buzzed in the room as three different conversations took place. Three days had passed since the attempt on Varius' life, and Quinn had settled into her new role, one that already took her places she hadn't been allowed as a handmaid. While she had learned little of the Empire's plans thus far, she hoped tomorrow's proceedings between the Council and city prelates would change that.

Master Sheen entered the room, trailed by three stewards, two with carafes of wine, the third carrying a pitcher of water. They circled the table and filled goblets until every person seated had a full cup. Quinn watched their hands the entire time to ensure nothing was slipped into a drink and that no knife was drawn from a hidden pocket. Her gaze drifted toward the face of the steward holding the water and her breath caught in her throat. The steward's green eyes met hers, locking in a moment of recognition before he turned and followed the other two stewards through the door.

Now possessing the freedom to investigate threats as she saw fit, Quinn crossed the room and exited through the same door. She stepped into the hallway and saw the back of the third steward fade from view as he descended the stairs. With a hurried stride, Quinn walked to the stairwell and scurried down, turning at the landing as the steward rounded the corner. Moving even faster, she sped down the stairs and reached the corner in seconds. She gasped when someone grabbed her and pulled her through an open doorway. The instinct to fight back had her hands on his chest in a flash, but she did not push him away, nor did his hands drop away from her arms.

"Are you following me?" Brandt asked.

She felt the beat of his heart beneath her palm. His hands released her arms, but found their way to her hips, providing a warmth that was both comforting and distracting.

Quinn glanced toward the open door and the empty hallway beyond it. "What are you doing here? It's dangerous."

"I never got the chance to say a proper goodbye when you left."

"You came here to say goodbye to me?"

He grinned. "A proper goodbye."

Her eyes narrowed. "What would that include?"

"Never mind. I plan to stick around for a bit. Someone needs to watch out for you."

"I can take care of myself," Quinn said. "Seriously, why are you here?"

"Same reason as you are here. Delvin sent me." His eyes flicked toward the floor, and Quinn found them more intense when they again met hers. "I have things to tell you...and I need you to tell me what you've discovered. We fear that time is growing short."

She considered her schedule for the evening and the following day.

"Meet me tomorrow night, an hour after sunset, in the garden beyond the western doors."

He released her and she backed into the hallway. A glance in each direction revealed it empty.

"I must return to the dinner or Varius will wonder what became of me." She turned back toward Brandt and gave him a nod. "Until tomorrow."

"Tomorrow."

The look in his eyes stopped her for a moment, as if he held her by a tether. Finally, Quinn moved down the corridor, cutting him from her view. She found herself smiling, happy to have a friend in Sol Polis. While climbing the stairs, she considered the new situation and adjusted her course of action. It was time for redemption.

With her hands clasped behind her back, Quinn stood before the Archon's desk while Varius finished the document. The woman put her pen back in the ink well and arched a brow.

"You are sure you wish to do this?"

Quinn's response was confident. "Yes, Archon. This is the right thing to do."

"I still don't understand why you feel like you owe her something." Varius cocked her head to the side as she stared at Quinn. "You agree to take responsibility? I cannot endure suffering her attitude or mistakes again."

"This is my idea and my responsibility. Things will be better than they were before," Quinn said. "In addition to easing my conscience, this act resolves a vacancy and frees us both to focus on other things… such as keeping you alive."

"*That* is an objective I support."

Varius folded the paper and lifted the candle from her desk. Tipping the thick cylinder of wax, the flame flickered while melted wax dripped upon the paper. She then pushed the signet ring on her right hand into the wax, holding it in place while the wax cooled. Lifting it away, she picked up the paper and held it toward Quinn.

Taking it, Quinn said, "Thank you, Meryl. You won't regret this."

"I suspect I won't." The woman stared at Quinn for a moment, her eyes measuring, calculating. "Compassion is a valiant trait, perhaps more so for someone in your position. Just be sure it doesn't prevent you from acting decisively should the need arise."

Quinn's gaze was rock steady. "As you witnessed with Warrick, you can trust me, Meryl."

Varius nodded. "I know."

Opening the door, Quinn stepped out into the corridor. She paused a moment and eyed the seal on the missive in her hand, marked by a circular rune within a flame. A guard walked past her, his sidelong glance cold and distant. The castle guards seemed to avoid her now, as if she were alien to them. *Do they mark me as an enemy because I killed one of them?* she wondered. *Or are they now intimidated by me?* Wyck had been in Sol Polis for two weeks, and many of the soldiers had likely sparred with the brute. Even more had likely thrown back ales with him. The man was a killing machine, and he surely would have bested her if not for Everson's Chaos trap. If the other guards knew of Wyck's skill and strength, maybe Quinn *did* intimidate them now.

Moving along, Quinn descended the stairs, turned at the landing, and continued downward, past the ground level, to the servants' level. Down the corridor, she walked. The porters she saw grew wide-eyed and looked toward the floor while they walked past, fear replacing any friendliness they had previously displayed toward her.

When she found the laundry room doors held open, she paused and stared inside while recalling her past visits. Mavis looked up and saw Quinn. When their eyes met, Mavis froze. Quinn smiled, but the effect was not what she had hoped. The woman flinched and turned away before scurrying between the rows of shelving.

Quinn was struck by a wave of loneliness, like a shadow crossing over her. The thin relationships she had built with the staff had been shattered, leaving her on an island. Then, she remembered Brandt. The image of his green eyes flared in her mind, joined by the memory of the warmth of his hands on her hips. Something about him brightened the gloom and gave her peace. His appearance at Sol Polis gave her someone to cling to while she was away from Everson. Perhaps longer.

With a sigh, she continued down the hallway, crossed an open area, and slipped through a pair of double doors. A dim glowlamp sat on a pedestal at the near end of the hallway and nothing but darkness waited beyond it. She picked up the glowlamp, shook it to activate the powder inside it, and the light bloomed to life, extending her view much further down the corridor. Lifting it high as she walked, Quinn counted the doors on the left until she found the one she needed.

It opened with a squeak, a rarely used door since the primary route down was at the other end of the building. The stairwell that waited behind the door was steep and dark at the bottom. A musty smell clung to the air, even that seeming like a relic from another age. She descended the long flight of stairs, unable to shake the feeling that she had somehow taken a path that led to the past. The walls around her seemed a thousand years old.

When she reached the bottom, a pair of double doors stood before her. She opened them and found herself in a graveyard of sorts, the space containing relics from regimes long past. A pathway had been cleared through the heart of the old weapons and furniture that surrounded her. Following it, she opened another pair of double doors and entered a long corridor with a dim light emanating from an open door at the far end.

As Quinn neared the light, she heard a deep rumble and paused, waiting as she tried to determine the source. Once again, the rumble rose up, coming from the lit room. She smiled when she recognized the sound as it reminded her of her father. When she entered the dungeon jail room, she found a big man leaning back in a chair, asleep with his feet resting on the desk before him. His heavy jowls vibrated as he snored again.

Quinn walked toward the man, grabbed his huge foot, and swept it off the desk.

"Wake up!" she yelled.

The man's eyes flashed open as he fell from his chair and landed in the dirt on his hands and knees. Spluttering, he climbed to his feet and grabbed the cudgel from his desk. When he stood, his full height proved to be a foot taller than Quinn, his weight likely three times her own.

"You best have a good reason to be down here or you're gonna end up in a cell," he grumbled.

Quinn eyed the man with a challenging glare. "I'm Glynnis Mor, the Archon's bodyguard."

The man's jaw dropped open, and he lowered his cudgel. "You? Well, I..."

She thrust her arm toward him, and he flinched back from the folded sheet of paper, as if it were a weapon. "I have a writ, signed by Archon Varius. I'm here for one of your prisoners."

He took the note and looked down at the seal before glancing back toward Quinn. When he broke it open, he squinted at it, his head moving back and forth while his lips silently said the words.

Finally, he nodded. "The prisoner is still here. Locked in cell three."

"Well, what are you waiting for? Open it."

He pulled a ring of keys from his belt and walked to the door. After inserting the key, he gave it a turn, and opened the door, the hinges squeaking at the weight.

Quinn moved closer and lifted her glowlamp. Light seeped into to the dark cell – six feet wide and twice the depth. At the far end, a woman was curled on a pallet, holding her hand up to shield her eyes as she whimpered weakly. When Quinn saw her, guilt snaked down her throat and twisted her innards until she thought she would vomit. The smell from the cell was horrid, as was the sight.

"Why is she naked?" Quinn demanded.

"Um...those were the orders."

"Well, the orders just changed. Get me something to cover her."

The man backed away, kneading his hands. "Yes ma'am. I need to run up to the barracks. Will you be all right with her free?"

Quinn pressed her lips together. Before she could respond, he added, "Never mind. I'll be right back."

The man darted out the door, and Quinn turned back to the cell.

"Water," the woman croaked faintly.

Turning, Quinn found a pitcher and a pewter cup on the desk. When she approached it, she found the pitcher half-filled with water. Using it to fill the cup, she returned to the cell where the woman waited, now sitting upright and hugging her knees to her chest. Quinn put her lamp down, stepped in the cell, and squatted with the cup held out.

"Here, Jeshica. Drink."

Jeshica reached for the cup, her hands shaking as she did so. With the cup to her mouth, she drank, draining the contents without taking a breath.

"Can you stand?" Quinn asked.

The woman nodded, but when she tried to stand, she stumbled. Quinn caught her and helped her to her feet. She then led Jeshica out of the cell and into the light. The softness was gone from Jechica's voluptuous frame, leaving the woman thinned to an alarming degree. Bruises and sores covered her elbows, knees, and back. Her skin was dirty and unwashed, the stink of sweat thick within the cell. Quinn fought the urge to wretch as guilt again welled up inside her.

"Stand here for a moment," Quinn said before she darted across the room and grabbed the chair. When she returned, she placed it behind the woman. "Please, sit."

Jeshica did as instructed, sitting and wrapping her arms about herself to keep warm. "Do you have more water?"

Without a word, Quinn grabbed the entire pitcher and gave it to the woman. She drank and drank, downing most of it, spilling some down her chin but not caring. When she finished, she handed the pitcher to Quinn.

"Why are you here, Glynnis?"

"I have a writ from Varius. You are freed from your cell and are invited to resume your previous position as her handmaid."

The woman blinked. "I will get my old room back?"

Quinn shook her head. "I'm afraid that won't be possible. Varius requires me to remain in the room beside hers. You will have to take a room on the lower level with the other servants."

"If you are in my old room, are you also her handmaid?"

Quinn gestured toward her leather jerkin and tapped one of the metal-plated bracers that encased her forearms. "Do I look like a handmaid?"

"No. More like a fighter, I guess."

"You guess?"

In the lull of their conversation, Quinn heard a whisper. "Help me." She frowned. "Did you hear that?"

Jeshica glanced toward a closed cell door. "Yes. I had heard it before, but I thought it was my imagination." She shuddered. "You don't know what it's like being locked away in the dark, alone for weeks. I would see things that were not there, hear things that could not be possible. Consciousness would come and go, reality melding with false moments until I was unable to tell what was real and what was not." She reached out and tentatively touched Quinn's hand before nodding. "Sorry. I wanted to make sure this is real."

The weak voice returned, "Help me."

Quinn stared at the cell door from which the call came. She moved close to it and put her ear to the wood. "Who's in there?"

Silence.

She tried again, louder this time. "Is someone in there?"

"Yes," a scratchy voice croaked, and then coughed. When recovered, he said, "It's Dalwin Pretencia. You must help me."

Quinn's eyes grew wide, her jaw dropping at the revelation. Everyone had assumed Pretencia was dead. She glanced at Jeshica and considered the woman's condition after six weeks of incarceration. *The man must have been locked in his cell for over twenty weeks now. Yet...he lives.* Quinn stared at the door as she wrestled with the idea that the man was alive...and what it meant.

"Who is in there?" Jeshica asked. "You look...startled."

"It is nobody." Quinn shook her head and stepped away from the door. "Merely a man who committed murder and wished to confess his sins to someone before he died."

Jeshica let the issue drop. Quinn, however, turned her thoughts toward a plan.

36

RESCUE

A sea of stars dotted the sky, one of them suddenly streaking toward the horizon. Brandt's eyes followed it as a voice arose from the shadows.

"Some say that sharing the sight of a shooting star means that your paths are destined to intertwine."

Quinn stepped out into the starlight.

"I normally prefer to take my own path," Brandt said. "In this case, I would be willing to break that rule."

"Break a rule? That is so unlike you," Quinn said. "You're late."

"Yes. Sorry about that. Just when I was about to slip away, Sheen sent me with a carafe of wine to Prelate Dorlan's room. The old coot claims he cannot sleep without it...as if he hadn't downed an entire bottle himself during dinner."

Quinn snorted in reply. "I assume you have things to talk about other than Dorlan."

He took her hands in his and pulled her close until their chests were nearly touching. Gathering his courage, his mouth drifted closer to hers until her warm breath mixed with his. His right hand found its way to her cheek, gently cupping her chin while the other hand slipped around to her lower back. She stared at him, her blue eyes challenging and defiant. Brandt found himself frozen in place by an unseen tension until Quinn's eyes drifted shut, her lips parting as his did the same. After months of thinking about it, wishing for it to become real, the kiss had finally come and his head swam in the glory of the moment. Her soft lips felt cold at first, likely from waiting out in the cool evening air. However, they warmed quickly, as did his pulse. His hand slid from her cheek, into her hair while the other moved even lower on her backside. With her pressed up against him, his body urged him to respond, his heart racing. Too soon, she pulled back. He opened his eyes to Quinn's smile, her white teeth appearing blue in the starlight.

"I should have done that before you left the Ward," Brandt whispered in a breathy voice.

"Why didn't you?"

"I…was afraid."

"I wouldn't have hit you."

He smiled at the comment. "I know."

"Why, then?"

Brandt's gaze lowered before looking back into her eyes. "Because…I care. I find myself wishing to be with you. That is…new for me."

A smile spread across her face. "I have that effect on people. They cannot get enough of me."

Brandt chuckled. "You sound like me."

"Good. That was the intent."

"I have something for you, from Everson." He withdrew two Chaos traps from his cloak pocket. Starlight sparkled from the etchings in the bronze disks.

"Two of them?"

"Yes. He said you may need them."

Quinn took them and slid them into her vest. "Good. I expended the one he had given me while saving Varius."

"There are wild rumors. Staff members are saying you saved the Archon's life. Some of the stories are…well, I'm sure you can guess. What really happened?"

She looked away and appeared upset. "It was Wyck. He tried to kill Varius."

"Wyck?" Startled, he realized he had said it too loud.

"Shh," she hushed him.

In a quieter voice, Brandt asked, "Why would Wyck be here?"

"He said that Firellus sent him to Cinti Mor to spy as a guard for Dorlan. Unfortunately, when Wyck foiled an assassination attempt on the prelate, he was promoted and relocated here."

"I'm with you so far."

"I was working as Varius' handmaid, so my room was beside hers. After hearing a commotion, I entered her chamber and found her unconscious with Wyck standing over her, about to kill her. I tried to reason with him, but he wouldn't listen. He attacked me, I fought back, and somehow…he died."

Hearing the pain in her voice, Brandt took her hand and gave it a reassuring squeeze. "I'm sorry it came to that. It must have been difficult for you, even if the man was an ass."

Quinn closed her eyes for a long moment.

In a quiet voice, Brandt asked, "I wonder why you chose to protect her?"

Quinn opened her eyes and took a deep breath before replying. "The Archon was the only reason the Empire has not attempted to extend their reach since taking Kalimar. General Kardan and half the council were pushing for war against the west. Varius took a firm stance to stop them, fearing the destruction it would yield. However… Wyck's attack on Varius changed the situation."

"How so?"

"She blames the kingdoms for the assassination attempt. Today, she spoke to the Council and the city prelates, in favor of war." Quinn's voice took on an edge of fear. "They are laying out their strategy and will likely attack soon."

"What more do you know?" Brandt asked. "I must tell my sister."

"Cassie?"

"Yes. There is something that few people know about us." Brandt lowered his voice even further, now a faint whisper. He was about to share a precious secret, one he hoped she would hold close. "She and I can communicate telepathically. I simply must think it, and she can hear me, the same as I can hear her. That ability is why I'm here, to help you and to act as a conduit between you and the Ward."

Quinn's brow furrowed as she stared at Brandt for a moment.

"They have weapons they intend to use against the kingdoms – explosive weapons made from something called flash powder. Explosives were used to blow up walls so they could quickly capture cities such as Sol Polis.

"Someone named Jarlish is developing a new weapon with flash powder. I fear what it might mean for the west and the destruction it might render. Imagine a Chaos-wielding army facing one armed with explosive weapons. What could a sword do against such power?"

Brandt wrapped his arms about her, and she squeezed him back while resting her head on his shoulder. It felt good to hold her and to be held. He wondered how she had managed to keep her edge, all alone in the stronghold of the enemy, hundreds of miles from anyone she knew. She squeezed him so hard that it was difficult to breathe. That alone told him more than mere words could convey.

"We will figure something out, Quinn," he whispered. "Together, we will find a way to stop this war."

Quinn relaxed her embrace and looked him in the eye. In that gaze, he saw a fierce determination and knew that she was about to ask something of him.

"Did you ever meet the king of Kalimar?

"King Dalwin?" He shrugged. "Sure. A number of times. The last was three or four years back."

"Good. There is something I must do, but I cannot do it alone," Quinn said. "I need your help, but it will be dangerous."

Brandt grinned. *She needs me.* "Danger? Danger happens to be my favorite."

Moving quietly, Brandt followed Quinn down the dark stairwell, the damp air growing cooler and carrying an ancient mustiness with it. He had visited the Kantar Citadel dungeon numerous times. The air in this stairwell rekindled memories of that place and the torture chamber it housed. His father said that he never used the chamber – that it only remained as a relic from Empire rule. Just thinking about that room – the instruments it contained, the horrors it had inflicted – sent chills down Brandt's spine.

Now, Brandt and Quinn were entering a dungeon under the control of the Empire. He shuddered at the thought of being captured and tortured. Gathering his resolve, he put his fears aside and placed his faith in Quinn. If what she told him was true, he agreed that the opportunity outweighed the risk. Besides, her plan had merit.

The couple continued their descent with Brandt following the dim glowlamp Quinn carried, an uncharged lamp that did little to fend off the surrounding darkness. When she reached the bottom, Quinn led him to a pair of ornately carved doors, the etchings in the wood covered in dust. She opened the door slowly and the hinges emitted in a groan. Without pausing, she led him across a room filled with junk. Cobwebs billowed overhead as she walked past the refuse and opened another door. They entered a corridor with light pouring through an open doorway at the far end. Quinn rested the glowlamp on the floor and turned to face Brandt.

"With any luck, the jailor will be sleeping," she said in a hushed tone.

He snorted. "It's the middle of the night. We should be sleeping as well."

"Hush. You agreed to do this. We must act, for we may not have much time."

"Fine. Tell me what you need me to do."

"Since there are only two of us, stealth should be used in favor of brawn. Besides, I have worked hard to get into this position, and I don't wish to toss it aside now."

"Fair enough."

"When we get to the room, I need you to sneak in and steal his key ring. It may be hooked to his belt. Once you have it, make a run for it, but head away from where we now stand." Quinn hefted the cudgel she procured. "I'll knock him out from behind and then we can proceed."

Brandt gave a nod and began to slip past her, stopping when she grabbed his arm.

"What?"

She pulled the dagger from the sheath strapped to her thigh and handed it to him. "Take this in case you need to cut the keys from his belt." She gripped his tunic and pulled him toward her until their lips met, warm and soft and wet.

When Quinn released him, she stared into his eyes. "Pull your hood up to hide your face. Stick to the plan and stay alive."

He grinned at her as he pulled his hood up. "You like me, don't you?"

She rolled her eyes. "Go."

Brandt headed down the dark corridor, lined with closed doors. As he neared the doorway to the lit room, the rumble of a snore arose. He peered around the doorframe and found the guard asleep in a chair behind the desk. The man was massive. Brandt pictured the man waking and pummeling him with his cudgel until he was an unrecognizable mess. He turned toward Quinn, who had trailed behind him.

"You didn't tell me he was a giant." He whispered.

"Hush. Just go get the keys." She waved him along.

Taking a deep breath to calm his nerves, Brandt snuck into the room. Each step of his boots in the dirt seemed amplified, the crunch bouncing off the hard walls and ceiling. Brandt's own pulse thumped in his ears as he neared the jailor, a drum that threatened to wake the sleeping giant before him. As Quinn had said, a black keyring hung from the man's belt, but the man's thick forearm covered the cord tied to it.

Moving slowly, Brandt crouched down and gripped the key ring. He tried to move it to expose the cord, but the man stirred. Rather than try and expose the cord further, Brandt lifted his dagger and began to saw at the bit wrapped through the key ring. The dagger slipped, the point going straight into the man's arm.

"Argh!" The guard cried out, at first pulling his arm away and then swatting at Brandt. The man's meaty hand struck Brandt upside the head, and he fell to the dirt with the key ring in his grip.

"You little thief!" the man growled as he scooped up his cudgel and stood.

Brandt crawled away from the man and had to roll to the side to dodge the descending weapon. The cudgel smashed into the dirt with a thud and a puff of dust. When the man raised it again, Brandt yipped and scrambled to his feet. He darted into the corridor and stopped just outside the door.

"Give me those keys, or I'll kill you!"

The jailor hefted his cudgel and lumbered toward the door. Brandt backed away slowly, moving down the hall opposite from where Quinn waited. As the towering man neared the doorway, his thick body eclipsed the light and darkened the corridor. He stepped through and turned toward Brandt. A loud *crack* sounded, and the man bent his head forward, stumbling to the wall. The man spun toward Quinn with a backhand swipe, which she dodged by spinning away. Alarmed, Brandt dropped the keys and leaped upon the big man's back. The guard twisted and backed Brandt into the wall, driving the air from his lungs as pain shot through his body. He slipped off and fell to the floor on his side. The man lifted his cudgel, and Brandt felt a stab of panic. A loud *crack* sounded when Quinn's cudgel struck the back of the man's head again, this time causing him to fall to his knees. Quinn swung with an overhead strike aimed at the top of the man's head. Another *crack* echoed in the corridor and the man fell face-first atop Brandt.

With the dead weight of a three hundred pound man atop him, Brandt squirmed and struggled. "Get...him...off...me."

Leaning hard into the man, Quinn was able to help Brandt roll the jailor over. Sitting upright with gasping breaths, Brandt stared at the man and hoped that he remained unconscious.

"That was close," Quinn said.

He nodded weakly. "Yeah. Too close."

"Do you think he saw me?" she asked.

"In this light? No way."

"Good. I'd rather not kill him. Come on. We don't have much time." She turned, scooped the keys from the dirt, and stepped back through the doorway.

Groaning as he rose to his feet, Brandt stumbled before following her into the room.

Without pause, she walked straight to one of the cell doors and began testing keys. With her third attempt, the key turned in the lock and made an audible click. Quinn glanced back at Brandt, pressed her lips together, and pushed the door open.

The cell was dark, too dark to see anything. The smell was worse than anything Brandt had ever smelled before.

"Grab the light," she said.

He walked to the desk, picked up the glowlamp, and shook it until the light brightened. At the back of the cell was a man, sitting on a pallet and leaning against the wall. With graying black hair and a scraggily beard to match, he appeared undernourished and the rags he wore were covered in splotches of dried blood and dirt.

"Are you all right?" Quinn asked.

The man squinted and blinked at the light. "Is this real or another illusion?"

Quinn entered the cell and squatted before the man. She reached out and squeezed his hand. "I assure you, I am real. What is your name?"

"My name?" the man coughed. "My name is Dalwin Pretencia."

Brandt moved closer to get a better look. The man's state, with unkempt hair, beard, and tattered clothing made it difficult to be sure, but Brandt saw the same eyes as the man he remembered meeting years earlier.

"I think he tells the truth. I'm not completely sure, but he looks like Pretencia."

Quinn gave Brandt a nod. "That's good enough for me. Let's get him out of here."

She put an arm about the man and helped him to his feet. Brandt hurried to help as they half-guided and half-carried the man out of the cell.

"Grab the water from the desk," Quinn said.

Brandt did as requested and held the pitcher to Pretencia, who drank eagerly, paused and coughed, and drank some more. Once the man was finished, Brandt replaced the pitcher on the desk.

"Who are you people?" the man asked weakly while staring at Brandt. "You look familiar."

"We met in Kantar, sir. You know my father."

The man's eyes widened. "Young Talenz?"

"Yes."

"We're wardens," Quinn replied. "And, we must get you out of the citadel...and out of the city." She turned toward Brandt. "I'll lead you to the courtyard and then you're on your own. Once you have him safely away, you can return to your room. The servant's quarters are never watched, so it is simply a matter of your getting back over the wall."

"That's all, huh? Just take the missing king to a ship without getting caught and then return over a guarded thirty-foot tall wall built upon a hilltop. Oh, and then it's back to work at dawn, Brandt, so good luck with that as well."

She smiled. "I have faith in you."

"That is reassuring. Luckily, I know what to do. After all, I've done it before back in Kantar," Brandt said. "How will you get back to your room without being seen?"

Quinn smiled. "Same way I got out – up the rope hanging from my window." She pulled a metal disk from the small of her back. "If you draw the rune, I can use this to make him lighter."

"I cannot weigh much now," Pretencia said. "I have eaten little the past few months."

"We need you even lighter for what I'm about to do," Brandt said as he withdrew a wedge of coal from his pocket and began to trace a symbol on the man's arm. When finished, he sketched the same rune on his own hand in preparation.

Quinn pressed the button on the case and a rod popped from it. "This may burn a bit, but it's necessary."

She touched the rod to symbol drawn on the king's arm. He jerked in pain, the hairs near the rod sizzled and smoked as the rune burst to life before pulsing and fading. She pushed the pin back into the trap and slid it into her pocket.

"Finished," Quinn said. "It isn't as powerful as a full augmentation, but it will help. Grab him and let's get out of here."

Doing his best to breathe through his mouth and not gag at the smell, Brandt scooped up the gaunt king. Already light, the king now seemed like an empty shell. Brandt resisted the urge to toss the man into the air.

"Let's go," Quinn said as she ran out the door.

With Quinn in the lead, Brandt ran down the corridor, the two retracing their steps back to the servant's quarters and up the stairs to the main level. Rather than running through the central hall, they ducked out the side door to the western courtyard. Quinn stopped and faced Brandt in the starlight.

"When will I see you again?" Brandt asked.

"Soon. I need you to send information to the Ward."

"Is that all you want from me?"

"Oh, stop. You know there is more between us than that."

Brandt chuckled. "I know. I just wanted to hear you say it."

"Be safe, Brandt. I'd be quite upset if anything bad should happen to you."

Quinn then darted through the shrubs and faded into the shadows.

Turning toward the wall before them, Brandt considered the drop on the other side. He then looked down at the man in his arms.

"Hold on a moment. If we are to make it over the wall, I'll need an augmentation as well."

Brandt shut his eyes and gathered the raw Chaos surrounding him, drawing it in as if he were inhaling a storm. He opened his eyes and channeled the stored energy into the rune drawn on the back of his hand. It glowed brightly, pulsed, and faded as a wave of exhaustion washed over him. A moment later, his stomach flipped as gravity loosened its grip.

"Hold on to me tightly, You Majesty. This is going to be a bumpy ride."

He burst forward with two long, floaty steps, and leaped, the two of them arcing high in the air. When they cleared the citadel wall, the breeze from the sea caught ahold of them, slowed their momentum, and began to push them backward as they descended. The wind drove them into the wall with Brandt's sore back colliding into it and causing him to groan in pain. His feet then struck the top of the hillside and he rolled forward, losing his grip on the man as the two bounced and rolled down the hillside and onto the open plaza that encircled the citadel. There, they lay for a moment, staring up at the stars like a pair of drunken fools.

"Perhaps I should have used a different augmentation," Brandt muttered.

"That was an interesting escape," Pretencia noted.

"I'm glad you think so." Brandt sat up and gathered the king in his arms. "If we make it to the ship alive, I do hope you'll remember this moment fondly. It was an honest mistake." He stood and began taking long, floating strides toward the harbor. "I may be known for my past hijinks, but this particular one was not intentional."

With the city asleep, the trip to the western wall was quiet and uneventful. Finding the gate locked, Brandt leaped atop a second story roof near it and eyed the wall. Considering the wind, he leaped with a lower angle this time, clearing the wall by a fair distance before the wind grabbed ahold of him. He bounced off a sloped roof, rolled, slid off the side, and landed bottom-first in a narrow alley with the king on top of him. Again, the Reduce Gravity augmentation made the fall irrelevant, and he was up and off again in moments.

Even on the docks, things were quiet. Running past a dormant glowlamp, Brandt headed toward the far end of the center pier. At the most distant slip, he found the vessel he had hoped to see, still docked right where she had been when he landed in Sol Polis three days earlier. He made one last leap, arcing over the railing and landing on the deck.

He put the man down. "This is it, Dalwin. The vessel that will take you to Kantar."

"Don't move!" A man moved in the shadows. He held a bow ready and pointed at Brandt. "If you're thinking of thievery, you picked the wrong ship."

Brandt smiled, recognizing the voice. "Hello, Parker. I hope you don't mind an extra passenger."

"Brandt?" Parker stepped into the light of the glowlamp. "What are you doing here at this hour? Who's with you?"

"Tsk, tsk, Parker." Pretencia said. "After all the years we spent together, I lose a few pounds, grow a beard, and you don't recognize me?"

"King Dalwin? You…you live?"

"I believe so. However, we best set sail soon or that may change. I also hope your galley is well-stocked. I'm starving and have much eating to do. But first, I believe I could use a bath."

EPILOGUE

The mid-day sun shone through open windows. People walked past, eclipsing the light as their shadows slid across the table. The Aspen Inn was quiet, displaying nothing of the energy when Ikonis had last visited the tavern with the prince. He looked across the table and found Percy staring out the window, seemingly watching the passing foot traffic, but Iko knew better.

After setting his potatoes aside, Iko picked the jackaroo leg off his plate and took a bite. The juice from the meat forced him to wipe his face with the back of his hand. He chewed slowly and listened carefully as the barkeep and a regular patron shared gossip at the nearby bar.

"...as you can see, the blast caused a lot of damage," said a man with missing teeth and graying hair. "It might take years to clean it up and rebuild."

The barkeep leaned close to the man, lowering his voice. "I heard worse." His eyes flicked from side to side, and he said, "Nearly a week has passed, and nobody has seen the king, queen, or the heir prince. Word is that they were all killed in the explosion."

"No." The other man shook his head. "My cousin is a porter at the citadel and he tells me the queen lives, but has yet to regain consciousness. Might never regain it. The king and the prince...well that's another story."

"One of the king's own guards told me that General Budakis was killed in his own bed, murdered. Two members of the elite guard were murdered as well. Yet, they say there was no sign of a break in. They suspect it was someone who lived in the citadel."

"What'll happen, now?" The patron took a drink of his ale, emptying it.

The barkeep shook his head. "If the queen recovers, I guess she will take over. If not...it will be either the younger prince or his sister, who were sent off to live elsewhere. Good thing, too, or they might be dead now as well."

"And what of this Empire we keep hearin' about?"

The barkeep snorted as he picked up the tankard. "Your guess is as good as mine. There's been talk of war for months. Now, with the king gone..."

"Methinks it's a bad time to be a soldier."

"Ain't that the truth?" The barkeep turned and refilled the mug with ale before setting it back on the bar. "Kantar is an awful long ways from Sol Polis. If the Empire's arm is that long and they are behind the king's death, what prevents them from attacking us...or taking over the entire continent?"

"I guess we'd be right back where we were twenty years ago."

"True. That'd be bad for Unchosen for sure. However, not much would change for the rest of us." He glanced around the bar. "This place was here before King Brock took over. I bet it wouldn't matter to most of us either way, so long as the rules are fair and the taxes don't go up."

Ikonis finished his meal, wiped his lips and fingers clean with his cloak, and spoke as he stood.

"I have what I came for," he said softly. "Let's go."

Percy gave a nod, flipped his hood up, and rose to his feet. Iko repositioned his hat, keeping it down to cover his face, and slipped outside with Percy a step behind him.

Iko paused, his gaze turning toward the castle overlooking the city. A gaping hole existed in the top floor and the ceiling had collapsed to fill it. The memory of the explosion replayed in Iko's mind, the shock of the blast, the heat from above. Debris had fallen down upon him while he dangled from the rope. Bruises on his shoulder and cuts on his hand remained as markers from the event. It had been a near thing, but he held on and made it to the ground safely. The commotion created had offered him the opportunity to escape. Nobody was watching the western wall when he used a grappling hook to scale over it and fade into the night. For six days, he hid in Percy's rented loft in Lower Kantar. Finally deciding that the manhunt had run its course, Percy made a trip to the harbor to secure them passage. Now, with a solid meal in their stomachs, it was time to leave the city.

The foot traffic was heavy and they melted into it, catching a cluster that headed toward Southgate. Caught in the wake of the crowd, Iko and Percy flowed through the city, passing several Kantarian soldiers along the way. Nobody seemed to notice two nondescript travelers. The only Kantarians who could identify Iko as Kony were those who had met him. Most of those people were now dead.

They exited the city and walked along the gravel road that led down to the harbor. As they had when Iko first arrived, the palm trees swayed in the ocean breeze and the seabirds circled overhead in search of food, oblivious to the rumors that swirled. Iko agreed with the men in the tavern. Regardless of the machinations of mankind, the world continued existing. An empire fades and a kingdom takes over. A king dies and a prelate replaces him. Nothing changes but a few laws. The citizens adapt and forget the past. Still, if Iko's actions could help erase the taint of Chaos, it could no longer threaten humanity, no longer tempt mankind with god-like abilities. The only god was Issal, and in Issal's name, Ikonis would see the end of Chaos.

Iko and Percy stepped onto the docks and headed toward their ship. Five silvers had secured them passage with the promise of five more when they reached Wayport. A heavy price, but one that was required to ensure silence.

When they stepped aboard, Percy turned toward Iko. "I'll go talk to the captain." He held a pack out, which Iko accepted. "You go down and get settled so nobody sees you. It's the first cabin on the left."

Without a word, Iko headed toward the narrow stairwell Percy had indicated. He found the door to their cabin unlocked, slid inside, and sat on the lower bunk with the two packs beside him. A deep intake of breath preceded a long sigh.

"I'll be home in a week, Mother," he said aloud, knowing that neither she nor anyone else could hear him. "You will be proud of what I have done, although it broke my heart." He recalled his friendship with Broland – a painful lie. "Still, it is time for me to be at your side. This is a war we can win...a war we must win." Even said aloud, the words, the very purpose of his existence, tasted acrid as they passed his lips.

He reached into his pack and withdrew a journal. Opening it, he turned to the last entries. General Budakis had rough handwriting, the lines jagged – a telling sign of his condition. Iko had to admit that the man knew how to plan for combat. His defense and counter attack plans against the Empire were solid, if not inspired. Those plans were now in the hands of the Empire, and the man who had crafted them was dead. Iko put the book down and looked upon his hands as they shook. A tear slid down his cheek and landed on his wrist. He had been groomed for war since he was eleven, dueling since he was thirteen. In the past three years, his skill with a sword was unrivaled by anyone he had faced until Broland. Even then, the prince was barely a match for Iko. In reality, however, war strategy and duels are not the same as murder.

The lives he had taken stained his heart. He had killed good people who had the misfortune of believing in the wrong thing. Chaos was a disease he wished to cure. The dark magic was responsible for the ruination of his childhood and the loss of loved ones. Growing up in a prison, toiling from dawn to dusk every day, and watching the people around him die had hardened him until he thought himself impervious to pain. Killing Lorna, Burke, Budakis...and Broland had cracked that shell and pain leaked from it – deep-seated pain he had buried years prior.

His father had been a big man, a strong man, and a leader among the prisoners. Iko recalled his father lifting him in his thickly muscled arms, hugging him and telling him that he must remain strong. The man had given young Iko a gift, a ball he had fashioned out of brambles that grew in the prison yard. When Iko threw it too far and the wind carried it to the canyon wall, his father ran to retrieve it. The man never made it that far.

The image of his father's back with arrows jutting from it remained etched in Iko's memory, the moment feeling as if it had happened yesterday. Vinay Eldarro died with his son kneeling beside him, crying hysterically until a guard scooped Iko up and carried him to a bunkhouse. The man who had shot Eldarro apologized to the boy, but hate filled Iko's heart, and he attacked the man, wishing to do him harm but lacked the ability to do so. Subsequent years of labor, growing, and training had resolved that problem, and now that Iko could fight back, he found himself wishing otherwise.

The tears began to flow in a steady stream as he fell to his knees and prayed for Issal's guidance.

NOTE FROM THE AUTHOR

If you enjoyed The Arcane Ward, sign up for my author newsletter at www.jeffreylkohanek.com and receive a FREE download of *ICON*, a short story that outlines the events that lead up to the forming of the Issalian Clandestine Operative Network. This novella will be EXCLU-SIVE to my newsletter subscribers until 2019.

Best Wishes,
Jeffrey L. Kohanek

11438115R00164

Made in the USA
Monee, IL
10 September 2019